00000081520 21prt

JUST NOT THAT INTO BILLIONAIRES

ANNIKA MARTIN

ONE

Francine

I'M LIMBERING up at the edge of one of the big rehearsal spaces at the Gotham Metropolitan Ballet complex when legendary choreographer Dusty Sevigny comes storming up.

He stops in front of me, bushy brows drawn so low they nearly blot out his eyes.

"You're to report to Rosemary's office," he says in his thick Russian accent, tipping his head toward the area where the company support staff toils away.

Sevigny is difficult to read, what with his brows, his Einstein hairdo, and his stormy *artiste* vibe, but it's safe to say he's upset.

"Right this moment?" I ask uncertainly. It's a strange request, considering we need every second of practice on "Plamya," his big comeback piece. Let's just say the breakneck time signatures trip up a lot of dancers. There are thirty arabesques at one point.

"Immediately," he says.

I plaster on a bright expression "On it!"

He crosses the expanse of hardwood and disappears out the door.

My fellow dancers are scattered all over, stuffing their pointe shoes and rubbing their muscles in preparation for our five-hour rehearsal, but now all eyes are on me.

I stand. Heart pounding, I walk toward the door, passing a horrified cluster of colleagues who clearly think I'm in trouble.

They're not the only ones.

I put my hand to the side of my mouth and do a quick stage whisper. "Sevigny so loves her performance, he can't *even*!"

People give me sympathetic smiles.

As pep talks go, telling a ridiculous story about the bad thing that's happening is probably not that effective, but it's what I do. I pass them but I'm not done. I turn and walk backwards, adding, "He's sending her to the back office to pick up a huge bonus and a brilliant bouquet of flowers!"

Somebody snorts.

I turn and go out the door and rush down to the stairwell.

The admin section of the massive refurbished building has a highly polished tile hallway that leads past old-world doors with wavy waterglass windows. Words like "administration" and "tickets" are painted on them. It's all very film noir.

What could be the matter? Why not wait until rehearsal is over?

This feels bad. Like dream-crumbling-before-my-eyes bad.

Being chosen as second soloist for this piece was the hugest honor of my life. Only the first soloist and principal dancer have larger parts. We're embarking on a European tour after our in-town premier, including three nights dancing at my dream theater: Mérida's Roman Theatre in Spain, a magical space surrounded by ancient marble columns and statues.

Rosemary's desk, like her office door, has that film noir feel, but Rosemary herself is very contemporary, one of the many hip and worldly fifty-somethings who work behind the scenes in the New York dance world. She was a dancer herself in the '80s. If I didn't know it from talking to her, I'd know it from looking at her —I can always tell an ex-dancer by the way they move.

"Mr. Sevigny said to come back and see you?" I say.

Her face turns grim and she sighs. "Right. Take a seat. We've got an issue. It's..." She shakes her head, tapping away on her keyboard. "It's...not good. Visa stuff."

"Visa stuff?" I ask, wracking my brains for what it could be. My passport is valid for another year almost, so it couldn't be that. "What visa stuff?"

She holds up a finger. I'm to wait while she hits more keys.

I look down at the black screen of my phone, not bothering to tap it to life. Not like I'd be able to comprehend anything with my pulse whooshing in my ears. What's going on? It has to be serious if I was asked to duck out of rehearsal. Every hour of practice is critical and precious right now.

"Here we go." Rosemary peers at me above stern reading glasses. "Your visa applications have been rejected by three out of the fifteen countries we'll be touring in."

"Rejected?" My heart pounds. "Why?"

She eyes me full-on now. "An EU visa requires you to state your correct civil status. You told us on the forms that you were single. Never married."

I nod. "That's right. That's correct."

She's looking at me like she's trying to figure out if I'm lying. "Are you sure about that?"

"Of course."

She glances back to the screen. "According to Social Security records, your marital status is married."

"Excuse me?" I say. "There must be some mistake. I'm not married. I never was."

"According to Social Security you've been married for nine

years, and the discrepancy is getting you flagged and rejected. The powers that be are very picky about that sort of thing these days. Terrorism and so forth."

"There has to be some kind of mix-up. Maybe somebody is using my Social Security number or something." I try a smile. "I mean, I'd know if I were married, right?"

She reads off my Social Security number and I confirm that that is, indeed, my correct Social Security number. She frowns at her screen.

"Who am I supposedly married to?" I ask.

She shakes her head. "It just shows your status here. As married."

"They can't straighten it out?" I ask. The company's tour office usually handles this sort of thing.

Rosemary informs me that only I can straighten out a matter this personal. I'm going to need a notarized marital status affidavit which I'm to get in person from the New York county clerk at the New York County Supreme Court.

"I'll head over first thing tomorrow morning," I say, eager to get to rehearsal.

"No, look," Rosemary says, voice softening. "Mix-up or not, if we can't get this worked out, we can't bring you along. Right now, you're not somebody we can bring to three of our host countries."

"But I'm not married! Obviously it's a typo or whatever."

"I know, I get that, but we need this nailed down. Daneen will be dancing in your place today."

"What?" I gust out.

"You need to make this your top priority. You have a month to get that affidavit. I've spoken with my contacts, and that will give me enough time to get those visas in order. They're holding it open; they just need to see the affidavit and then they'll clear you."

I can barely feel my face. I might not *go*? After all this, I might not go? "Well, can we just change it to married and then deal with the problem when I get back?"

"Too late," Rosemary says. "It's a big deal when you sign your name to false information on that type of official document. At this point, you need to prove that the information is correct." She gives me the address for the New York County Supreme Court. It closes at 4:30.

"I'm on it," I say.

"Report back right away. We need to know that you can do this. If you can't get it straightened out, there's no sense..."

No sense in even rehearsing with the company. She doesn't need to finish the sentence. "I will get you that affidavit. I will do what it takes. And I'll let you know how it goes every step of the way. This is getting fixed. You can tell Mr. Sevigny that, too."

Thirty minutes ago, the worst problem in my life was my knee injury, whether to ice-heat-ice it or heat-ice-heat it.

And now all of my most cherished dreams are threatening to crumble.

TWO

Francine

NOT AN HOUR later I'm riding illegally in the passenger side of Noelle's mail truck as we buzz down Canal Street. She insisted on coming and picking me up when I called. She wants to go with me to the county clerk.

"You really feel like you have pull with the county clerk?" I ask. "Just from being a letter carrier?"

"I wouldn't say I have pull," she says. "More like a kinship. These are my people. And I'm good at cutting to the chase."

I hold on tightly as she rounds a corner. "Are you saying I don't cut to the chase?"

She gives me a quick grin, navigating efficiently around an obstacle course of delivery trucks, and double-parked vehicles, honking fiercely. "You can sometimes have a dramatic presentation, Francine, whereas a government employee is going to want the *when what where* and *why* presented simply and without fanfare."

"Are you calling me fanfare-ish?" I ask.

She shrugs and rounds another corner. "Court's on the next block."

I nod, and there's this silence where all I can think about is the devastating possibility of me not going on this tour.

"We're gonna fix this," she says.

"I've been literally floating on cloud nine for months," I say. "And being so careful. No just-for-the-hell-of-it cartwheels. No leaping puddles. Every time I so much as step into a crosswalk I'm obsessively scanning for speeding bikers and peds on phones. Who knew it would be some bizarre bureaucratic blunder? As if I'm married!"

"You are definitely the last person that I would ever imagine getting married. You would be like, screw this piece of paper!" she says.

"When and if I fall in love, I will not need a piece of paper to cement the deal," I declare. "No offense to our married gal pals of course. Even if they are married to *billionaires*," I say, trying not to let the word drip with all the derision in the world.

Noelle snorts. "Tell me how you really feel about billionaires."

I laugh. "You know how I feel about billionaires."

"Yeah, but I want to hear you say it," Noelle teases.

I beam at her, grateful for her teasing me and getting my mind off my problems. Whatever happens, I'll have my gal pals at 341 West 45th Street. "You are such a good friend."

She reaches out and grabs my coat sleeve. "Backatcha," she says.

It turns out to be amazing having Noelle along. She gets a front-and-center parking place reserved for official vehicles. She gets me to the exact right floor without so much as glancing at the building directory whereas I would have had to study it for an hour. She's cheerful in line.

When we get up to the front, I really do have the feeling

that there's a kinship between her and the county clerk, a man with salt-and-pepper hair and thick glasses.

"Pinoy?" I ask him.

He gives me a questioning look.

"Never mind," I say. Noelle gives me a stick-to-the-topic look and launches into explaining things, casting the situation as if it's all of our puzzle to solve together, like we're on the same team, like it's not anyone's fault.

"They have you as married..." he says, tapping keys.

"You can imagine how shocked I was to hear such crazy news!" I tell him, rooting through my purse. "I'm not even sure how I feel about marriage in general. I haven't decided. I can see some advantages, of course—"

Noelle clears her throat and I hand over my many forms of identification. The clerk types some commands into the keyboard.

"Did you travel to or reside in Las Vegas nine years ago?" he asks.

I stiffen. "I lived there for a summer," I say. "I guess that would be nine years ago."

He swivels around, grabs a sheet of paper from a printer, and slides it across the desk. "Does this look familiar? Is that your signature?"

I blink as my mind interprets the words. It's a Nevada marriage license. It has my name on it. And yes, my signature.

My eyes scan to the other column.

To the name of my husband.

Benjamin Stearnes.

I stare at the letters, heart racing. *Benny.*

I can see him in my mind's eye like it was yesterday. His sandy, wavy hair puffed up on one side from frenetically running his fingers through it. His intense gaze through too-huge-for-his-face glasses—said intensity coming, more often than not, from his high level of annoyance at me. I imagine him grabbing a sheaf of papers off the pit table with his angular, uncoordinated movements, more gangly than graceful. And those lips—so expressive and beautiful, even if they were usually in a frown.

"What do you think?" the clerk asks.

"There's gotta be some mistake," I say.

"Does that look like your signature?" he asks.

"It looks like my signature," I say.

"Do you know Benjamin Stearnes?"

I can feel my cheeks heat with shame like they always do when I think about Benny. I can feel Noelle's gaze boring into the side of my face.

"Do you know who that is, Francine?" she asks.

"Well, I *knew* him," I say. "But I don't remember marrying him. I think I would have remembered. There would have been a wedding. Flowers. A dress, preferably a decent gown—"

"Did you two date or anything like that?" she asks before I elaborate further.

"No, not really."

She narrows her eyes. "Not really?"

She wants more but I don't know if I can give it. I have no idea how to characterize what Benny and I were. "We worked together. We were more like work frenemies than anything."

"Look," the clerk says. "I can't give you a notarized affidavit of single status until I have proof that this marriage is invalid. And I'm sorry, but I honestly don't see anything that suggests to me that this is not a currently valid legal document."

"I need my affidavit of single status for some overseas travel ASAP," I plead.

"Then you'll need proof that this document is invalid," the clerk says. "My suggestion would be divorce papers. Download some divorce papers and track this guy down to sign 'em. You show me that and I'll give you your affidavit."

"How long will that take?" I ask.

"It's something I can turn around right here, but getting a judge to sign off on your divorce decree, if that's the way you go, it could be a few weeks. Assuming there are no disputes."

"Benny...probably isn't my biggest fan," I whisper as I watch my world crumble.

"Don't be crazy. Everyone loves you." Noelle pulls on my sleeve. "Come on."

"Not that I would even know where to *find* him..." I continue.

Somebody grumbles behind us. I'm aware of Noelle and the clerk exchanging glances.

"Come on, let's figure this out while he takes the next person." She pulls me out of the large, now stuffy-feeling room. We sit in plastic molded chairs out in the hallway. I'm staring at the paper, mystified.

"Look, this still works," Noelle says. "We know how to fix this. You have to find him right away and get that signature, and then we hope for a judge who can clear it right away. It can happen!"

"I only have a month," I say, "or they'll use another second soloist!"

"There's no reason it can't happen," she says. "Right?" She gives me a little hug. I'm sure it feels like hugging a large mummy from her end.

Benjamin Stearnes?

"This is doable!" she says. Sweet Noelle. Always so positive. It was her positive thinking that completely saved our building from demolition.

But she doesn't know Benny.

"He will not be thrilled to see me," I mumble.

"Who could not be thrilled to see you?" Noelle asks.

"Benny could."

"So he was your co-worker?"

"He was the backend tech guy for the show I danced in, completely nerdy and scowly and antisocial, and I was this out-of-control social butterfly at the time and...it was weird between us."

"You didn't get along?" Noelle asks.

I think about this for a while, watching all the people go up and down the hallway to all their various courthouse appointments. "I actually had a crush on him. It was one of those weird sorts of crushes. I mean, he *so* wasn't my type at the time. And he definitely didn't return my affections. I really, really annoyed him. I guess I didn't know what to do with that, so I would kind of turn it up to eleven with him. Sort of like poking at a beehive. It was a kind of compulsion. I was a little bit fascinated with him."

"Is it possible that on one night you weren't haterators?" she asks.

I'm staring at the piece of paper. "Umm...it's possible," I say.

"Gulp," Noelle says, waiting for more. "Do tell."

I trace the little fiberglass lines in the molded chair. "We had a drunken escapade."

"Like a one-night stand?" she asks.

"No, we didn't have sex. It was more that we were both really drunk at the closing night party, and we had this kind of fun, wild night together. Benny was singing this really hilarious version of 'Alejandro'—the whole show was built around 'Alejandro,' that Lady Gaga song—and Benny singing it, in my mind, it was the most wonderful thing ever, and then there was more tequila. And then Benny and I were somewhere else, having energetic conversations, and everything was fun and funny and new and exciting. Then I woke up in his bed the next morning."

"But you didn't..."

"No, I had my clothes on. He was on the couch. I tried to make the moves on him, though. It was so...Uhh! He was not into it!" I cringe at the memory of him peeling my hands from his chest like they were giant barnacles. "I was so mortified when I remembered what I'd done! The show was over anyway and I definitely didn't want to hang around waiting to see whatever snarky, annoyed thing he'd have to say. Or worse, his pity or disgust. I got out of there as soon as I woke up."

"You left?"

"Well, the show was over and I was mortified! I moved up my plane ticket, even."

"Is it possible he liked you?"

"No way. Benny was all about computer games and robotics and making it clear I annoyed him. Or vexed him—that's the word he'd use for things that annoyed him. 'This router is entirely vexing,'" I say in my exasperated Benny voice. "'This router is ninety-eight point five percent pure vexaciousness!'"

"Come on, Vexerella," Noelle says, pulling me up from the seat. "I have to get back to my route, and you have a husband to find."

"A husband," I say, following her to the ancient courthouse elevator.

"I can't believe you were married all these years and didn't even know it! That is so you." She hits the down button and turns to me. "But in a good way," she adds in the face of my frown.

"If I'm even married to him. Maybe this is just somebody's idea of a joke?" I say hopefully. "Maybe one of our mutual friends from the show out there arranged it."

"A bit much for a joke," she says. "Filing fraudulent documents and so forth."

"I have to fix it," I say. "This tour is everything."

Married to Benny!

We step out onto the busy sidewalk. It's late April, that blissful time before the heat starts baking the dumpsters.

"You thought he was Filipino," she observes. She knows about my trick, that whenever I see somebody who I think is Filipino, I ask "Pinoy?" and if they look confused, I know that they aren't, but if they grin and engage me, it's a connection and maybe even a fun conversation.

"I thought maybe," I say.

"I completely forgot you had spent time in Vegas," Noelle observes once we're in her mail truck and on our way back. "You never talk about it."

"It was just a summer," I say, googling Benny. "My thirty-four-month contract with Nevada Met had ended, and I had my sights set on Gotham and some of the other companies out here, but auditions weren't until winter, so I had a summer to work and save up money. Beau Cirque Fantastique was hiring and they paid really well."

"Is that like Cirque Du Soleil?" she asks.

"Yeah. A ballet-heavy version of Cirque. More leaping, less trapeze. Super glam with elaborate lighting." I scroll through the endless Benjamin Stearneses. "This is bad. There are a lot of Ben Stearneses out there! How is that name so common?"

"There are 365 million people in the US," she says. "Pretty much every name is common that's not Podunk Kurtzweiler."

"Who would name their kid that?" I ask.

"You don't wanna know." As a mail carrier, Noelle knows these things.

"Maybe he's still in Vegas. Maybe if I try Facebook..." I google Ben Stearnes and Las Vegas on Facebook. I find a few, but the pictures are wrong. A lot of the accounts have no pictures. What if one of them is Benny? He'd be just the kind of guy to not have his picture on Facebook. Maybe he's not even on Facebook. He was never big on social interaction.

"Isn't his Social Security number on the marriage license?" she asks.

"Oh, right," I say. "How do I search with that?"

"We'll get Willow on it," Noelle says. "Or even Lizzie. Cookie Madness hires people all the time. She probably has a service that does background checks."

"How could this happen? It's probably my fault. I was super crazy then."

"We're all crazy when we're twenty-one," she says. "But, dude! You were in a big glam Vegas show? That is unbelievably cool!"

"I was just a backup dancer. Benny had the big job—he ran the technical stuff. There's a crazy amount of robotics and computerization involved in a massive light show like what we had at Beau Cirque."

"Do you think he could still be in the theater world?" Noelle asks. "Maybe he moved out to Los Angeles or something."

"I don't know. He hated being told what to do, hated working for other people. Most people hate bosses, but Benny..." I find myself smiling at his surly awkwardness. "Benny hated people in general."

Even the idea of touching him seemed strangely forbidden, as though he had an intense force field all around him. A force field that I could never breach. Until that night I acted like a sex-addled asshole.

"All I know for sure is that he probably ended up doing something totally technical. And I definitely can't imagine him married with a family or anything like that."

"Well, Francine, according to the piece of paper you have, he's married to you."

"No, that's not real."

"It's real, and what's more, a current marriage is the sort of thing that would have gotten caught if he'd applied for a marriage license. Just like with your visa. He'll probably be as surprised as you are."

I hang on for dear life as she rounds a corner.

"Don't you think?" she shouts over nearby jackhammers. "Maybe he'll be surprised. Maybe he'll even think it's funny!"

I sit there, watching the buildings go by. "He won't think it's funny."

THREE

Francine

TABITHA STANDS over me with a pitcher filled to the brim with sparkling pink liquid. She gestures for me to hold out my glass. "Come on, Francine," she says.

"Yeah, you're drinking for two," Mia says. "This is your bachelorette party *and* your wedding shower."

"And your pre-divorce party!" Tabitha says. "And the congrats on your one-night-stand Vegas wedding that you totally don't remember."

"Ummm, thanks?" I say. I hold out my glass. I only let her pour an inch, and then I fill the rest with bubbly water. Hot Pink Barbie, her signature cocktail, has lord knows what in it, and it tastes like candy. I avoid alcohol when I'm in rehearsal mode. I like to stay sharp.

There's a knock at the door and Noelle pops up to answer. News of my nuptials has traveled quickly around the building and even beyond to our friends who have since moved out. I'm kind of glad. It's taking my mind off the possibility of my dream being utterly crushed.

Lizzie bursts into the room clutching her coat and a large white box. "I understand congratulations are in order!"

I raise up a hand. "Please," I say. "I don't even know what to say."

"Don't worry, we're going to track down that missing Vegas husband of yours!" She sets the box on the coffee table and flings open the lid. It's full of frosted cookies in the shapes of double bells. "Happy wedding! And impending divorce! Woo-hoo!"

Antonio, our resident hot Italian model, strolls in with a six-pack of beer and an eight-pack under his shirt. "Off the market," he says sadly, adding something in Italian. He claps a dramatic hand to his chest. "My heart breaks, *stellina*!"

"Only a million girls left for you to serial-date," I say. "Whatever will you do?"

Mia grabs a cookie. "The good thing about Hot Pink Barbies is that it's the kind of alcoholic drink that goes perfectly with cookies. You have to appreciate that in a drink."

"Agree!" Tabitha grins. "I appreciate it very much."

Lizzie sets up her laptop at the kitchen table. "Okay, I brought all my stuff for a background check. You got his social for me?"

I slide the paperwork over to her and take a chair at the other side of the table.

Kelsey comes over and sits next to me. "Don't worry, we're going to figure this out. You're gonna go on your tour."

"I don't know what I'll do if I can't," I say.

"Well, if you don't go, at least your knee will be happy," Kelsey says.

I give her a dirty look. "The knee is happy now. The knee is eager to tour."

"Yeah, sure," Kelsey says. "On the bright side, you got an unexpected day off!"

Kelsey's a dancer, too—she's in the big production of *Anything Goes* with Mia. She knows how brutal a dancer's schedule can be—hours of classes and rehearsals, back-to-back. She knows what a knee injury can mean, but nothing is going to get in the way of my international tour. Unless we can't get this divorce paperwork pulled together in time, but I don't let myself think that.

Noelle is telling everybody what I said about Benny and his nerdy ways. I fill in with some additional Benny details. His glowering glare when I'd laugh with the other cast members. His sullen attitude at the morning meetings. The different types of extreme annoyance he would exhibit. "There was DEFCON level, nuclear level, quantum level, platinum level, though that's not the order of extreme-ness."

"You had names for his levels of annoyance?" Tabitha asks. "Hardcore!"

"We need a picture! Was he cute?" Kelsey asks.

"I can't say."

"How can you not say?"

"Because he was so..." So *Benny*, I want to say. "He was just this perfect grump, glaring out at the world through those big glasses. He didn't give you a chance to decide if he was cute, you know? Even the way he spoke—no niceties, just so abrupt and rude. And he moved with zero grace."

"Clumsy?" Antonio asks.

"No, more like, weirdly efficient and without grace. He typed hard and freakishly fast, and you'd look at the computer screen and it was all these crazy lines of code, like something from another planet. When he adjusted his little robotic things, his fingers would just fly, all knuckles and hard angles."

I look down at my drink, remembering the way he moved

through the world, all gangly intensity. But then he'd come up with such brilliance. People saw him as this nerd, but I knew his abruptness grew out of one-pointed intention, a singular passion that excluded everybody.

I could relate. Fixating on something to the exclusion of all else is the way I'd lived my life since the tender age of five. It's how you have to be to rise to the top of the ultra-competitive ballet world.

So I spent a lot of time wondering what it would be like to be friends with him, wondering what it would be like to be lovers with him. I couldn't help it. Something about all of that harsh passion.

"Features vaguely symmetrical?" Mia presses. "Hair color?"

"Umm...dusty-brown hair, bedhead style, like he'd fallen asleep at his keyboard and woke up with five minutes to spare. Tawny skin that would get bronze in the desert sun. Light brown eyes. He kind of had this whole tawny, dusty-brown color scheme going except for his oversized and very severe black glasses, all the better to glare at you through."

"Literally glaring?" Lizzie asks.

"He even hated my weird T-shirts."

"How can anyone hate your weird T-shirts?" Kelsey asks.

"You'll have to ask Benny. Or maybe not." I smile, remembering it all. "He hated nonsensical T-shirts the most. He'd be like, 'What does that even mean?' And I'd be like, 'I know you want this T-shirt so bad.' Whatever he hated, I'd pretend he wanted it so much."

"I bet you did," Tabitha says.

"The only time we really related was when he would say annoyed things to me. Well, we also had these fake humblebrag children that would compete."

"Wait, what?" Kelsey asks.

I'm not sure if I should try to explain, but everyone's staring at me now.

"One of our really mean stage managers would humblebrag all the time, so then I started humblebragging about my daughter, Monique, that I pretended to have. 'Oh, I stayed up all night knitting while Monique translated the works of Balzac into Chinese for her third-grade project. She just wasn't happy with the current translations on the market. She's such a picky child!'"

"Seriously can't imagine you doing that," Noelle says —sarcastically.

"I'm lucky I didn't get fired. But it was totally hilarious and people would always ask me about Monique whenever they were mad at this jackhole stage manager. Of course, Benny would just glare. It's not that he liked this guy any better than the rest of us liked him, it was just annoyance. And then one day, Benny seemed so angry with me when I was humblebragging..." I'm grinning thinking about it. "I was going on like, 'it's so hard to know what to do with a child as brilliant as Monique —people don't understand how problematic a gifted child can be. The French studies alone...' And suddenly Benny goes, 'My boy, Igor, is so creative he doesn't want to have anything to do with French so I have enrolled him in Klingon language studies. It is so tedious, though, to have such a precocious child who doesn't care to follow the herd.' We were all totally shocked because he never engaged with us. And suddenly he's humblebragging back to me. And it was good humblebragging, too."

"And he never talked to you before that?" Kelsey asks.

"Not much! We were all stunned, like, does Mister Socially Awkward have a sense of humor? And it went on from there. We'd humblebrag-compete. I thought it was fun, but for him, I think it was more like an extension of his extreme displeasure with me."

"Huh," Antonio says.

"Sometimes, like if Benny was glowering at me, I'd do this fake concern about Igor having Victorian diseases. Like I'd ask about Igor's scurvy, and he'd be like, 'We were only grateful that Igor's very mild condition didn't become a case as tragic as Monique's rickets. No offence, of course, we were all very concerned.' I was stunned," I say. "Chronically annoyed Benny Stearnes joining in on the joke!"

Noelle narrows her eyes. "So the main communication between you two was that you had imaginary children that would compete with each other?"

I nod.

Mia flops back on the couch. "So basically you were both weirdos with a weird sense of humor. That's what I'm getting here."

"Pretty much the only communication! Though there were also glowers and grumbles," I say. "And I asked him to coffee this one time and he was like, 'Huh?'"

Mia widens her eyes. "You asked him to coffee?"

"I just liked him, I don't know. We had that quirky Igor and Monique thing going. Considering that he was the opposite of my type who found me annoying, I don't know what I was thinking. I blurted it out one day. I was like, 'That coffee place is having a two-for-one, you wanna go?' and he was stammering out his no. He couldn't say no fast enough."

"So you asked him out even though he was the opposite of your type," Mia clarifies.

"Yeah, I couldn't help it, and then I felt like an idiot. My attraction to him was weird, anyway. And of course it would've deprived him of being able to criticize my dates when they came to pick me up."

I explain how Beau Cirque had this cheap-rent deal with this apartment complex for the workers, so we all lived there.

Benny liked to do work out in the courtyard, escaping a building full of loud theater people.

"I could always count on him to roll his eyes when guys picked me up," I add.

I have everybody's attention. I never talk about my Beau Cirque days, mostly because of how they ended: shamelessly glomming on Benny.

"You think he was jealous of your other dates?" Tabitha asks.

"No, it's just how he was. He'd make these little comments like, 'Somebody needs to check the hair product factories for recent robberies!' Or, 'Nice douchebag shirt.' And I'd be like, 'I love that shirt, and we're going to have a fabulous night on the town.'"

"You goaded each other," Tabitha observes.

"I guess." I shove at the half-melted ice in my drink. "Or he'd be especially scathing if they came in limos. He'd be like, 'Oh, look, you're getting picked up in a low-self-esteem mobile... I mean a limo.' He definitely ruined a few dates with his jackass opinions."

"Record scratch!" Lizzie says.

"What?"

Everybody is just staring at me now.

"You dated guys in limos?" Mia asks, shocked.

"It was a weird time for me," I say.

"I'm sorry, this is completely blowing my mind," Mia says. "You think rich guys are the worst. All of them—millionaires and especially billionaires. In fact, I seem to remember you saying last year that billionaires are the scourge of the earth!"

My face goes hot. I did say that billionaires are the scourge of the earth, which is super embarrassing now that a few of my friends have hooked up with billionaires. "I don't hate *your* billionaires," I clarify. "Just the rest of them."

Noelle snorts. "What do they care too much about?"

"Shut it," I say. "I'm not gonna sit here ranting on your menfolk."

Mia throws a pillow. "Tell us! What is the problem with billionaires?"

"Well, seriously!" I say, laughing. "I mean, a billion dollars? That's how much money you had to make? This is what you've spent your time on?"

Noelle's laughing and clapping.

"Have you ever heard of charity?" I continue. "A simple and honest day's labor? Working with your hands? However" —I turn to Noelle— "you know I always make an exception for Malcolm. In spite of his rocky start, he is clearly one of the good guys. And fine, Theo. Max. Rex. The billionaires you have chosen, clearly they're awesome. In fact, their good taste in choosing you somewhat redeems them."

"But just *somewhat*," Tabitha teases.

"Just somewhat," I say.

Noelle is grinning. "Poor Francine. Every time you look away, a billionaire grabs up one of your friends!"

"It's true! Is it too much to ask that maybe one of my friends picks a thousandaire? Thousandaires are amazing! Sexy bartenders, hot musicians, sweaty construction workers, amazing veterinarians. I mean, *pullllease*. Millionaires and billionaires."

Everybody's laughing. "That's why we love you, baby!" Mia says.

Kelsey says, "I'm still having a hard time picturing you with a guy in a limo."

"Seriously, I didn't know which way was up! I'd been in strict ballet boarding schools since the age of ten." I point a baby carrot at them. "While you all were going to prom and football games and keggers and sleepovers. The only music I knew by heart was written two centuries ago by men in powdered wigs. Suddenly I'm on my own in the city of sin without a ten-hour-a-day regimen? And there are no weigh-ins? I was ready to go to clubs and date glamorous men and eat whatever I wanted."

"Like Rumspringa," Lizzie observes. "When Amish kids go into the real world and sow their wild oats."

"I guess, yeah," I say. "And the dancers in Beau Cirque were so hip and fun and I wanted to belong, and suddenly I did. Unless of course you asked Benny, sitting there zeroing in on me, all scowly and judgmental. I knew I could crumble or could turn it up to eleven right back at him."

"You know he was probably in love with you," Mia says. "You know that, right?"

"No way," I say. "You had to be there."

"You're the beautiful, vivacious, wayward dancer. He was the sullen misfit, desperately in love with you."

"Totally not how it was," I say.

"The nerdy frenemy, pining for you," she continues.

"He was not thinking along those lines, I promise you. His all-consuming focus was on his little inventions and his nerdy pursuits."

"And you," Lizzie puts in.

"And then like a fool I get drunk and throw myself at him. Because I guess I love being rejected by him."

"And don't forget marrying him," Kelsey says.

I'm shaking my head.

"I still can't get over you riding in limos," Mia says.

Lizzie looks up from the laptop where she was doing her research. "You just would die a grisly death before you'd date a billionaire, wouldn't you?" she asks. "Did you not say that once?"

"Well, it's true," I say. "I would die a grisly death before I dated a billionaire."

Lizzie fixes me with a huge grin. "But would you marry one?"

"Hardly!" I snort. "Again, nothing against your guys!"

"Would you die a grisly death before you married a billionaire?" she asks me weirdly. "A grisly and horrific death?"

I shrug. "What can I say?"

"Well, Francine," Lizzie crows, "not only is this your wedding shower and your bachelorette party, but I'm afraid it's your funeral as well!"

"What do you mean?" I ask.

"Benny Frederick Stearnes, born in Detroit, Michigan..." She fixes me with a big grin.

"Right, that's him!" I say. "He was from Detroit."

"Here's *Forbes Magazine*, an issue from five years ago—*Tech entrepreneur Benjamin Stearnes unveiled his new microrobotic particle scavenger last month to a frenzy of excitement. The reduction of its energy source is a significant advantage for the tiny robots, which are designed to clean particular matter in manufacturing and industrial environments. This new innovation is sure to cement the billion-dollar company's market share over the next five to ten years.*"

"You are so full of shit," I say. "You are making that up!"

"I'm not making it up! You think I could make something like that up on the fly?" Lizzie turns the laptop toward me.

I scan the article. "Maybe there's another Benjamin Stearnes from Detroit."

"There may be another Benjamin Stearnes from Detroit," Lizzie says. "But no other Benjamin Stearnes shares your Benjamin Stearnes's Social Security number."

"No way," I say. "I'm gonna need to see a picture. This is just...no way. Benny?"

"Gasp!" Tabitha says, staring into her phone. "Heart-eyes!"

"What?" Mia goes over and sets her chin on Tabitha's shoulder. Her eyes go wide. "Erp!"

"Let me see!" I say.

Kelsey crowds in. "Francine! You've been holding out. Your secret billionaire husband is quite magnificent. He might be hotter than Antonio himself."

"*Stellina*, you kill me," Antonio says, clutching his heart.

I hold out my hand. "Come on, lemme see."

Tabitha keeps it hidden, clutching her phone to her chest, eyes sparkling. "Francine, my friend, I shall now present your husband, billionaire industrialist Benny Stearnes."

I take the phone with a *harumph*.

And time stops.

There in front of me, glowering out at me from the sparkly frame of Tabitha's phone, is my long-lost frenemy, Benny.

He holds himself erect, gazing down at the camera lens with his same old annoyed scowl, his wonderful lips in their annoyed configuration, which means they're extra-plumpy in the vaguest of frowns. He's all filled out—strong jaw, thick, corded neck, jaw set hard. And where did those cheekbones come from? Did his entire face undergo a tectonic event? Those glasses that were too big for his face, giving him the look of a beetle—a large, gangly beetle—have been right-sized and switched to pale brown clear frames that look amazing on him. He's managed to tame his dusty-brown hair. He's...objectively hot.

Benny.

"What's an industrialist?" Kelsey asks, as if from faraway land. "Wouldn't he be more of a microroboticist or something?"

"I don't know, I just wanted to use that word," Mia says, also from a faraway land, possibly a faraway planet.

"Entrepreneur," Lizzie suggests. "Tech entrepreneur."

At this point, I've basically stopped processing language. I don't know what to make of this Benny that I'm seeing before me. I can't quite square this guy with my old frenemy, pondering some little robotics thing, rambling on how he's 72.5% sure some component will fall apart.

Tabitha comes up behind me. "Nerd no more."

Lizzie reads on: "*We caught up with the notoriously publicity-averse Stearnes one afternoon while he was directing the launch of a new product, marshalling his troops with the demanding perfectionism that he has become known for—a remote, driven, intensely private visionary at the helm of one of the fastest growing firms of the year*. Wow," she adds. "One of his homes is right here in New York City."

"Really?" I say.

"*Stearnes is based in New York City, with residences in Los Angeles, Manhattan and Lucerne*," she reads.

"He's right here in New York?" I ask.

"Lucerne must be where he has the chalet," Kelsey says, reading her own phone. "Where he keeps his mentally enfeebled wife."

I frown. "Mentally enfeebled wife?"

"Where do you see that?" Lizzie asks.

"The comments?" Kelsey says. "It's all the comments are about."

"You're reading the comments?" Noelle asks, aghast. "Why are you reading the comments?"

"Because they're the most interesting part?" Kelsey says, reading on. "It's what everyone's saying in the comments. *Keeps his wife locked in his Swiss chalet. Why doesn't that jackass free his wife? The photographer should go in there and free the wife*."

At this point, we're all gathered around Kelsey, reading the comments.

"*Ask Billionaire Bluebeard about his trapped wife*!" Lizzie reads. "*Journalistic malpractice*!'"

Mia slings an arm around my shoulder. "Married to Billionaire Bluebeard! How about that?"

"Not. Funny."

"What's Bluebeard?" Jada asks.

"It's a folktale," Noelle says. "Bluebeard is a rich dude who has a closet full of dead wives. He marries them and kills them."

"And you question *our* taste in billionaires!" Mia teases.

"I'm sure the enfeebled wife trapped in a Swiss chalet is just bull," Tabitha says.

"No, there's a reporter taking the search for his wife seriously," Kelsey says. "One of these blogs has aerial photos...lemme find it again..."

"A Vegas wedding doesn't count," I protest. "You can get a drive-through wedding in Vegas as easily as you can get a cheeseburger and an order of fries." I stare down at Benny's picture, blood racing. "What if he doesn't want to give me the divorce?"

"Oh, I'm sure he'll be more than happy to sign for a quickie no-strings divorce," Lizzie says. "I highly doubt you two signed a prenuptial. Some women would take him to the cleaners, sue him for a big chunk of his billion-dollar empire."

"Agree," Mia says. "If you present him with a no-strings divorce, he won't be able to sign it fast enough."

"I'm gonna need a really messed-up T-shirt for this," I say.

FOUR

Francine

I STAND in front of Ventoux, a farm-to-table restaurant, wringing my hands. I should go in. I should just do this. But my legs won't move. I use my phone to touch up my lipstick. I'm wearing my "I'd tap that" tap dance T-shirt with fun flowered pants and a sweet spring jacket.

Thanks to the mad Google skills of my gal pals we have determined that Benny eats lunch here alone every Friday. It's across the street from one of the many cutting-edge, decentralized workspaces that make up his apparently very cutting-edge company.

I tuck a stray hair into my updo. It's stupid to care how I look. A nice hairdo has no impact on how ashamed I feel for the way I acted back then. A perfect coat of lipstick won't make Benny think I'm less annoying.

Spine erect, I push open the door and sail in.

"Do you have a reservation?" the woman at the hostess stand asks me.

"No, I'm here to see somebody," I say.

"Can I check if your party is already seated?"

"Well..." I lean in and peer into the elegant dining room, everything very mod and tasteful. There's a sea of white-tablecloth-covered tables and a row of booths down one side.

At the very end, alone in a corner booth near the window, I catch sight of him. Benny.

My heart races. It's that old fear and excitement.

He's frowning at his phone, light brown hair in an attractive and coherent style, but I'd know him anywhere. I'd even know his hands, what with their highly knuckly knuckles. How much time did I spend staring at those hands during interminable meetings? And of course, his lips, more beautiful than a man's lips should be, powerful and expressive if not downright sculptural.

"I see him," I say to the hostess. "We're good." I head into the dining room before she can stop me, because I get the feeling this is the kind of place where they don't let people walk in from the street.

A voice behind me. "Wait, if I could just get the name of the party you're meeting."

"It's fine," I toss over my shoulder, speeding up.

I'm just a few tables away when Benny looks up, as if he sensed me coming. His stony gaze is a punch of awareness to my soul—a punch that has me reeling, unsure.

I stop in front of his table, feeling weirdly vulnerable. "Okay, so you might not remember me. We worked together at Beau Cirque one summer, back in twenty...uh..."

"I remember you," he says.

Still that stony expression. *Really* not happy to see me.

I'm secretly panicking at this point. "He's sooo happy to see her," I say.

Benny deepens his glower.

"He's been dreaming of this day!" I add.

Silliness is probably the wrong approach to take, but that's how nervous I am. I swallow and pull myself together. "Seriously, though, I come bearing news."

A pair of men have materialized by my side at this point. One lightly touches my elbow. "Mr. Stearnes isn't to be bothered."

"It's okay," I say, and then I turn to Benny. "I have news. News of the weird and it's very important, Benny. And it'll just take a sec."

Meanwhile, the hostess has caught up to me. She's apologizing profusely to Benny, as though he's an active volcano liable to freak out and explode at any moment.

The men are gently trying to steer me toward the exit without touching me. "Mr. Stearnes is lunching now. You'll have to make an appointment," one of them says.

I spin back around. "Lunching?! He's lunching?" I'm grinning, because is there honestly a call for *lunch* being a verb?

Benny sighs darkly, like I'm being tiresome, and maybe I am, but I'm so nervous seeing him again, and of course there's my dance career hanging in the balance.

Benny waves a hand, all cool and composed.

I almost can't believe my eyes for a second. What's up with the Mr. Suave thing? Where are his abrupt, awkward movements?

The men scurry back to their table and the hostess returns to her stand.

I slide in across from Benny, trying to look serene.

"Well?" he says.

"So nice to see you, too," I say nervously. "Oh, me? I've been fine—thank you for asking!"

A waitperson sets down a bowl of tomato soup and a plate

with half of a sandwich arranged artistically on a bed of greens. "Can I get you anything?" she asks me.

"Ummm, I already ate," I say. Not that I could eat anything right now—my body is using all its energy to pound my heart like a bongo.

"Carbonated water with a lemon twist," he commands darkly, avoiding my eyes. "Berry flavored, if you have it."

I blink. "Wow, yeah, I'd love one," I say.

The waitress walks off.

"You remembered," I say.

He takes his napkin off the table and settles it into his lap.

"I guess I shouldn't be surprised, considering your famous memory," I add.

He watches me strangely. "It's a beverage."

I pick up a napkin and twist it, and then I fold it with maniacal perfection. "Well, anyway, I'm sure you're wondering why I'm here. As I said, I have just learned some very shocking news." I hold up a finger, feeling a smile break out on my face, because this really is so outrageous. "I do believe that there's one thing that you did not take a very good photograph of in your famous photographic memory." I go into my purse and slap a piece of paper down on the table between us. "And that thing would be our freaking marriage certificate." I widen my eyes. Maybe we can be allies. Allies fighting together against the craziness that is our Vegas marriage.

He gazes at the piece of paper for a long time, but he doesn't pull it to himself to read up close. He doesn't even seem curious.

"We are married!" I say. "Officially!"

I can't read his expression, but he doesn't seem pleased. I'm sure he's thinking about that night where I ruined our fragile new friendship by trying to ravish him.

I stay grinning like it's no big deal, even though deep down I want the farm-to-table booth bench to swallow me right up.

FIVE

Benny

HER HAIR IS as glossy as I remember, eyes sparkling. Attitude mischievous.

But she doesn't remember us getting married? Now that's surprising.

Not that I spend a lot of time dwelling on the past. Dwelling on the past is for losers. But at least I remember we were married.

When I woke up to find her gone that morning ten years ago, I figured the wedding was some kind of a drunken prank of hers, the ultimate practical joke. She skipped town after that without so much as a second thought, because that's Francine—people are simply an endless parade of amusements for her beautiful life, and she's the river, sparkling brightly, flowing through with effortless ease.

She doesn't even remember.

And now she thinks it's weird and funny. She's waiting, staring at me, expecting me to be surprised.

The only surprising thing is that it took her almost ten years to realize she was my wife. Though I shouldn't be surprised at that, either, being that this is Francine.

"Right?" she says again. "Can you *even*?"

"I knew," I inform her.

Her eyes widen. "Excuse me? Be serious, Benny. We are *literally married.*"

"Yes," I say.

"Literally," she repeats.

Francine always misused the word literally. *My eyes literally bugged out of my skull! I literally lost my mind!* For once, she's using it as intended.

"Literally," I confirm.

She narrows her eyes, pretty features taut with pretend suspicion, pillowy lips puckered. "Soooo...you knew all this time?" She seems stunned, as if the unusual aspect here is that I remember we're married, whereas it took her an *entire fucking decade* to discover the fact for herself.

That, too: very Francine. Nothing really matters to Francine unless it has something to do with ballet.

"All this time?" she asks, incredulous. "How is that even possible?"

"I utilized a cognitive faculty called *memory*," I tell her.

She gives me a humorous scolding look now, hands on her hips. Even seated, she's in full physical expression mode. "You're telling me you knew?"

I stare down at the paper. "You don't remember...anything?"

"Well..." She jiggles her head while making a funny face, a playful gesture she used to dramatize the concept of "umm-mmmm wuuuuut?" which happened to be a favorite phrase of hers. It was Francine's expert way of making light of an awkward situation, or getting out of a difficult question. And people would gladly let her off, because she's beautiful and fun.

"You remember nothing of it?" I ask again.

"Bits and pieces," she says, looking down. "And I remember waking up at your place. You were on the couch. I remember it was a bit of a drunken night. And let's say I haven't touched tequila since. Benny, I just need to say—I'm so sorry—"

"Don't," I say. "Nobody cares. It was nearly ten years ago."

"Well, Social Security cares. Only Vegas, where you can get a marriage license out of a gumball machine, right?"

A gumball machine marriage. The naive kid I was back then would've been crushed to hear such a thing. The man I am today doesn't give a shit.

I pick up my spoon and draw it through my soup.

"So you've just been going with it?" she finally asks when I don't bother to chime in.

"Why not?" I say coolly. "Our marriage has been extremely convenient. You're an excellent tax break."

She swallows, rolling the corner of her napkin. Francine was always excruciatingly easy to read, but even if I couldn't read her, the state of her napkins always gave her away. She's nervous now. If this particular napkin weren't made of cloth, she'd have ripped it to little shreds.

There was a time when I hated that I made her nervous—hated that I made people nervous in general. I didn't know how to put people at their ease. I didn't understand back then that I didn't have to care about those things. I didn't understand that this very thing that I hated about myself could be a strength.

"Well...I had no idea, personally," she says. "But I know now. And here's the thing—I really, really need us to *not* be married." She looks up at me, searching my eyes, back and forth. "I need an affidavit of single civil status as soon as humanly possible. If you would be so kind."

I set my spoon on its napkin, lining it up precisely with my knife. "An affidavit of single civil status," I say.

"Exactly." She produces another piece of paper and sets it on the table next to the license. It looks like the type of divorce decree you'd download from the internet. "The affidavit I need requires a divorce. This is a simple one—no strings, no fault. I mean, it's not as if we're actually married, right?"

A divorce, then. This is her quest. This is why she's come.

Then again, why else?

The waitperson sets down her drink.

"Thank you," Francine says brightly. She swishes the peel. "My dance company leaves on an international tour in January and it's the chance of a lifetime. If I don't have an affidavit of civil status that shows me as single, I'll look like the liar of the year on a bunch of my visa applications."

Here she lowers her voice, fixing me with a serious gaze. "Apparently I signed a lot of documents saying that I'm single when I'm not, and it turns out that embassies get *tres* uptight about that kind of thing these days. Due to terrorism and all." She stirs her drink. "Thanks a lot, terrorists. Like, that was the hobby you had to choose? It couldn't have been macrame? The sketching of fruit bowls? Woodworking? You went with terrorism?"

She looks up with a humorous little smile that I don't bother to return. I'm not exactly known for my sense of humor. I'm good with that.

"So that's how you found out," I observe coolly.

"Yup." She looks back down at her glass, stirring with the spoon, now, clinking it softly against the sides. "Okay, I know what you're thinking, Benny."

There's zero chance of that, but I play along. "What am I thinking?"

"You're thinking, what a tragic ending. I mean, great as it was, right? Our amazing honeymoon to the Bermuda triangle. Monique and Igor will be crushed, naturally. I think it would be best if we don't tell them, don't you? It's best that they continue to practice their acrobatics and juggling, don't you agree? If they ever have a hope of getting into the French circus, they'll need to keep up on their skills. And you know Igor, what with his tragic issues."

Igor and Monique. Of course she'd use them. There was a time when invoking Igor and Monique would have affected me deeply.

That time is past.

She slides the divorce decree closer. I stare down at it.

An international tour was a dream of hers. Back in the Beau Cirque days, she'd tell anyone who would listen. She had visions of a grand dance recital performed against the backdrop of Mérida's Roman Theatre in Spain. Maybe that's where they're going.

"If you could just sign there," she adds. "I researched it online, and if you don't have kids together or property together, it's just this form filed and done, and then a judge has to sign off. Really simple and straightforward. It keeps the status quo. Aside from, you know, us as a married couple, which, well, clearly we're not."

Again she points at the line where I'm to sign, or more of a fluid flourish, because even in this she's graceful. A dancer right down to the bone. I used to marvel at the way she moved through the world, so graceful and confident.

"You would sign right here."

A line for the signature. A line for the date. And with that our marriage will be over.

Even as a naïve kid, it's not as if I thought it was the solemn and hallowed affair that other weddings are. Tequila, a wild idea about Igor and Monique needing a stable family. Singing. Running through the streets, laughing like bandits. I saw it as special, somehow. Singular. Like us.

"Just ye old *John Hancock,*" she says, trying for humor.

It comes to me here that I simply don't want to. And why should I? People have been speculating about my mysterious wife. Why not give them a look at her? I'm the last person to give a shit about my own press, but it is convenient that she's turned up.

"Right here," she says again.

What if I keep her around a bit? Make her put in a cameo or two?

I breathe in her familiar scent—it's a type of jasmine called Sampaguita, the national flower of the Philippines. She traveled there once with her family to meet distant relatives. The trip had a profound impact on her, judging from how often she talked about it at Beau Cirque. She's worn the scent ever since.

The more I think about it, the better I like the idea.

I read a lot of business books back when James and I were building TezraTech. One of the themes that struck me was that most successful business leaders have the ability to make decisions quickly and firmly. It's a lesson I embraced.

Making big, bold decisions has worked for me over the years. Sometimes I don't know why I'm deciding a thing, I simply decide it and go with it, moving forward with unstoppable force—no deliberating, no second-guessing.

In other words, I go with my gut.

I've found that a gut call is usually a correct call. Your gut knows things before your brain does. It's just how humans work.

Whenever people question me on my gut decisions—decisions that I may not have a rationale for yet—I simply inform them that I don't require a rationale. In fact, the best response to somebody questioning a gut call of mine that I can't quite yet articulate is a big fuck you, though maybe not in those words.

"Just right here," she says again.

"I see where I'm supposed to sign," I tell her. "But I'm not going to."

She stiffens. "Right, of course. You would never sign anything without a lawyer reading it. What am I even thinking?" She tries for a smile. "Though it's super time sensitive, that's the thing here. But if you need a lawyer to look at it, I understand," she continues. "But if you could be quick, it would mean a lot. If I don't get my shit together on this like yesterday, I won't get to go on tour."

She gazes at me, waiting.

"A lack of legal advice is not why I won't be signing your paper," I say.

She frowns. "Well...what's the problem?"

"There's no problem," I say coolly. "I'm not planning on signing it, that's all." I sit back.

"Why not? Why wouldn't you..."

"Why *would* I?" I ask her. "Give me one good reason to give away something of mine for nothing."

"Wait, what?" She sits up. Blinks. "Give away something of *mine?* Did you literally just say that?"

This is a rhetorical question that I don't bother to answer.

"Are you trying to be funny?" she asks.

"Do I seem like I'm being funny?"

Her dark brows draw together and she cocks her head at a new angle. She's beginning to see that I'm in the driver's seat now.

"Give away something of *mine,* though? I mean...*mine*?" Here she pauses. "*Something of mine, Benny*? So I'm something of yours?" She's waiting for me to hear how ridiculous it is.

Newsflash: That won't be happening.

"Mine!" she echoes again, as if that's the part I'm not comprehending. When in fact, it's the part of this that I like the best now. "Be serious, Benny. On what planet..."

"This planet." I tap my finger on the copy of the certificate. "The planet of this document. I take my contracts very seriously."

She snorts. "Come on, Benny!"

I sit back in the deeply cushioned bench. Now who's amused? I am. "Ask me, Francine," I say to her. "Look at me and you ask me, whose wife am I?"

She regards me with a look of shock.

I wait.

"Dude," she says. "*Dude.*" Maybe she's getting the picture that she's not dealing with that awkward, smitten nerd anymore. True, I had a lot of feelings about her complete radio silence that first year after we married.

And then I moved on.

I forgot about it.

I put her and the whole thing behind me.

"Go on. Ask," I say. "Whose wife am I, Benny?"

"Did you get a concussion or something?"

I shift my posture, sitting to one side, play-acting her asking me. "Whose wife am I, Benny?"

Her lips part. She can't believe what she's seeing.

I shift to the other side, as if to answer myself, but here I gaze right at her. "Mine," I say.

She raises her eyebrows, eyes wide under dark lashes.

It's rare that anything but ballet captures Francine's full attention, but I have it now—I should know; the study I made of Francine is more exhaustive than the study I made of robotics, and I made my fortune in robotics.

I tilt my head, give her an ice-cold smile, a negotiating technique hammered out over the years. "Mine," I say again. "That's whose."

"Dude, the 1800s called," she says. "They want their sad freaking mentality back!"

I pick up an imaginary phone. "Hello?" I say. "Why, yes, this is Benjamin Stearnes. What's that you want back, 1800s?" I shift my gaze to her. "No, I'm sorry. You can't have it back." I shrug. "Why? Eh. I suppose keeping it suits me. Yes, thank you. Good day to you, too, sir." I hang up the pretend phone.

She's gaping at me. "You're not even funny right now."

I pantomime picking the phone back up. "Oh, and by the way—consider investing in steam locomotives. Just a quick tip!" I put the phone back down again.

"Why are you being like this? It's a piece of paper. Why would you even care? Why would you even want to be married to me?"

"Why would I want to be divorced from you when you've been the perfect wife?" I ask.

"Be serious, Benny," she says.

"I am being serious. You've been an amazing tax break. You make no demands. You're a handy keep-out sign to the legions of gold diggers out there."

She stiffens, and then she smiles. She's laughing. "Omigod, Benny!" she says. "You are the most hilarious. Were you like, ready with this whole spiel the whole time? Lying in wait for the day I realized we were married? Planning this?"

She's grinning, still hoping that this is all a joke. If there's one thing that Francine has always possessed a great deal of, it's wishful thinking. As a stunningly beautiful woman, she could misjudge reality in her delightfully hopeful way and people would scurry to rearrange things to keep that delight going.

"Dude," she continues. "Come on."

"I'm not in the habit of signing away things of mine for nothing," I inform her.

"But aren't you glad that I only want you to sign this paper? Some women would try to get money from you."

"Some women would try, it's true. And my lawyer would rip them apart like a lion would rip apart a feather pillow."

Her pretty lips part.

There was a time when I would have given Francine the world. It would have never crossed my mind to say "no" to her, to deny her anything. That time is gone.

I find, in fact, that there's a certain pleasure to saying "no" to her.

More than pleasure; it's a stone-cold rush crackling through my veins.

"You can't just make me be married to you," she says.

"Actually, I can," I say. "Isn't it awesome?"

"*Why* are you being like this?" she asks. "I need this."

I taste my soup. It's more delicious than usual. Rich with tomato and pungent basil, just the perfect amount of salt. I crumble in a thick artisanal cracker.

When I look back up, her rosy lips are again parted, this time in not-so-friendly surprise. "Benny," she cajoles. "I'm sure you can find another...*tax break,*" she continues. "Another shield from the gold-digging hordes of females."

"Why should I get a different wife when I already have *you*?" I wipe the crumbs from my fingers, movements smooth and slow. "Weddings are a bore. I'm so glad we eloped, aren't you?"

"Benny, please," she says. "If I don't get a judge to sign off on this thing in thirty days or less, I won't get the affidavit or my travel papers, and I'll be kicked off the most important dance tour of my life! There's never going to be an opportunity like this again for me. I'm thirty-one now. Dancers start retiring at my age and..." She looks down, not finishing her sentence. She wouldn't have lined up anything else. Francine goes for broke.

"Travel papers in thirty days," I say. "Piece of cake. But you'll have to do a few things for me."

Francine looks up at me, shocked. "Excuse me?"

"I'll do this thing for you. I'll use my connections to get a judge to sign off on divorce and travel documents, but you're going to do some things for me first."

"What are you? The Godfather?"

I wait.

"Like what?" she asks.

"For starters, you're going to attend a few business functions with me," I hear myself decreeing. "As my wife. People haven't met you, and there's a good deal of strange and ridiculous speculation about us. It'll be good for people to meet you. Nature abhors a vacuum and all of that, including a vacuum of information. This wife of mine that nobody has ever met..."

"Strange and ridiculous speculation about us?" she asks, eyes twinkling. "I totally can't imagine, considering your sunny disposition."

"I'm looking for a yes or no answer here; not a character assessment."

She tilts her head, studies me some more. "You want me to pose as your wife," she says.

"You *are* my wife," I say. "Now you'll start acting like it—in public, at any rate; I don't care what you do in private."

She's shaking her head in disbelief.

"It's not a difficult assignment."

"And if I don't?"

"Then you don't get your visa papers," I say. "This is a simple *quid pro quo*."

She stiffens. "This attitude of yours? Not loving it!"

"But you're gonna pretend to love it, aren't you?" I say. "You're going to pretend to love my attitude and everything else about me. You will pretend to love me to utter distraction if you want to go on your tour. Play my charming wife for three weeks, convince people we're married, and my people will get you any documents you require."

"Your people," she echoes. "Because you have people now."

"I have people," I say.

"Are you sure that's not cutting it close?" she asks. "The guy at the clerk's office said it can take thirty to ninety days to get a judge on board."

"I could get it for you tomorrow if I wanted," I say.

"But you prefer to jerk me around," she says.

"I told you what I want." I push the paper back across to her.

"Why, Benny?"

"Leave your address with my guys on the way out. My car will pick you up at seven tomorrow night. Wear something nice." And then, just because I know how she can be, I add, "Not a T-shirt. Something stylish. A stylish and pretty dress."

She looks aghast. Maybe even disgusted.

It makes no difference to me.

"Stylish and pretty," she repeats. "So now you're telling me what to wear. I play adoring wife or I can kiss my tour goodbye."

"Now you're getting it." I pick up my spoon, stir my soup with measured movements, letting the lumps of crackers get coated with the rich soup.

Moving in a smooth and measured way didn't come naturally to me. It's certainly not how I moved or interacted with the world as a youth. But people grow out of things. Sometimes people grow out of things naturally; other times it takes a great deal of effort.

I stir my soup in a smooth and measured way, savoring her deliciously white-hot glare.

SIX

Francine

LIZZIE ARRIVES with her shapeless prairie dress.

"Oh my god!" I am just laughing, imagining showing up at a fancy restaurant in that.

"It would serve that asshole right!" Mia says from where she's lying on the couch throwing M&M's up and catching them in her mouth. She misses one and it bounces across the floor.

Kelsey grabs the bag from Mia. "No more M&M's for you."

I take it and hold it up on its hanger. "I don't know. It's neither pretty nor stylish," I say.

"Somebody thought it was pretty and stylish at some point," Lizzie says.

"Did they, though?" I ask.

"The Amish, maybe," Tabitha says.

"Eye on the prize!" Noelle says, coming out with my red print wraparound. "This is what you wear. This is your prettiest and most stylish dress. It looks gorgeous with your hair."

"Why should I look good for him?" I take the hanger with the red dress.

Mia grins from the couch. "You shouldn't."

"Right? He's decided to push me around just because he can? And now I have to wear a nice dress for him? Screw that!"

"I get it. He's a jerk and it's not fair, but you need to focus on your goal," Noelle reminds me, playing the voice of reason. "You need to do what it takes to make this tour happen."

I sigh. "I know, I know..."

"But what fun is that?" Mia taunts from the couch, ever the devil's advocate.

"Maybe it's a blessing in disguise for your knee," Kelsey says. "Tell him to buzz off and divorce him on your own terms. I mean, a ten-city overseas tour with that knee..."

"Pullllease!" I point the finger of hypocrisy at Kelsey. "You'd go on the tour of your dreams with this knee in a minute."

"Doesn't make it a good idea," Kelsey says.

I sniff, though in truth, I'm sometimes terrified that I'll be busted for hiding this injury and get kicked off the tour, and everything I've worked for and dreamed about goes up in smoke. Other times I'm terrified that I'm too good at fooling them, and I don't get kicked off the tour, and my knee will blow out in Croatia or something and I'll be alone in a medical center where I don't speak the language, alone with my crumbled career.

"Does he think you're going to fall into his bed again with this whole wife pretense?" Lizzie asks. "Do you think that's his secret hope?"

"No way. Sleeping with me is the absolute furthest thing from his mind."

"Disagree," Kelsey says, tossing M&M's into her own mouth now. "Sleeping with you is on the mind of nearly every hetero man who meets you, Francine."

"And you did get married," Noelle says. "You're sure there's nothing there?"

There was something on my side, but that's not what she's asking. "He was drunk. I've seen drunk people eat fish eyes and dive into empty pools, you know? Anyway, the man I saw today is only interested in pushing me around. He was like, 'power trip? Yes, please! A chance to make Francine sing for her supper? Yes, please!'"

Lizzie folds her arms. "He wants to toy with the pretty dancer."

"Something like that," I say.

"Wife locked away in a gloomy chalet in the Swiss Alps," Mia says. "What does that say about you that people would think, yes, a mentally enfeebled wife locked away in a Swiss chalet, yeah, that seems like a thing Benjamin Stearnes would do."

"It's a step up from the attic," Noelle says hopefully.

"Hold up," Lizzie says. "Do you know Janice Schembechler? Isn't she on the first floor?"

"I think she's in 106," Kelsey says.

"Isn't she in the 'Sound of Music' weekend sing-a-long thing in the arts theater thingy by the river?" Lizzie asks.

"Are you proposing I deprogram him with mid-century musicals?" I ask as Lizzie heads out the front door without explanation.

"Noelle deprogrammed Malcolm with videos of our apartment building," Mia says.

"I think Noelle deprogrammed Malcolm with her magical pussy," I say, and Noelle promptly hits me over the head with an India print throw pillow.

I drape the prairie dress over the couch and examine the pretty red dress. "And who are these legions of gold diggers going after him? What's up with that?" I ask.

"Well, he is a handsome, rich billionaire," Kelsey says, popping another M&M into her mouth under Mia's fake glare.

"They can have him," I say. "Here's a guy who eats alone at a restaurant, and he has employees who sit nearby whose entire job is keeping people away from him? And they act all nervous when they fail him, like he's gonna lock them up in some gloomy Swiss chalet along with his enfeebled wife? And his old co-worker needs the tiniest favor, and he's all, *You will obey me now?*" I shake my head. "The gold diggers can have him."

"But you've decided to play along," Noelle says. "Because you want him to cooperate. And you'll go on your tour and it'll be so amazing."

Lizzie bursts back in, clutching a bundle of fabric. "We have to promise to have this back by Sunday but..." Here she unfurls a dress.

I press my fingertips to my lips, eyes wide. "Oh. My. God."

It's not just any dress. It's got gathered cap sleeves. A lederhosen pinafore, all very Swiss Alps meets Sound of Music meets St. Pauli Girl.

"Imagine walking into the restaurant wearing *this*!" Lizzie exclaims. "Does it look Swiss or what?"

Mia claps. "Evil!"

"No!" Noelle is laughing. "Timeout! You cannot!"

"With all these rumors about him keeping his wife locked up in a Swiss chalet?!" Mia says. "Oh my god you have to wear it!"

"Think of your tour," Noelle says. "You can't take chances."

"He said stylish and pretty," Lizzie reiterates. "Were those not his words?"

"Yes! Those were his words," I say. I'm grinning. I feel... excited. Happy. "This is definitely stylish. And it's pretty. We had an agreement, and he can't say I'm not holding up my end.

And it would teach him a lesson for pushing me around and making me play his doting wife!"

"You guys, it's not like people in Switzerland wear dresses like that," Noelle says. "People in Switzerland wear completely contemporary outfits."

"But a wife trapped in a Swiss chalet by Billionaire Bluebeard might just be forced to wear such a thing," Mia says.

"I can't imagine people really believe that rumor," I say.

"People believed that Richard Gere put gerbils up his butt," Mia says. "People love to believe weird things. They probably think it's some kind of a fetish. Maybe Benny was deeply affected by a bottle of Swiss Miss hot chocolate as a child. With that cartoon Swiss girl. It happens."

I take the dress from Lizzie and hold it up to myself. "I really shouldn't," I say. "I really, *really* shouldn't! But if I did, I'd need to walk into the restaurant with something over it, like a coat or a wrap so that I could pull it off for a big reveal. Because Benny would never just take me into a restaurant wearing this."

"Brilliant!" Mia says.

"It's pretty. It's stylish. And best of all, it'll make him sorry," Lizzie says. "I'd say that's a pretty good dress."

"Fuck with the bull, you get the horns," Mia says. "And if you make Francine be your fake wife, you will get some free-spirit fun in your face."

"Is it just me or does that just sound the slightest bit dirty?" I ask.

"He's not gonna like this," Noelle warns. "This is not what Benny had in mind, and you know it. Maybe this is not the right time for fun."

I hold up both dresses, heart pounding like mad. I should be angry and upset about this whole thing, but I imagine his sullen gaze, and something lifts in me.

And weirdly, for the first time in months, I'm not horribly stressed out about my knee.

I WAIT under the canopy outside our building.

A night out is the last thing I need after a grueling day of classes and rehearsals; my usual nighttime routine is sewing pointe shoes while soaking my feet in ice, followed by a salad and then toe and ankle exercises.

But then Benny's sleek gray limo slides up in front of the building and I'm just grinning.

A limo. How perfect! Because who can forget his snarky comments about the limo guys I used to date in Vegas?

Not me!

I'm wearing one of my favorite spring coats, a bright red number with black embroidery along the collar and around the buttons. It has a black belt, and I love it to death. And it perfectly covers the Sound of Music/St. Pauli Girl dress.

I tighten the belt, feeling excited and just a tiny bit nervous as Benny's driver comes around to the back and pulls open the door.

Benny's in there. The half of him that's facing me is so deeply shrouded in shadows, I can barely see his expression. His profile and the outer edges of his white collar are outlined in a pale glow by the streetlights behind him, along with a sprinkling of dirty-blonde whiskers on his cheeks.

I slide in next to him and the door closes behind me, shutting us up together, me and the shadow side of Benny. Though, he's all shadow side, apparently. A nerd in wolf's clothing. But more—the wolf has totally taken over the antisocial nerd, chewed it to pieces.

Still, I can't quite hide my grin. Benny in a limo. Oh, how the mighty have fallen!

"What's so funny?" he demands as it lurches out into the honking cacophony of traffic.

"A limo is funny," I say.

He stares down at his phone with a *harumph.*

"I seem to recall a certain somebody calling it a low-self-esteem mobile," I tease.

"I seem to recall a certain somebody who enjoyed the billionaire trappings at one point," he says.

"Well, like you say, people change," I tell him. "I'm just not that into billionaires these days."

"You're not?" he asks.

"They just don't work for me," I say.

He doesn't reply, just scrolls darkly.

"And here you are, riding in the hated limo. How'd that happen?"

"It happened because only imbeciles continue to operate on information that's ten years old. As it turns out, when you're a business owner like I am, a limo is a tool that aids in client management, client acquisition, and a host of other functions."

I'm still smiling. There's no way I'm letting him slip out of this. "Do you ever wonder if people watching you drive by are just scowling at you?"

"As a matter of fact, that's how I measure this limo's mileage. Scowls per gallon," he says coolly, barely bothering to look up. "This one gets five scowls per gallon. I'm hoping to upgrade to seven in the near future."

I suck in a breath. He was sullen and antisocial before, yes, but he's added a snarly dimension to his personality.

I study him discreetly, wondering about that night together. What possessed us to get married? Aside from my shameful behavior, I remember vague flashes of scenes. Us talking excitedly in some dark cavern of a bar. Feeling excited out on the strip.

I want to ask him, but I'm a little afraid to.

Did I confess something embarrassing to him? Like my fascination with him and his gangly hands and gorgeous lips? Or other inappropriate things I would sometimes think about him after he made it clear he was off-limits?

"What?" he grumbles, feeling my attention upon him.

"So...is this the first time you've met these people?" I ask, like that's my big concern.

He grunts something that is clearly a yes in the direction of his phone.

I swallow. Maybe I'm just part of the furniture to Wolf Benny. Maybe I'm just another tool in client management—limo, contract, annual holiday gift, wife.

I sit back and fold my arms, feeling even happier about my dress.

If the back of his limo is like a small living room, we're sitting together on the main couch. There's a pull-down tray between us that currently holds a crystal tumbler of what is probably horrendously expensive scotch or whiskey.

Across from us is a smaller seating area, and right in the middle of the two seating areas is a console that is like a small coffee table, except it has a screen set into it.

According to the screen, Pandora is running the current musical selection—something soft and ballad-y—Radiohead, if I'm not mistaken. I remember him liking alt rock of that era. All except Dave Matthews Band. I smile at the memory of him leaping across Beau Cirque set pieces to get rid of a Dave Matthews Band song during lighting blocking. As head of AV, he exerted fanatical control over the music as well as the lights. And he so hated Dave Matthews Band. I never understood why. I always liked them.

"What's so funny?" he asks.

"Nothing," I say.

He gives me a look. "Don't screw this up."

I give him a pouty little frown. "I'm not the one conscripting a fake wife for a business dinner."

"Real wife." He goes back to his phone. "My actual wife."

I snort. "A little hard to forget."

He gestures at the small door that forms the base of the fancy limo coffee table. "Beverages. Help yourself. It'll be a while."

I pull on the discreet handle and it turns out to be a luxurious mini fridge, complete with lots of snacks and beverages, including, much to my delight, a couple of mini cans of zero-sugar black cherry carbonated water and chilled glasses. "Don't mind if I do," I say. "Don't mind if I do at all."

I never drink sugary stuff when in rehearsal mode. When you're doing seven-hour days of dancing—ten if there's a performance—you have to manage your energy.

When I'm done pouring, I toss the can into a discreet compartment with a recycling logo. This place is like a cockpit, except way more high tech, and definitely more luxurious, and it smells woodsy and spicy like him, not that I'm keeping track.

"So who are these personages that we're going to be dining with?" I ask.

"It's the president, vice president, and a few of the operating officers from a company called Arcana Protech," he says, not bothering to pull his gaze from his phone.

"Never heard of it."

"It's an international conglomerate based in Rio de Janeiro, with offices in Dallas," he says to his phone. "They're all about industrial engineering. The Texans we meet tonight may act like they are in charge, but it's actually one of the Brazilians who makes the decisions. A woman named Juliana."

"And Juliana wants to buy your company, which makes little machine-cleaning microrobot thingies."

"Somebody's been doing her homework," he mumbles, scrolling onward.

"A girl likes to know who she's married to," I say. "So when the robot takeover happens and artificial intelligence exterminates all of the humans, will your microrobots be like tiny little Renfields? Obediently shuffling after our overlords while catching and eating flies?"

"Machines create human leisure," he says. "We humans are the overlords of technology."

"Somebody needs to re-watch the Terminator franchise," I say.

He simply grunts.

"Is there anything else I should know? Don't you think it would be customary for me to be up on this stuff?"

"You don't bother yourself about the business. You're deeply infatuated with me. That's what our marriage is based on."

"Deeply infatuated," I tease.

"Deeply." He looks up at me now. His face is in shadows, but his eyes are burning out at me. In a rumbly voice he says, "You can't get enough of me. Something just comes over you whenever I walk into the room. Though I have to say, a man has his limits, Francine."

I snort. "Omigod. Can't even."

He doesn't smile, of course, but I can feel the jerky pleasure radiating off him in waves.

"We met in Vegas doing Beau Cirque, of course," he says. "We're both extremely private, and very independent in our pursuits, not always on the same coast. Best to stick close to the truth."

"Right, of course, this all really sounds like we're sticking with the truth."

The car slows. Benny glances at the console thing—the picture on the console changes from the Pandora display to a map and an address.

"Are we there?" I ask.

"Picking somebody up," Benny says. "Aaron. He works with me."

I nod, thinking about the Wikipedia article on him. Benny founded his company with his friend, James, and the two of them brought on this lawyer, Aaron. Benny figured out the inventions, James figured out the whole business side of it, and Aaron did the legal stuff. James was hit by a car a few months back on Thanksgiving weekend—he was on his bike. It was a hit and run—they never caught the guy. Now it's just Benny and Aaron.

I can hear the driver getting out up front. I suppose everybody who rides in this car needs the door opened for them.

Does Benny miss James? Were they friends or was it just a co-worker thing? Benny is such a loner, I can't imagine him being really close friends with anybody, but he's so different now. I want to ask him, but he doesn't seem to want to communicate whatsoever with me.

The door opens and a stout man with a thick pelt of brown hair, a thick little mustache, and wire-rimmed glasses slides into the seat across from us.

"Aaron. Francine," Benny says, because he can't be bothered to do a proper introduction. His phone pings and he's back tapping and scrolling.

Aaron eyes me in a way I don't love, and his smile isn't exactly friendly, either. In fact it's not hard to imagine that disdainful little mouth ripping apart a feather pillow. Lizzie told me that Aaron has a reputation for playing hardball.

He turns to Benny. "Perfect play. Trotting out the wife."

Benny grunts, eyes still glued to his phone.

"Perfect timing, too," Aaron continues.

"And a dream come true for me," I say breezily, though in truth, I'm a bit apprehensive about the dress thing now.

Aaron fixes me with a hard gaze. "She gonna play nice?"

"She'll play nice," Benny assures him, thumbs flying over his phone.

I give Aaron a sassy smile.

Aaron addresses me directly while simultaneously speaking to me in the third person and possibly even threatening me. "She'd better play nice," he says. "This is an important deal."

"I can't imagine why she wouldn't play nice," I say, also referring to myself in the third person. "I mean, being threatened with the loss of something I've worked my whole life to attain?"

As soon as I say it, I regret it. I can see the gears turning behind his eyes and I don't like it. You never show people like Aaron what's important to you.

I go for a smile. "Who could resist?"

"Don't worry, she can charm people when she wants," Benny grumbles.

"She certainly can..." I turn to Aaron now, all sassy, and add, "When she *wants*."

Aaron frowns.

Benny finally looks up. "And she wants."

"Oh, I'll charm the stuffing out of them—don't you worry about that," I assure them. "Considering I have no choice."

"All you gotta do," Benny says, going back to the phone.

"So they want to buy your company, and this dinner is to talk about that?" I ask.

Benny says, "We're not really sure what their agenda is. They've requested a social dinner. It's likely that Juliana, our decision maker, just needs to meet me face to face, or maybe somebody else from the team wants to green-light who they'll be dealing with."

"Why would it matter?" I ask. "If she and her group think your tiny-robot-making company is worth buying, why do they need to meet you?"

"Because they want me to stay on for a year, overseeing the team that adapts my tech to different industrial environments," he says, ever so bored and annoyed with me.

"Hold the phone. You'd stay on and work for them?" I ask. "As an employee?"

"Yup," he says.

"For a *year*," I clarify, trying not to laugh.

"What's so funny?" he asks, like he's so weary of me already.

His whole freaking attitude is giving me a complex, but I soldier on. "You," I say. "You're funny in the way that you're not using your cognitive faculty of memory."

"Meaning what?" he asks.

"Meaning you hate working for other people. You thought the Beau Cirque bosses were idiots."

"They *were* idiots," Benny says.

"You think that about everyone—you know you do, Benny! Everybody in Beau Cirque knew it, too. You were practically unemployable at the age of twenty-two. And now you've made a bazillion dollars and your big prize is...drumroll...working for other people, a thing you absolutely hate!"

Benny frowns at his phone. Is he even listening?

"He won't hate working with the Protech team," Aaron says.

"And you've witnessed him being an employee when?" I ask.

Aaron gives me a dark look. "And you got your business degree where?"

Benny is finally looking up from his phone. "That's enough," he says.

"I know what I know," I inform Aaron, getting in the last word. I turn back to Benny and his whole U-Can't-Touch-This forcefield. "And, dude, you were literally apoplectic every time they gave you an order, but I'm sure you've completely mellowed now. I'm sure you have a way better disposition. So much sunnier," I say.

Benny's focusing on me now. He has this ability to hyper focus with his full attention to the exclusion of the whole world. It was one of the things that made people think he was rude, but I got it. I knew what it was to focus like a demon—it's how you get good at things. Needless to say, it was something about him that I secretly loved. I sometimes wondered what it would be like to have that intensity turned on me.

"You sell your company, and your big prize is that you get bosses, something you hate. What could go wrong?"

"You almost done?" he asks.

"Oh, right, I forgot. We're not supposed to go by what was true ten years ago. My bad," I say.

The way he's watching me, it's absolutely unnerving. I focus right back at him; I will not be cowed. We're focusing weirdly on each other, now, like Clash of the Hyper-focusing Titans. It probably shouldn't feel as hot as it does.

It's hot to me, anyway. I doubt it's hot for him.

"In the world of business," Aaron begins from the other side of me, employing the most infantilizing tone possible, "a business owner staying on during a transitional period is part of how a sale like this gets done."

Benny and I are still in our gaze-lock, but now I smile prettily. "It was unbelievably entertaining to watch you get bossed around," I say. "It was physically excruciating to you, but entertaining to others."

"A company isn't like a car where you just hand over the keys," Benny says, pulling out his newly minted measured cool-guy tone. "My presence in the company ensures that it retains its value through the transfer."

"Good luck with that," I say.

"I don't need you to be on board with this sale," he says. "I just need you to go eat dinner and be charming."

"Oh, don't worry, I'll be charming."

"You'd better be," Aaron chimes in annoyingly.

I'm just watching Benny. I forgot about his honey-colored eyes, how mesmerizingly saturated with light brown they are.

The limo stops yet again. The driver gets out.

"Are we there?"

"Aaron and I have to go up and sign something," Benny says. "We'll be back in ten minutes."

"And what? I just sit here like a rutabaga?"

"Think you can handle that?" he asks.

I try to think of a good retort, like something about rutabagas being awesome, or at least I'm not a banana, but before I can come up with anything, the doors are shutting, and I'm alone, aside from the driver up front on the other side of the privacy panel. He comes on the intercom and asks me if I need anything.

"I'm fine, thanks!" I say. Because I'm not a jerk like Benny.

I finish my fizzy water, then I pull out my phone and do a selfie where I'm making a jaded face at my limo environment. I send it to my girl gang.

And I sit back and wait.

A new song comes on Benny's Pandora mix. Something by Blur.

I slide up and check his Pandora. We're listening to a mix that Benny created called Radiohead radio. I got a lot of my pop music education that summer in Vegas. I especially got an education in Benny's specific tastes via the playlists he'd play before and after rehearsals and performances from his seat of power as head of lights and audio.

The way Pandora works is that you pick a few songs and bands you like, and Pandora creates a station with a heaping helping of that exact music plus other songs it thinks you'd like, and you thumbs-up or thumbs-down those songs, allowing Pandora to become smarter about what songs to play.

I click into the station history, and all the usual ones he always liked are there, largely unchanged from ten years ago.

It's here I get my brilliant idea: I add a few of his hated Dave Matthews songs as "seeds."

Surely he still hates Dave Matthews Band! I switch the view display back to the normal screen and wait. Sure enough, a Dave Matthews song comes on. Benny would have a fit!

This probably shouldn't make me as happy as it does.

I give it the ol' thumbs-up and sit back. Two songs later it plays yet another Dave Matthews Band song. I enthusiastically thumbs-up that one, too. More of this, please! That's what my thumbs-up says.

Rutabaga for the win, bitches!

Eventually, Benny and Aaron are back. The limo takes off again.

I wait excitedly, hoping Dave Matthews will come back on.

No such luck.

Never mind. Good things come to those who wait.

The rest of the ride is completed in phone-scrolling silence.

Twenty minutes and two loud-honking Saturday night traffic snarls later, the three of us are walking into a lovely and very chic restaurant done in an elegant style, all white finishings and silver crystal and potted palms. Beautiful people crowd into the bar area and linger over candlelit tables across in the dining room.

"Ah, there's our party," Benny says nonchalantly, gazing across the place.

I look at him, surprised. This sophisticated new Benny is really throwing me for a loop. Is it a natural thing that he grew into? Or is it something he has to concentrate on really hard? I suppose it's nice for him in business and things, but I miss my old awkward Benny.

Somebody offers to take our coats. I keep mine. "Just in case I'm chilly," I squeak.

"Are you ready to behave?" Benny asks me. "I'm expecting some convincing adoration. An altogether adoring wife."

"Well, we know people are always at their most adoring when under duress," I say.

He smiles. "That's one of the things duress is good for—promoting adoration," he informs me. "It's one of my favorite uses of duress, in fact."

"Ugh," I say.

"Is that a yes?" He's clearly enjoying bossing me around. It's like I'm in a real-life drama of "Revenge of the Nerds." Or more like, "Revenge of the Sullen and Antisocial Nerd From Your Past, Whom you Drunkenly Married."

"Waiting," he says.

"I think you should've given me that divorce when I asked for it," I say casually.

His eyes twinkle. "And miss all this fun?"

"You make a good point," I say, trying not to grin like a madwoman.

Benny narrows his eyes, suspicious at my agreement. Erp!

"Bringing the wife to dinner. Stroke of brilliance," Aaron says, trying to echo Benny's debonair tone, but it just turns out asshole-ly, because that's Aaron.

Benny still has that suspicious look. "You *are* planning on behaving..."

"I wouldn't dream of disobeying any one of your orders!" I say.

"Good girl," Aaron says.

The host arrives and we're led to a large corner table. Two women and three men stand as we approach, watching me with friendly curiosity. There are greetings all around and everybody agrees that it's great to finally meet face to face instead of Zoom.

Benny turns to me, gazing into my eyes with a look of superiority tailor-made to irk me. "My adoring wife, Francine."

Oh the fun he's having.

Aaron looks on confidently.

"Hi, everyone!" I say, trying to act natural. "So great to meet you!" I give smug Benny my most adoring smile—I really pour it on. "I've been so excited about this dinner for so long. I don't get out much. Barely at all, in fact."

Benny cocks his head, maybe wondering why I would say such a thing.

Heart racing a million miles an hour, I start to undo the buttons of my coat, slowly revealing my dress. I smile innocently at him as I pull my coat off, baring the gathered sleeves, the embroidered apron, the full Swiss Miss madness.

Benny's expression has shifted from smug pleasure to something far more delightful—let's call it energetic surprise.

I was worried, but now...worth it!

Innocent as can be, I look around the table at the baffled glances of the Arcana Protech people, who have clearly heard the rumors about me being locked in a Swiss chalet.

"Uh...cute dress," Juliana's pink-lipstick-wearing Texan colleague says. Other people startled. One of the guys is a deer in headlights.

"Thank you! It's one of Benny's favorites. Pretty and stylish, he always says." I drape my coat on the back of the chair. "This is really fun already. Seeing new people and all! It's such a rare treat for me!" I sit and take a menu from the waiter. "Thank you," I say brightly.

I turn to Aaron, who's seated next to me and looks like he's about to lose his mind. "This place looks amazing," I say. "Did you pick it, Aaron?"

"No," he says, managing to pack an astounding amount of growl into that single syllable.

I ask the leader of the small group, Juliana, if it's her first time in New York City. It's not, and we strike up a wee conversation about the different airports. For the record, I am being totally charming, as promised.

I can feel Benny's gaze on me. I'm almost glad I came, now. I turn to him and smile. Our eyes meet. My pulse races.

His gaze lowers to the bodice of my dress, which plumps up my breasts in a super sassy and sexy way. When he looks back up, he's still all cool and hard on the outside, but I know he thinks it's hot. He can't hide it from me.

And I think it's hot that he thinks it's hot.

"What is it, honey?" I ask innocently.

He gives me a heated look, his face hard planes. The way he's looking at me, it's like a very sexy arrow that goes right into me, right down to my curling toes.

My gaze drops to the side of his neck where his pulse pounds away. That place seems so unbearably alive; it's the wild, beating heart of him, his highly annoyed molten center, and I have this crazy impulse to brush my fingertips down along his throat, right there, just to touch him, to breach the foreboding force field of Benny.

Would I be able to feel his pounding pulse? Would his skin feel hot? Or cool and smooth like his new personality?

It's right here that I realize I *can* touch him. I'm his charming wife now, aren't I? This is what he requested, is it not? Me to play his charming wife?

"Oh, Benny," I say. Tentatively I reach up—I want so badly to touch him, skin to skin, to maybe slide my thumb over his mind-bendingly masculine lips, so thick and expressive, but I chicken out and straighten his collar instead, movements light and unsure.

His chest rises minutely, as if with a sudden intake of breath.

"My Benny," I say, and then, as if my fingers have a mind of their own, they graze his neck, right over his thrumming pulse point, a slide of skin on skin, alive like fire.

My heart skips a beat. The floor seems to tilt.

His gaze is stony. Does he not like me touching him? Because I love it. I'm shocked at how much I love it. Touching him is strangely addictive. His skin is kind of...wonderful. Beckoning.

I pretend to rub something off of his jaw with my thumb. His eyes flare minutely.

I need to stop this madness—I really do. I'm literally helping myself to his face and neck.

I settle my fingers back on his neck, smiling at him like I'm so thrilled with life. I can feel his pulse, strong and hot as a war drum, this hard-pounding center of him. The pale brown crackles in his irises seem to glow.

Heat seems to rise between us.

Before I can even think what I'm doing, I brush the pad of my thumb over his bottom lip. It's soft as I ever imagined—rosy and soft but strangely commanding.

Benny, I chant in my mind. *Benny, Benny, Benny.*

What is happening? What am I even doing?

"There," I say, as if there was some kind of purpose to this whole melodrama. Like he had a crumb there or something.

Quickly I remove my hands from his person.

SEVEN

Benny

SHE TOUCHES MY THROAT, fingertips like wicked butterflies, gazing at me the way that only she can.

The bright intensity of her radiates through my core.

I suck in a steadying breath. *Calm. Cool. Collected.* I say the words. I count backwards in my mind from 237, a technique that usually keeps me steady.

It doesn't work. She looks unbelievable. Her breasts look unbelievable. Her lips. Fucking unbelievable.

I focus on a color in the room. I imagine my arms heavy and warm. I have a whole arsenal of techniques to stay smooth and controlled, to keep the awkward, frenetic nerd at bay. He's a relic of the past.

She's worn the worst possible thing she could wear. Clearly she's heard the rumors. It's clever, I'll give her that. Devil-may-care Francine, dancing across the stage like a firebird, setting the very scenery ablaze. She's hot as hell in the dress. And she's touching me. And I'm hard as concrete.

She removes her hands.

I pull my gaze away and glance over her shoulder. Aaron's gaze is hard; he looks like he's having a coronary event. I don't blame him. Francine's actively jeopardizing a deal worth hundreds of millions of dollars with her bullshittery.

I fix her with a glare. Sleek braids twist around her head. She always wore elegant ballet hairdos; this one is more complex than usual. She looks gorgeous, yes, but if she thinks I'm still that kid from Vegas, she's in for a rude awakening. That kid is dead and buried with a stake through his heart.

Gary, one of the Texans, is expounding upon the subject of taxis versus Ubers and Lyfts, and everybody is chiming in. The center of gravity of the table is elsewhere, being that everybody has an opinion, but it could be that they're just seeking escape from the awkward and downright bizarre situation of Francine playing the part of my captive Swiss wife. And perhaps my inconvenient and entirely momentary enchantment with her as well.

I lower my voice. "You think you're funny?"

"Very," she whispers.

"Do you think that this puts me in the mood to help my wife with her problems?" I growl.

"I think your wife is wearing something pretty and stylish, just like you asked," she breathes, leaning close. "That was our agreement, and I take my contracts seriously."

She pouts theatrically, like she just got a new and distressing idea, and draws even closer. "Do you suddenly not like having a wife? I could see where having a wife isn't all it's cracked up to be in certain situations. You just never know what will happen. You can never tell what she'll do."

"Is that a threat?" I ask.

"More like frenemy...ish...ly advice," she says. "As to what might be best."

I can't believe the way she's pushing back. It's been years since anybody has thought to push back against me, particularly when I hold all the cards. "Best for whom?"

"Best for you," she says.

I breathe in her jasmine scent and whisper, "This is not a game you want to play with me."

Something dangerous gleams in her eyes. She turns to the waiter. "Do you serve cheese fondue here, by any chance? I don't get out much, and that's the food that I'm accustomed to eating. Swiss cheese, ideally."

Our dining companions go still.

I gaze at her, stunned, as the waiter assures her that they do not serve cheese fondue.

"There's no fondue!" She turns to me. "You said there would be fondue, honey."

Behind her, Aaron's looking stressed, blinking too much, or maybe he's squeezing out Morse code messages like a desperate hostage.

And I can't help it—I just start laughing.

Suddenly Juliana's laughing. "Swiss cheese fondue! I get it! Oh my goodness," she exclaims. "Priceless! You two had me going!"

Her colleague Juan says something in Portuguese. She replies, also in Portuguese and Juan claps, saying something that I'm thinking is Portuguese swear words. He turns to the Texans. "A joke."

All the Protech people are laughing now.

"We all kept hearing this bit about the Swiss chalet," Gary says. "And here you come waltzin' in here dressed like that! You could've knocked us over with a feather!"

I smile. "Well, that rumor is just so ridiculous. And really, why a chalet?" I beam triumphantly at Francine. "Keeping her in a chalet? Why would I?" I slide my arm around her shoulders. "I wouldn't want my beautiful wife anywhere else but by my side."

"Except when I'm on tour, of course," she says.

"Of course," I say.

"I can't tell you how relieved I am," Juliana says. "I'll confess that we had reservations about your being too serious and somber to fit with our engineering group. We didn't think you had any sense of humor whatsoever!"

"Benny has an amazing sense of humor when you get to know him," Francine says. "He loves practical jokes."

I growl softly, tightening my hold on her.

She looks up at me. "And puns. If he's in a crabby mood, a pun will always lift his spirits."

"Oh, I don't know about that," I say.

"You'll see," she says, grinning at everybody. "The more stormy he acts, the more he's enjoying the pun. You'll see."

"The team loves jokes," Juliana says. "I'm sure you'll fit right in."

The team loves jokes. *Grrrrreat.*

"Coulda knocked me over with a feather," the Texan says again.

"I can't take credit," I say. "It was Francine's idea. My wife is one in a million. Truly."

She searches my eyes. What is she thinking?

"We've heard that you dance, Francine," Juliana says.

"Yes, that's how we met," she says. "When I was early in my career as a dancer, I did a summer at Beau Cirque Fantastique, one of those huge Las Vegas extravaganzas, and Benny was doing lights and sound."

Juliana's excited. She was in Vegas a few years ago and she saw Beau Cirque Fantastique. She's excited that Francine was in it once. Francine tells her that her part was akin to being a tree in a play.

"She's underselling herself," I say. "The part was *not* like being a tree in a play."

She looks at me, surprised. "It was a little."

"She had a small part, part of the background dance corps, but she stole the show every time she was on stage. I guarantee you, a full eighty-seven percent of that audience was mesmerized by her and her alone."

Everybody's beaming at me, enjoying my husbandly devotion. Even Francine is watching me intently.

"Benny is extremely supportive of my career," she says. "I'm going on a European tour with my ballet company soon and he's so excited for me."

"Do you have an interest in ballet and acrobatics, Benny?" Juliana asks. "Is that why you got a job there?"

"Applying with Beau Cirque was more about the tech, I'm afraid," I say. "It was an interesting challenge for me. There are a lot of moving parts to a live light and sound show. A lot of robotic moving parts, actually, in terms of the lighting and some of the props."

"It was an entire stage show built around the Lady Gaga song 'Alejandro,'" Francine says. "You know that song?"

It turns out that everybody knows that song. People all over the world know Lady Gaga. The group is discussing the song now.

I'm focusing on Francine's hair, elaborate twists coiling around like a map of my current state of mind. I imagine tracing one with a finger, around and around.

She didn't even know we were married. Ten fucking years.

Who does that?

Francine, of course. She's an artist with zero detail orientation whatsoever, unless it has to do with ballet. Anything having to do with ballet, she's as serious as a general conducting a mission behind enemy lines. I can't even begin to contemplate the tax trouble she might be in. Will she have to redo her taxes for the last ten years? Probably. Eventually I should probably inform her of this.

"This I need to hear," one of the Texan women says to me. "Come on, do the song, Benny!"

I straighten up. "What? What are we talking about?"

"Francine says you can sing a funny rendition of 'Alejandro.'"

I turn to her, surprised. She remembers my singing that, but not our marrying. I guess I shouldn't be surprised.

I can't believe I sang that song. One second I'm having the end-of-the-production-run punch and the next thing I know, I'm singing that ridiculous song—not just singing it, but singing a mocking version I only ever did in my head. Her intense delight at my singing was like the best drug in the world, blazing through my veins, and I wanted more of that. More, more, more. So I kept on with it.

"I wouldn't even know the words, now," I grumble.

"Oh, do the song, Benny! You have to!" she begs. "And don't pretend you don't remember it." She turns to the group. "You have no idea, it was so funny, the way he can sing it. You'll die. Literally."

"I don't know about literally," I say.

She grins. "They literally will!"

It's here I realize that she's using it on purpose, to annoy me, another arrow in the quiver of ways to make me sorry I'm forcing her to go around as my wife.

"He completely remembers every single word and every single intonation," she continues. "We only heard the song a million times. Nothing gets more embossed in your memory than a song you do a show to. Juliana, you should totally make the purchase of this company contingent on him singing it to you at some point. He would love to sing it, but you'll have to press him."

Barbara the Texan claps her hands together. "This I need to hear." Everybody's enjoying themselves a great deal at this little dinner of ours—except Aaron, of course. Aaron is not a fan.

They're all waiting.

"Somebody is engaging in some extremely fanciful thinking," I say.

Francine hums the first few notes. *Hm-hmmmm-hm-hmm.*

I shake my head. *Drop it,* that's what the headshake says.

"You know you have to now," she says.

I give her a hard look.

She hums onward, unperturbed.

My heart pounds.

As the tune swells, she raises up her hands.

Our dining companions are laughing. They're getting quite the opposite-world idea about me at this point.

She's humming, raising her arms up, orchestra-conductor-style.

I grab her hands. Her skin is soft and warm, pulsing with life.

Her eyes widen and she stops humming.

I'm gripping her hands, suspended between us.

Our dinner companions are still laughing merrily, but my ears have stopped working thanks to the connection of us, skin on skin. That's how much she's fucking annoying me.

I raise her left hand to my lips, holding her gaze. Is she running this show? No. I press my lips to one knuckle, brushing my lips over her knucklebone.

Her nostrils flare, eyes wide with shock.

"Aww," somebody says.

I pull back with a cool smile, ignoring the rush of sensation, keeping hold of her hands. If she thinks she's the one in the driver's seat here, she's sadly mistaken.

This close I can see the sooty lashes that rim her deep brown eyes, see the places where they're just a little bit clumped together thanks to the eyelash glue that dancers use as part of their stage makeup. It was a major dancer complaint back in the Beau Cirque days, getting eyelash glue off the eyelashes.

Her eyes begin again to sparkle and I know she's going to do it—that's how fucking predictable she is.

She hums a few more notes—*Hmm-hmmmm*. Because that's Francine. She just never quits. *Hmm-hmm-hm-hmmmm*.

I kiss her next knuckle. People are laughing. We look like quite the comedy team.

She keeps on humming, but she's going to have to work a hell of a lot harder to make this into a problem for me. So far, in fact, it's working out brilliantly. A tax break and now this expert image resuscitation. I really might become a proponent of marriage after all.

"Consider this a rain check," says Juliana, laughing. "A rain check that I plan on cashing."

I realize here that I'm still holding Francine's hands. I let her go. What were we even talking about before?

Francine turns to Juliana. "Hold him to it. Because he totally thinks he just got out of it."

Right, the song.

Talk at the table turns to business. Juliana has questions about some of the files we sent. Tablets and phones come out. Drinks and appetizers come and go.

Aaron is answering questions, looking distinctly unhappy. It didn't help that she made that comment about my hatred of working for others, which is...entirely accurate. Or was at one time.

But then, he's been uncomfortable with this whole thing all

along, ever since Francine appeared at Ventoux asking for the divorce.

I'd texted Aaron after she left, and he came directly across to the restaurant. Aaron had been worried she'd appear someday; he'd been warning me that we needed to prepare a robust legal offensive for her return. There were times over the years that he'd suggested we become proactive about it, by which he meant digging up some dirt on Francine, working up some kind of shady leverage to force her to agree to a no-strings divorce. Or locating her and paying her off. He wanted to hire somebody to locate her.

I always strictly forbade it. I knew she was in the New York dance world and that I could find her if I wanted to. But why would I want to?

True, I was pretty heavily focused on the idea of her turning up that first year out from Vegas. The year the minature robotics stuff really blew up for us. The year of money falling from the sky. I really thought she'd show, and I'd be ready, but then... nothing. I figured out exactly where she was and went to school on her social media and discovered that she was just...living her life. As if none of it had ever happened. I stopped focusing on her, put more effort into the business, put her out of my mind. If she wanted to pretend it wasn't real, that was her business.

James always took my side on leaving the Francine thing alone. It's still shocking that he's gone. His death was so sudden, it feels unreal, somehow.

I was braced for the Protech gang to say something about him, or ask if I think the driver who ran him down on his bike will ever be caught. I was relieved that they didn't, but it also feels wrong not to invoke him. The company was half his baby.

I stare at the small bowl of olives, remembering James's easy smile with a sharp twist of grief. The way he'd clap me on the shoulder.

He was a big, rugged guy who wore man buns and hiking clothes, as out of place in corporate leadership as I was. It was against his better judgment to let the Francine thing hang out there, but we were friends, and we always had each other's backs, especially against Aaron, whom we trusted less and less as the years wore on.

Aaron got a chunk of shares when James died, but I got more. I make the decisions alone now.

Still, Aaron thought I'd lost my mind, not signing her quickie divorce papers.

"All this time I've been pressing you to do something about your Vegas marriage and this is what you decide?" he'd demanded. "To refuse this immense gift that she's offering you? Do I have to tell you again what she could do to us?"

I'd sat back and crossed my legs, still buzzing from the surprise of her turning up after all these years. "She won't try to do anything. Francine's not like that," I'd assured him.

"What about the people around her? She could get some crafty advice. Maybe her folks out in Podunk North Dakota fall on hard times and press her for a payday."

"Then you'll handle it, won't you?" But I knew it wouldn't come to that. It's not in Francine's nature.

"This is bordering on criminal mismanagement." He'd said it lightly, presenting it as a joke, but there's always a hint of threat with Aaron.

But this little gambit with Francine playing my wife has turned out to be a stroke of genius. Especially considering the revelation that the Arcana Protech people were worried about my sense of humor. How did we not know about this potential objection of theirs?

Well, now it's been addressed.

Business talk has been tabled, with Juliana insisting that this is a social dinner, not a working dinner. They're talking about

Brazilian politics and Brazilian dance. Eventually—and unsurprisingly—the center of gravity moves back to Francine; people want to know about her upcoming ballet tour, which leads to her talking about that Roman theater of hers. She tells them that it's an archaeological wonder constructed in 16 BC, and that she's always dreamed of dancing there surrounded by tiers of ancient marble steps and statues. "Now it's really happening," she says.

So the tour is going there. One of the reasons it's so important to her.

Her phone comes out. She's got pictures, probably the same ones she'd pass around in Vegas. The Beau Cirque people were big on all-company meals and hangout spaces—some shit about dancers, musicians, and us AV people forming a cohesive unit. Even so, I was never included in the circle when phones got passed around. I was usually happy to be free from the obligation to react appropriately with others watching, but I looked it all up online later.

"It looks like a film set of ancient Greece!" Juliana exclaims.

"Right?" Francine looks over at me. "Benny's probably sick of hearing me describe it."

"Not at all. It's going to be amazing. And not only will she dance there but she'll be one of the main soloists," I say, demonstrating my knowledge of her life, not that they'd question us being married at this point.

She beams at me, and something strange flows through my chest. I suppose because at one time, this was my naive dream. This whole scenario.

She tells them about the dance, the fast flow of movements, the constant injuries.

"These dancers will dance with broken bones sticking out of their ankles if you let them," I say.

"Well, that might be a little extreme," she says, "but we do push through the pain a lot. I have a knee injury that's threatening right now but I've been icing it like a demon."

She has a knee injury? She was battling a knee problem ten years ago in Vegas.

People make concerned noises and she assures them that it's nothing. She proceeds to launch into the rest of the fantasy—they stay at a specific hotel that's a restored 15th-century building. She walks around the Old Town early in the morning all by herself. She stops at a specific piazza coffee shop, orders a café au lait, and reads the Spanish paper. She has photos of all of it.

She tells our dining companions how, as a little girl in rural North Dakota, she had those pictures on her bedroom wall—that specific town, that specific coffee shop, that specific theater.

I take this moment to give Aaron a pleased look. Surely he sees the wisdom of the plan now.

But he's frowning. Even his mustache seems to turn down at the edges. Aaron is a lot more invested in nailing down this Protech deal than I am. I'll have other paydays, but it's unlikely that he'll have other paydays anywhere near to this level.

Not that I don't want the deal. This company was built to be led by two friends with complementary skills and now it's just me; Aaron's only legal support. We gave him a chunk of the company early on when we were too poor to pay him, a decision we definitely regretted over the years.

I look at her ridiculous traditional Swiss dress or whatever it is that she has on. Where did she even get it? She's lucky it worked out, that's all I can say.

I twist up a bite of linguine, remembering things I hadn't thought of for years. Those late-night cast dinners, post-performance, the giant group of us at a long table. She'd flit from cast member to cast member, laughing, irreverent, dark hair cascading over her shoulders, having deep conversations here, telling a silly story there.

The cast at Beau Cirque viewed putting up the show as a punishing and exhausting endeavor, but to Francine, it was a walk in the park, and she'd be running around after every show, trying to get people to go out dancing or exploring. She never asked me to go out, except once as a confusing joke.

She's poking me. "Benny, Benny! Tell them."

"What?"

She's grinning. "He does this. Lost in thought. Cogitating," she says, eyeing me, maybe wondering if I remember.

Of course I do—she once accused me of daydreaming, and I'd felt embarrassed and informed her that no, I wasn't daydreaming, I was *cogitating*. There was no end to how pathetic I was in those days. I'd use stupidly big words. I didn't know better.

"You must never say he's daydreaming. He doesn't like it. Cogitating, bitches!"

Juliana smiles. She likes Francine. People always do. The Beau Cirque staff would clamor for her attention. I remember just rolling my eyes and shaking my head at the whole thing. It was so annoying.

"We have our baby names picked out," she says. "It's okay if I tell them, right?"

Over her shoulder, Aaron looks aghast.

I'm not exactly pleased. I cast her a warning glance because, Igor and Monique? These people aren't idiots!

She tilts her head questioningly, like she's actually my wife or something. "No?"

I shake my head minutely.

She settles a hand on my arm. "That's enough. He doesn't want to tell."

"We won't use them, promise!" Barbara exclaims. She's had too much to drink, but also, Francine has a way of pulling people in and making them feel like they're in an enchanted bubble with her. Like that last night.

Something grinds in me.

"I'll tell, I'll go first," Barbara says in her Texas drawl. "Katarina and Arthur." She sits back happily as people praise the names. Katarina is a bigger favorite than Arthur, but Francine likes Arthur—she tells the group that it reminds her of Artie Shaw, the jazz clarinetist. If there's one thing I learned in my summer in Vegas, it's that most dancers have a deep knowledge of the history of music. It's part of their training.

She turns to me, beseechingly.

No—just no. While Monique is a believable name, nobody in their right mind would name their kid Igor. It was supposed to be a funny thing just between us. "I'd like to keep them to ourselves," I say.

She studies my eyes in the beat of silence that follows. "Okay, then," she says softly. "Benny is an intensely private person," she adds. "My very own oyster." Suddenly I don't know if this is for show, or if it's a little bit real. All I know is that I'm feeling chaotic.

"You bring him out of his shell," Juliana says. "I can tell."

I lose myself in my linguini. The Brazilians are complaining about not being able to get tickets to any of the shows they wanted to see, including the big Reno Sweeney revival, and my high-achieving wife offers to snag them premium seats at a matinee. It turns out she knows the star. Of course.

"Have you seen it?" Juliana asks. "It would be fun if you and Benny could come along."

I shove at Francine's foot under the table. Hopefully my communication is clear: no, we will not be accompanying them.

She looks over at me and then smiles sweetly at Juliana. "I hear it's really an amazing show."

I shove again, just to reiterate...no. I'd stick needles into my eyeballs before I'd sit through a three-hour show and she knows it.

She smiles wickedly.

She wouldn't.

"Benny? Have you seen it?" Juliana asks me from somewhere in the distance.

I'm boring into Francine's eyes as the din of the restaurant seems to grow fainter. I can't believe she's pushing it like this. But that's Francine, she always had to be the little rebel.

"I'm much too busy with performances and rehearsals, and Benny's not a musical theater guy," she says, swooping in at the last minute for the save. "He would just be sitting there crabbily multitasking in his head."

"You need to relax more," Juliana says.

Francine puts her hand over my wrist, beaming at me. "Tell me about it!"

My gaze lowers to where her hand rests upon mine, the point where skin meets skin like a ghost at the table.

EIGHT

Francine

BENNY IS BARELY SETTLED into his plush limo seat next to me when he and Aaron start grumbling in business-speak over a melodic background of Velvet Underground, another of Benny's moody favorites, played dutifully by his Pandora station.

"Seriously, how is a social dinner the first we hear about some pretty major objections?" Benny says as the limo slides like a sleek fish through the honking and chaotic Saturday night traffic.

Aaron grumbles back, something about his point person not having full access.

It's so Benny to be angry about not knowing something. Benny's one of those guys who likes to know what's happening at every moment. If he ever had his appendix out, you know he'd demand a local anesthetic so that he could stay awake and monitor every move the doctors make, whereas I would be like, send me to La-la Land, the faster the better!

They're analyzing the dispositions of the Brazilians and discussing the attitude of the Texans. And then Dave Matthews Band comes on.

I bite my lip and wait for him to notice.

It doesn't take long. "What the fuck!" Benny exclaims mid-sentence. He leans in and stabs the console screen with excessive speed and force. *Stab! Stab! Stab! A million thumbs-down!*

It's his old abrupt movement style, and it does something to me, just seeing it. Maybe it's the *déjà vu* of it, but my heart beats a little bit faster.

"What the fuck!" he says again.

"Clearly it's a sign," I say. "The powers that be are angry that you're dragging me around like this."

He mumbles something about algorithms and returns to his conversation with Aaron, now with a furrowed forehead of annoyance above his stylish billionaire glasses.

I sit there innocently, hoping against hope that another Dave Matthews Band song comes on, because that was...exciting. Wonderful, even.

We drop Aaron off at his high-rise.

The door isn't even closed behind him when Benny turns to me. "You think you're pretty funny, don't you?"

Whereas my old Benny had a voice that would once in a while drop to a deep timbre, new Benny lives there, with a voice growly and deep. The voice does something to me. What's more, I'm highly conscious of us being alone in this small, private space. The butterflies in my stomach are doing their own fast tempo ballet, complete with fluttery arabesques.

He drops his tone even deeper. "You think that whole thing was funny?"

"Umm, a little?" I say. "You didn't?"

"I did not," he bites out. "And you shouldn't be taking these kinds of stupid risks, considering you need my signature for that tour of yours to happen. And that thing with the Broadway show? You're pushing it."

"What? I'm playing your wife, and as such, I wear interesting fashions and I take a large role in managing your social schedule. You're just so impossibly grumpy—sometimes it's good for you to be socialized with other people."

"I'm not a dog," he says.

"Of course not," I say.

He's more like a wolf—that's what I'm thinking. I don't know how to feel about him—I just don't. Benny's presence has always put me off-balance, ever since the Beau Cirque days when I was so acutely aware of him sitting there in the smoldery shadows, sexy lips pressed together in total concentration, his large, awkward hands flying over the controls, lighting the stage on fire with his robotic innovations buzzing along the cavernous ceiling.

"You are not here to manage my social schedule," he says.

"That's too bad," I say. "Because I was going to see if Juliana and the gang would like to go with us to a Dave Matthews concert."

The momentary horror that suffuses his face is priceless. "Not. Happening," he rumbles.

It's all I can do not to squirm with delight. Instead I put on a face of innocence and sigh dramatically. This shouldn't be so fun but it *so* is. "Well, you know your wife is just so full of surprises. It would be a shame if we arranged something and got their hopes up and then cancelled. But if you don't want a wife, you know what to do. It rhymes with *gavel vapors*."

He grunts, annoyed.

"He was so grateful for how his beautiful wife saved the day that he decided to release her from this charade and get her visa stuff in order. He set his whole legal team on it—that's how grateful he was."

"Ah yes, the famous Francine Janea wishful thinking." He grabs a beer from the posh little fridge. "Your visa problems will disappear when I decide to make them disappear."

"He so wished he had a wife just like her, but all his money couldn't buy such an amazing wife, so he *made* her be his wife by threatening the one thing she most wanted."

He gives me a hard stare—his Wolf Benny stare. This new Benny feels a lot more dangerous than the old Benny. It's not just the way he puts me off-balance. It's something more—something ineffable.

"Such a sad tale," I continue.

He holds up his ice-cold beer bottle, watching it catch the lights from the cityscape outside the window, reds and blues and flashing neon.

I go into the limo fridge and grab a fizzy black cherry water for myself and a few cans of bubbly for my friends. I stuff them in my purse. "A little something for my friends. Your better half is very generous to her gal pals. You don't mind, right? Oh, and of course, you're welcome for the amazing job I did playing your pretty and charming wife."

"You want an Oscar?"

"You know what I want," I say.

"You nearly blew it with that outfit."

"This outfit killed," I say. "And for the record, it is extremely stylish, and I think it's pretty, too, don't you agree?"

Naturally his expression is shrouded in shadows.

"Don't you think it's pretty?" I repeat, because I know what he thinks of it. I might be playing with fire, but I can't stop. "What's your favorite part of my outfit?"

He turns to me, all smoldery.

My pulse races. "Do tell."

His eyes darken.

I give him a witchy grin. I can't stop goading him, pressing him. I feel like one of those granite-boring machines they use for mining, like I have to bore down through his rock-solid armor, down to the beating heart of nerdy Benny.

"Tell me," I say. I want to make him say it.

There's this beat of silence there in the back of the limo, and I'm pretty sure he's not going to tell me his favorite part of my dress.

Then he tilts his beer bottle so that the bottom edge is pointing to the ruffle at the top edge of my bodice. Before I can make sense of what's happening, he touches one ice-cold corner of it to the bare mound of my breast, right above the ruffle.

Heat blooms low in my belly.

He slides the cold finger of glass along the bare top of my breast toward the center of my chest, tracing along the top of the bodice.

My breath hitches.

With a smoldering gaze, he keeps on, tracing the top of my other boob, drawing a freezing and excruciatingly slow line of wickedness across my wildly heated skin.

I can barely think.

This is pure Wolf Benny and I don't know what to say. Wolf Benny has me reeling.

"This," he whispers.

And then the bottle is gone, and I'm secretly panting.

Still watching my eyes, he takes a long swig. A bit of foam stays behind on his upper lip. I'm focusing on it. I want to put my lips there and lick it off, maybe even suck it off. But then his tongue darts out and he licks it off himself, looking at me smugly.

"Uh..." I begin. "Well, I like the embroidered roses on the apron."

He's examining the beer bottle. He doesn't even seem to be listening.

"The beautifully embroidered vines as well," I say.

"My driver is going to drop you off at your place," he says finally. "You'll have the night to collect your things, and tomorrow you're going to move into my penthouse."

"Wait, what?" I do a highly theatrical double take. "Excuuuuuuse me?"

"I can't exactly have my wife living across town in some piece-of-shit apartment building," he says.

"I can't stay at your place!"

"You can and will," he says.

"I have six a.m. yoga and then class and rehearsals. We're literally rehearsing seven hours a day. And I have Pilates afterwards."

"The day after tomorrow, then," he says.

"I have just as much stuff that day, too!" I protest.

He shrugs. "Alverson can drive you to those things."

"Seriously," I say. "After I did this amazing thing for you?"

"It's a start." He takes a swig and sets his beer in the cup holder.

"Are you trying to punish me or something?"

His gaze changes—just a bit—like something flaring deep inside of him, some emotion that I can't read. "You're working for me, Francine. I'm not in the habit of providing my employees with rationales or explanations. If you want your travel documents at the end of this term that you have agreed to, you will follow the rules as I set them."

I can barely breathe. "Me living with you."

"That's right."

"And what exactly do you have in mind here? Because if you think you're gonna seduce me—"

"Sorry to disappoint you, but no. You'll have your own bedroom," he says. "And that's non-negotiable, so don't get any big ideas."

"Oh my god, you think *that's* where my mind went?"

"I mean it." He puts on an uber-serious expression. "You are specifically to stay out of my bedroom. You are not to pester me or go near me unless I require your services for public appearances."

"I'm not to pester *you*?"

"That's right."

Is he messing with me? "Are you forgetting you're making *me* do this idiotic charade?"

His expression is stony and distant. "We clear?"

"On the fact that you are an unbelievable jackass? Crystal," I say.

"Alverson will give you his direct number. You'll text him tomorrow morning when you're all packed up, and he'll come and get you."

"I'm an athlete in training!" I say.

"And?"

"So in the middle of the most grueling series of rehearsals of my life, as I prepare for the most important tour of my life, while desperately trying to not put extra stress on my hurt knee, you have decided that I'm to be ripped from my comfortable home where I have all of my friends and support system and move in with you as some kind of an employee?"

"That's about right," he says.

I sit back, heart pounding. I've never felt so powerless. I hate it. "Well," I begin, "I'm assuming it's alright with you if I bring my wind chime collection?"

He glowers anew.

Benny hates wind chimes. There was one in the palm tree in the courtyard of our building that drove him crazy. He'd drag chairs over and climb up there to tie things around it, but the groundskeeper would always get rid of his wind chime-muting fixes.

"Because I've become an avid wind chime collector," I add.

"You may not bring wind chimes," he says.

"Even if it's one of your wife's passions?"

"No wind chimes."

"Fine," I say. "But surely you won't object if I use your money to commission a massively expensive portrait of myself to hang in a prominent place in the living room? Because that's another thing that I must have. In addition to other things that I'll soon think of. A gown, possibly."

He pulls out a credit card. "Go crazy," he says.

NINE

Francine

NEWS of my impending forced cohabitation with Benny travels quickly around 341 West 45th and beyond, through our far-flung friend group.

My girlfriends stop by one after another to theorize about this strange turn of events. Even Vicky has dropped by; she's staked out the comfortable corner chair while Smuckers makes the rounds of people's laps.

Lizzie speculates that wealth has made Benny power-mad, and that I'm his new shiny toy. Jada thinks maybe he's turned embittered from years of females rejecting him when he was in his nerd phase.

"So messed up!" I say. "Shouldn't he be happy with all of his success?"

"Maybe he really has been in love with you all these years," Kelsey says, because clearly she still hasn't let go of that idea. "And it crushed him that you didn't even care you were married."

Scenes from last night flash through my mind like a montage of film clips, and it's safe to say that him sliding the cold edge of his beer bottle over the hot mounds of my breasts as he gazed into my eyes is the headline feature. It's up on the marquee of my mind in giant letters surrounded by blazing lights.

It's a side of Benny that I wouldn't have imagined—a sort of dommy side that's all about being in control. Technically hot, yes. Okay, it was very hot. But so unlike the Benny I knew and adored.

I wish he would let me apologize for how idiotic I acted. I want to tell him how truly ashamed I am about having made those unwelcome advances and then blowing town the next morning after he was so kind to let me sleep in his bed while he took the couch. "Nobody cares," he'd said. But that's not true—I care.

But then he goes and acts so jerky. Maybe he doesn't care.

"Whatever he was before, the man he is today just wants to push me around," I say. "It's all about a powerplay with him. And I promise you, he's acting like the opposite of somebody who is in love with me."

"Like the schoolyard bully who pulls a girl's pigtails?" Kelsey says. "Is he being mean in that way, possibly?"

I give her a dismissive wave. Because, no.

"So sucks," Noelle says, collapsing into the seat next to me.

"It's fine. I'll handle it. You know me, I'm all about resilience." I raise a finger up in the air. "'Instead of wallowing, we Pinoys pick ourselves up with a smile and keep going.' That's what my mom always says." Mom loves to talk up the determination of our peeps.

"You do love a challenge," Noelle agrees.

Unlike Benny, my girlfriends think that my wind chime idea is hilarious, as well as my idea for a giant portrait of myself to be hung in the living room.

"You should totally do it!" Vicky says.

"I don't exactly have time to sit for a portrait," I say.

"Give me a picture of yourself and I'll have somebody at the makers studio do it," Vicky says. "We'll make it really big and outrageous and charge it to him! I'll handle it. I love this kind of project!"

Noelle snorts. "We know you do, Vicky. Dog throne, anyone?"

"The whole point of this is to get me out of there, not start decorating the place."

"Well, either way, you'll be making him use one or two thousand dollars out of his vast wealth to commission some original art," she says. "He gave you a green light, did he not?"

"Can you make it diamond-encrusted?" I joke. "Have me wearing a tiara in it, and there are real diamonds in the tiara?"

"How about cubic zirconia-encrusted and we say they're diamonds?" she says.

I'm laughing now.

"I know," Mia says, "do the fake diamond-studded portrait and have it sent to his place with a fake invoice that says it cost millions of dollars. That would be hilarious."

"He did say go crazy, did he not?" Vicky asks me.

I can't help but smile. Vicky loves her art projects. She scrolls through her phone and finds a photo of me from my redhead phase, which I veto, and then she finds a good bunhead one and I give it the big thumbs-up. Why not?

"New idea," Mia says. "Francine needs to have a lavish party at his penthouse and invite all of us so that we can all observe him up close, and observe him interacting with Francine, and then we'll all regroup and have more informed discussions about this situation."

I find I don't like the idea. I don't want this complicated situation made into some kind of a gal pal parlor game…even though, why should I care?

"Fly in some blue crab and Trenton tomato pies!" Mia says, and everybody groans because she is always on a New Jersey pizza cuisine.

"I wouldn't mind seeing what his place looks like," Noelle says. "Is it a super dude place or did he hire a designer? Is it sentimental, full of mementos?"

"Hmmm." I fold my arms, trying to decide. All I know is that it would feature at least a few Star Trek things.

"Now I want to know too," Vicky says. "You have to have the party, and also, I'll bring Smuckers over to meet him. Smuckers will totally growl at anybody he doesn't like. Smuckers is a great judge of character."

"Benny is allergic to dogs," I tell her. "Or else that would be a good idea."

ALVERSON PICKS me up at the appointed time.

It turns out that Benny lives in West Chelsea, which is one of my favorite areas to take visitors to, full of amazing museums and fun-but-pricey restaurants. It's got the High Line, too, a magical park built on elevated tracks that went out of use.

But my eyes nearly pop out of my head when Alverson pulls up in front of the Zaha Hadid building.

There must be some mistake! The Hadid building seems too fabulous and otherworldly for somebody I know to live in.

Alverson comes around and opens the door. I get out. "You're telling me Benny lives *here*?"

"Yes." He goes to grab my suitcases.

Breathlessly I gaze up at the flowing and harmonious lines of the steel and glass structure—the place looks as if it were swirled into existence with a spatula rather than built with cranes and concrete. I pointed it out to my parents when they visited from North Dakota. In a sea of harsh lines and severe angles, the Hadid building is beautiful and sculptural, and I love that a visionary female architect created it.

All this time Benny lived here? I find it...unexpected. Impressive.

"The Hadid building!" I say to Alverson.

"Oh, yes, Mr. Stearnes was extremely proactive in securing a penthouse here." He motions toward the lobby door. "Right this way."

A doorman is holding open the door. I follow Alverson in. I never imagined I'd get to set foot in here.

We ride up to the top floor. Alverson knocks once on the polished wood door and a dog starts barking. He opens it up and deposits my luggage just inside the foyer.

"A dog?" I say just as a fluffy brown and white dog bounds in.

"Down, Spencer," Alverson says giving him a quick scratch behind the ears. "Don't worry, he's friendly."

Spencer is a medium-sized dog who looks to be a whole mix of breeds.

"Benny has a dog?" I say. "I thought he was allergic."

"It's not his, or...well..." Albertson trails off here and switches gears to information about locks and building codes, and with that he leaves me standing there alone with Spencer, closing the door behind him.

Because of course Benny hasn't come to the door to greet me. Is he even here?

And whose dog is this? Does it belong to a girlfriend? That's the kind of thing a boyfriend does, taking the girlfriend's dog when she's traveling. Could that be why he told me so explicitly and insultingly to stay out of his room? But then why have me step in as the wife? Why be Mr. Sexy with me?

I swallow, turning around, looking for signs of cohabitation, but who even cares? Let him be in a relationship. Let him be as jerky as he wants to be; I'm finally inside of the Hadid building.

"Come on, Spencer!" I say, heading into the main room, which is stunningly bright, not just because of the floor-to-ceiling windows, but the furnishings are bright and simple—all light woods and earth tones with the occasional pop of blue to match the blazingly bright blue sky. There's a magnificent porch outside with seating like a posh restaurant.

Further exploration turns up a spa-like bathroom with amenities that I don't even understand, but the jet tub will be amazing for my knee. The view is insane here, too.

Spencer is following me around. New friend alert! I rub his ears and we head into the kitchen where all things are stainless steel and wood and glass, and it's mind-blowingly beautiful. The feel is that of serenity and simplicity, of harmonious flow; these things greatly appeal to me as a dancer.

Stepping out onto that stage alongside my fellow dancers and embodying the feelings of classical music is pure bliss. It's like transforming into emotion and energy and beauty.

So while I'd have chosen this building in a heartbeat, I'm surprised Benny would have chosen it—he always seemed all tech and hard angles and anti-social abruptness.

So unexpected!

Just for a second, I forget the bullshit he's pulling, and I have a picture of us bonding over the beauty of this building. And he twirls me around and we'd go out on the porch and look over the High Line. And I'd reach up and touch his beautiful Benny lips, and then feverishly, he grasps my arms—abruptly and passionately like I always imagined back in the Vegas days—and we'd kiss.

I spy a bookcase. And I smile. Bingo!

I head over and excitedly scan the spines of the books for his collection of Star Trek novels, and specifically the bright orange spine of his favorite, *Spock Must Die*. My heart sinks when it's not there. It's a lot of photography books and tomes on coding and tech stuff.

No Star Trek novels. I shouldn't feel sad about it. Why should I care?

Benny was reading *Spock Must Die* that summer—I remember standing out waiting for one of my dates to pick me up, and Benny was at his favorite patio table reading this dog-eared copy. I asked him about it, and he told me there are two Spocks in it, and one had to go. I teased him about reading the book version of a TV show, and he said he read it every year. He was all serious and annoyed and flustered, a bit pink at the tops of his ears. He had asterisk-style stars next to passages that meant things to him.

I think I teased him about talking a little bit like Spock. I would sometimes do that, not because I found it laughable, but more because I found it cute, the way he'd use brainy words like "vexing," the way he'd quantify things with weird specificity, like he was 93.5% sure the batteries on one of the adhesive lights were going to run out.

And then my date picked me up, and Benny had some judgy thing to say about the limo.

I get this rush of affection, thinking about the guy he was. People misunderstood him, but in the end, I was the biggest asshole of all to him.

"You made it," Benny says, jolting me back to reality. He's strolling in from the direction of the foyer, Spencer jumping at his side.

"I can't believe you live here!" I say. "This is literally one of the coolest buildings in the city. I mean, you know, for a weird blackmailing kidnapper to live in."

Benny shrugs, expression carefully neutral. Spencer the dog nuzzles his hand.

"And I thought you were allergic to dogs," I say.

"People grow out of things," he says.

"You grew out of your allergy?" I ask.

"People grow out of things," he says again, more tersely this time. If his words had hands, they'd be shoving me away. Why force me to be his wife just to shove me away?

"Okay, fine. However..." I gesture at the bookcase, grinning. "Where is it?" I ask. "Because I know it's here somewhere. Because yeah, you can say that people change, but some things don't change."

"*What's* here somewhere?" Benny asks.

"I'm looking for it on the bookcase and I did not see it...but maybe you have a different bookcase where you keep your most hallowed books."

He furrows his brow.

I cross my arms. "*Spock Must Die*?"

"Are you talking about the Star Trek book?" he asks.

I give him a look. "I don't literally think Spock must die."

"You think I still keep those books around?" he asks.

"Don't tell me you got rid of them! Even your precious taped-up paperback? With all your little margin notes and stars and things?"

"Why would I have that?" he says.

"Because you read it every freaking year because you love it so much!" I say. "You told me you read it every year and you planned to continue doing so for the rest of your life."

"Sticking to every decision you made as a kid isn't exactly a recipe for a successful life," he says.

This makes me so sad. Stupidly sad. I loved that he did the

whole yearly reread. I loved that he told me about it. It meant so much to me. I felt like he was showing me another side of himself, letting me into a place he shut other people out of. "S-so you didn't even keep *Spock Must Die*?"

He shrugs. "It's just a ratty paperback."

"Oh," I say.

Is it stupid and childish to expect Benny to still read *Spock Must Die*?

And why do I care?

"I'm running a massive corporation and inventing things that ten-X the efficiency of machines," he says. "I hardly have the time to sit around reading a book I already read."

I can feel my face heating with emotion. "I don't know what's worse," I say with a casualness I don't feel, "the fact that you no longer have the book that you used to so love or the fact that you just used the term ten-X unironically."

"We can't live in the past," he says.

"Are you suggesting that I'm living in the past?" I demand.

He gazes into the distance, as though carefully composing his answer. He seems to have a slight case of the sniffles, and his eyes look irritated, like he's been rubbing them. "I'm suggesting that *I'm not*," he says.

"Okay, well, good for you," I bite out. "So do I get my tour? When am I to see my servant wife quarters?"

He leads me down a hall I hadn't explored, past one interesting-looking room after another. The place really is as magnificent from the inside as the outside. And Benny lives here! God, he's objectively handsome, and he lives in this building, and he's all angry and closed off. No wonder women go after him, I think with an unpleasant twist in my gut.

We turn down the hall, passing by a doorway that opens into a large bright space with gleaming hardwood floors. We're a few steps down when the explosiveness of what we just passed registers in my mind.

"Hold up." I stop, processing a moment, and then I spin around and start back in the other direction.

"Where are you going?" Benny says. "Your room is this way."

Like he can stop me.

I head into the huge workout space, gliding across the expansive gleaming hardwood floor that screams up to a massive window overlooking West Chelsea. Benny seems to be using the space as a weightlifting and boxing area; there's a heavy bag hanging at the center of the empty part of the room, as well as benches and a few mats strewn about.

My mind boggles at the extravagance of such a vast, nearly empty space in a private residence.

And piled up at the far interior end, opposite the window, is a mountain of boxes. You can't even tell how far back the space goes, that's how tightly piled up the boxes are. It's floor-to-ceiling boxes opposite floor-to-ceiling windows, and we're talking twenty-foot-high ceilings here!

"What's up with all of those boxes?" I ask. "Do you not have storage in this building?"

"That *is* my storage, and this is my space for boxing and weight training," he says, directing my attention back to the bright window side of the large room.

"This seems like a lot of wasted space," I say, looking back at the boxes. What in the world could possibly be inside of them?

"You're to stay out of here. Come on," he says, beckoning me back to the hall.

"There's the ballet class I teach with my friend Kelsey," I say, "and we're constantly fighting for a practice space at the arts center. Like *Hunger Games*–level battles for an hour of studio time. If we could move aside your bench and some of these boxes—"

"You are not to touch those boxes," he says pointedly. "You are not to be in here whatsoever."

"But I'm your wife now. This is our shared space, and you're so excited to make accommodations for me."

"But you're excited to go on your European tour, and you don't want to do anything to threaten that," he says. "So you won't set foot in here ever again."

I stiffen. "Are you suggesting to me that if I set foot in here, you won't sign off on my papers?"

"No, I'm stating it outright." He comes to me, stands in front of me—so close I can feel the annoyance radiating off of him.

My core goes hot. All I can think of is us in that limo, and the cool edge of his bottle, the harsh heat in his eyes.

"Got it?"

I take a step backwards toward the window. "What if I want to lift weights?" I ask. "And I don't even touch anything and you don't even know I was here?"

His gaze locks on to mine. My skin buzzes with aliveness. "I'll know," he says.

I suck in a tiny breath. "Have you become a Bluebeard re-enactor? Because you're doing a great job of it. You know that's what they call you, right? Billionaire Bluebeard?"

His eyes gleam. I wish I could read his expression. Does he find all this amusing, or is he being serious? He stretches his arm out toward the door, pointing the way back to the hallway.

"What if I just want to stretch?"

He takes a step closer. I move backwards and hit the window, cool against my sizzling skin. He says, "Any wife employee of mine who goes in there will be punished."

My breath hitches. My mind scrambles. *Punished*?

"Understand?" he rumbles.

There are a lot of words for the wild montage of X-rated images now racing through my mind.

"Understand" is not one of them.

"Uhhh..." I say.

He comes in a bit closer. I can barely breathe. "And I guarantee you, I'll know." Again he points at the door. "Now."

I whisper a faint "Aye, aye, Bluebeard" and head toward the door and out into the hall. He closes it behind us and leads me onward.

"Wow, you *really* don't want me to know what you're keeping in those boxes, do you?" I say, trying to sound normal and not mystified and strangely excited.

"You heard the rules," he grumbles.

"Whatever could be in those boxes..." I say in a singsong way. "Probably not dismembered body parts. You'd need to refrigerate or ideally freeze that sort of thing. Maybe strange dolls? Maybe it's blow-up dolls made to look like that Swiss Miss cartoon girl from the hot chocolate. Hundreds of them, all in their own boxes."

He stops and turns, gazes down at me, eyes glinting in the low light of the hallway.

I grin, excited and a tiny bit light-headed. "Late at night he creeps into the room and opens one of the boxes," I say. "He extracts the lucky doll, and in the darkness above the city lights, they begin to cavort, dancing wildly across the floor, man and doll."

"Are you almost done?" he asks.

"Dude, you have a massive room full of secret boxes. I'll never be done," I say. "You know what would guarantee I never look in your secret boxes? Your signature. On a certain set of papers."

"Let's go." He turns and leads me onward. What's in the boxes? Maybe it's robotics stuff. But then why the secrecy?

I grit my teeth as we pass a large corner bedroom that is clearly his. "Your forbidden bedroom, I presume?"

He keeps on walking. He passes one door. He passes another.

"Off-limits to my kind?" I continue.

He keeps on.

"The forbidden bedroom where I'm not supposed to go and pester you," I say.

Punished. Was he being funny? I can't even tell! It's just like Benny to be funny in a way where you're not sure if he's being funny.

"How will I restrain myself from bounding into your bedroom if I don't know which room it is?"

"It was my bedroom." Finally we reach the end of the hall. "This one's yours."

He leans back against the doorframe. He's got this really serious look, but then he points toward his room. "No matter what happens. No matter what—" He puts in a dramatic pause, then, "No matter what state you may get into." He points at his room, shaking his head ominously.

My jaw nearly drops to the floor. He *is* teasing me! "Whatever you say, Billionaire Bluebeard!"

He gives me an unreadable look and right there I'm thinking about it—I go in and surprise him in the middle of the night. He's sleepy and awkward and instantly consumed with passion, and he pulls me to him, unable to restrain himself, kissing me with those rough-and-tumble lips. His light brown hair is all messy like it used to be. And he maybe says something quintessentially nerdy and Benny-ish, like how entirely vexed he's been with me stuck in my own room, and he 100.5% needs me now.

I shake the thoughts from my mind and I walk past him into my wife quarters.

I see that my suitcases are already deposited in the corner.

"How did these get here? What, do you have a butler or something?" I ask.

"He's a butler-slash-personal assistant. Mac's his name. He's out right now, but he'll be back." He pulls out his phone.

"Hold on. So you literally have a butler."

"I *literally* have a butler-slash-personal assistant," he says.

I grin. Is he a little sensitive about that? Yes! So of course I push it. "Literally a butler!"

"A butler is more focused on household management whereas a personal assistant is more focused on bills and calendars and administrative-type things. It makes sense for some people to combine them. I'm texting you his number. If you need specific food items or toiletries or if you have questions about the operation of things like Wi-Fi and AV stuff, he'll deal with it."

"Gloss over it all you want, Poshface. You. Have a butler." I feel like the old Benny in the courtyard would be horrified by something like this. "A limo, a butler. Give you a little hair gel and you'd be one of those guys who used to pick me up for dates in Vegas."

Benny regards me with the unreadable expression that is beginning to drive me a little batty, though his jaw looks a bit tighter than normal.

"Well?" I say.

"Are you done?" he asks.

"For now."

He blinks. "You'll want to give Alverson your schedule of dance practices and things so he knows when and where to pick you up. He won't hold you to it, but he likes the general schedule, and then you can text him when it gets closer to the time and adjust accordingly."

"Okay." I walk around touching stuff. Naturally, the lowliest guest room that Benny can find is far grander than my bedroom at home. "I can't believe you live in this building! You know it's one of the places that I point out to visitors." I go to the window, feeling his eyes on me. "I can't believe you live here!"

When I spin around, this morose darkness has come over his tawny personhood.

"What?"

"We good?" he says in the manner of somebody really, really wanting to end the conversation.

The humorous connection between us is gone now. "So you do boxing?" I ask, wanting to talk some more.

"Why else would I have a heavy bag?"

"Yeah, right," I say. "Okay."

"You'll be free to use the kitchen as much as you want, of course."

"Are you sure there's no danger of running into me? The annoying wifely employee?"

"I typically take my meals at my desk at work. In fact, I'm heading to the office." With that he turns and leaves, sneezing as soon as he's out the door.

I stand there feeling hurt and dismissed. I hate when people shut me out. I hate being kept in the dark. As the youngest of seven children, I was always the last to know everything, always the clueless one. And then not going to a normal high school. Missing so much because of constant rehearsals.

"Suddenly remembering why billionaires suck," I mumble, closing the door after him.

I put away my stuff, and then I text Mac to get instructions to the house, which happens to include the password to the sound system and his precious Pandora account.

Score! I put it on and skip over a bunch of songs until I find a Dave Matthews Band song.

TEN

Francine

I'M SITTING at the corner of the studio after company class among scattered piles of wraps and sweatpants and water bottles.

It was a good class today—my barre buddies and I gave the dudes such shit about their push-up contest during barre. Then we changed into pointe shoes and began center work; people were on fire. We ended with grand allegro exercises. Watching my peeps, it gave me shivers. I feel like I'm in the best company in the world. Technically we're not the best company in the world—that would be the Paris Opera Ballet if you ask me—but in terms of heart, we absolutely are.

I'm wrapping my knee, fueled for a day of rehearsal. My friend Annie is next to me, slathering her legs with arnica gel.

Sometimes I wonder if my amazing resilience could be the undoing of me. The pain I can handle, but am I taking it too far? What happens in ten years? Will I still be able to dance? To do yoga?

Sometimes I wake up in the middle of the night with this image of me steering a ship, and I've been sailing in this one direction all my life, but am I actually steering the ship into a bunch of rocks? Do I even know how to steer at all?

Then again, the human body has amazing recuperative properties.

Annie nudges me, and I look up to see Rosemary beelining over to me looking determined, reminding me that I have bigger problems than this knee; namely, rules and regulations and entry visa red tape.

I stand up in one fluid motion. *No serious injuries here!*

"You really brought in the big guns," Rosemary says, amazed.

"What do you mean?"

"We have an assurance from Piper and Pearson, one of the biggest law firms in the city, that you'll have a work visa in every destination on our itinerary by the deadline. We're pulling Daneen off of rehearsing your part. She'll still be your understudy, but clearly your papers aren't going to be a problem."

"Great!" I say.

Annie clutches my arm and squeezes. "Paris, here we come!"

"Do you have some rich uncle we should know about?" Rosemary asks.

"It's just a friend helping out with a bit more firepower than needed," I say.

"Nice friend to have," she says and heads off.

Friend is a definite stretch. Friend suggests a person who likes you and doesn't use you as a prop against your will while finding you annoying.

And you don't moon over his lips and want so bad to kiss him. And you don't inappropriately fantasize about artless yet passionate sex with him.

I sit back down and go back to fussing with my knee wrap.

The billionaire brings a gold-plated sledgehammer to kill a mosquito, I think reflexively, but a second later I'm thinking how Benny always *was* good for his word; he always did follow through on things. Back at Beau Cirque, the director sometimes asked for things that seemed impossible, and Benny would receive the request in his sullen and antisocial way, and the next thing you knew, he would have created some little robotic wonder of ingenuity. People would compliment him on it, and he would just be all grumbly.

Now here he is, pulling out the lawyer big guns.

It's amazing to see Benny in this incarnation. Yes, he's become harder and more wolfish and conventionally hot where he was more nerdishly hot, but it doesn't surprise me that he's become so effective in the world. Like the end of a story that you finally get to read and you kind of knew what would happen, but it's satisfying all the same.

Another dancer, Shasta, settles in next to Annie and me. "How is it?" she asks. We're all really aware of each other's ailments, and mine is one of the company's worst, though people don't realize how much worse.

"I think it's better," I say hopefully.

A few other dancers wander in from lunch, depositing phones and water bottles around the edges of the rehearsal space.

Sevigny comes out in his usual outfit, which is a really tight black shirt and black workout pants that have white lines down the sides. He claps twice to let us know that there is to be an announcement before practice begins.

Phones get shut down. Snacks get put aside.

He tells us that ticket sales have been exceedingly strong and we're nearly sold out in Berlin and getting there in Paris. There's also been some amazing pre-tour press coverage. He tells us where to find links. Annie grips my arm. Shasta does a little dance from where she's sitting. We are all incredibly excited.

Even so, I feel this twinge in the pit of my stomach. The responsible thing to do would be to let people know the direness of my knee injury, and that it's not getting better. If only so that Daneen can really apply herself to rehearsing my part. I love my company so much. I don't want to let them down, but I don't want to screw myself out of this role of a lifetime.

"Now..." He delivers a couple more swift claps and lays out the schedule for the day, starting with the crazypants allegro the dudes had trouble with yesterday. We go through that and other trouble spots, cheering each other on.

An hour later I'm back in Hell's Kitchen, gearing up to teach the girls' class, the 42nd Street Twirlers. I rush up three flights of steps and burst through the door; screams erupt as a dozen little girls all run toward me, jumping and punching the air. "Miss Francine!"

Kelsey eyes me darkly from across the room where she's setting up the iPhone speaker, but she's just kidding. It's a big joke with us that the kids like me the best, but one thing's for sure: I'm crazy about them. Especially this ten-to-twelve age group.

"Okay, slackers, circle up!" I clap my hands and extend them out to either side. A flurry of girls in colorful leotards gather around, holding hands in a circle. I wait for them all to hush and stop fidgeting. I start them on warm-ups, painting a picture of the amazing class we're gonna have. One of my favorite things is to connect with the girls this way, on the level of the magic of ballet.

We watch the kids go through their paces to the music, hanging back.

"How goes it at posh central?" Kelsey asks, because of

course I texted the full photo array to our girl-gang-plus-Antonio text loop.

"Kind of weird," I say under my breath. "I just don't know what he wants from me."

"Do you need a hint?" she asks. "I can give you a hint."

"No, it's not what you think. It's almost like he's angry at me, or like he's punishing me or something, but then we'll have a fun or sexy exchange and I feel connected with him, but then he does something to shove me away..."

"Interesting," Kelsey says. "If he can't have your love, he'll flex his power over you."

I roll my eyes.

"I'm just working with what you give me," she says. "You really do need to have that party. We need to evaluate this guy as a group."

"Not happening. It's enough that I'm playing wife to Billionaire Bluebeard; I'm not going to be adding socialite hostess."

"Fine," she says. "But you wanna know what's so ironic? You do sometimes date people that are like how Benny sounds. Nerdy techie creative types. Or at least, pre-billionaire-status Benny."

"I wouldn't say the guys I date are like Benny at all."

"The orchestra sound guy?" Kelsey suggests. "Socially challenged techie in the arts? And that one Canadian who did all those little inventions? He was also a little bit gruff, as I recall. Without grace but fun—remember how you said that?"

I dismiss her assertions with a wave of my hand and catch her up on company news.

"Honestly, I was kind of glad they had Daneen rehearsing in parallel to me. That way I knew that, even if my knee blew out, somebody would be able to hit the ground running. I kind of wanted to tell them to keep her on my part, but I don't want to alarm them and get booted from the tour. I also don't want to let people down. I mean everybody understates their injuries but..." I look over at her to see what she's thinking.

She shakes her head. "I can't tell you what to do."

The kids are flagging and I run out onto the floor as hyena teacher, which means I scream and claw the air as I run toward them, and they all scream and step it up.

"I don't have to decide now," I say when I rejoin Kelsey. "About the knee."

"You don't," she says. "You'll know when you know."

I focus on the class, and that lifts my spirits. Nothing gets me down when I'm teaching with Kelsey. She and I sometimes talk about opening our own little school because there's not a lot of money in teaching for somebody else.

Class goes on. We start in on some barre work.

We have a big recital planned and we're not ready at all. Kelsey and I sometimes discuss working with the group in a park, just to try to catch up, but park rehearsals suck—you always get people watching and commenting, and random kids race into the middle of things and sometimes they even try to dance along. I'd do anything to be able to bring the girls to Benny's home gym to practice—even not moving the boxes, it would be workable.

If only.

ELEVEN

Benny

SPENCER RIDES in the back of the limo with me to the dog daycare, a vast dog playground that occupies the upper floor of warehouse space on Tenth Ave. I'm saying excited dog things to him.

My eyes are itchy and my head feels wrapped in gauze, but somehow it doesn't bother me; I feel this strange sense of optimism about life that I haven't felt in a long time. My thoughts drift back to the exercise room yesterday, to the way Francine's breath quickened when I teased her; to the sensation of her challenging gaze. The clever taunts directed at me.

It was strangely...enlivening.

Not that I'm looking at this situation with rose-colored glasses. She's here to get what she needs—nothing more, nothing less. Once she gets it, she'll be gone in a flash, just the way she was before.

Still, it's interesting. The way she jars me out of the malaise I've felt. The way she looks at life.

"Hey, buddy," I say, scratching Spencer's ears. He licks my wrist.

If James were here, he'd confront me to no end about this thing with Francine. *What the fuck are you doing?*

James was brutally direct, which suited me after a lifetime of people delicately dancing around me, misreading my expressions and my silences.

James and I got each other. It meant a lot. I'd never had such a good friend, and I know I never will again.

We were opposites in many ways—I was a small-picture thinker and James was big picture. I'd tease him about being a hippie, but he had incredible business savvy and he was loyal as the day is long. With his Patagonia clothes and Mediterranean good looks, James attracted women left and right. He was a massive serial monogamist—he'd fall hard and get bored two years in.

I wasn't particularly interested in dating, especially not in that first year after Vegas when I was so ridiculously emotional about it all. Plus, I was technically married, even if it was a fake bureaucratic paperwork marriage where we'd never had sex and it was only a drunken farce for Francine.

My paperwork non-marriage became a handy "keep-out" sign. I liked getting naked well enough, and even went through a phase where I worked on my moves rather diligently, hell-bent on replacing my old romantic technique, which I might describe as "hungry, out-of-control nerd," with a more cool and dominating style. But I liked that nothing could come of any romantic relationship—no strings, no emotions.

The Swiss chalet thing actually started as a joke that I made to a reporter. It took on a life of its own, that's for sure, and definitely reinforced my "keep-out" sign.

That was fine with me; I actually thought it was funny, but

James didn't. He felt strongly that I should get a divorce and find a true mate. He didn't believe that I liked things the way they were.

It was one of the few things we didn't see eye to eye on.

I check Spencer in at the front desk. This is something that Mac should be doing, but it's important to me that I do it, at least for a while longer. Spencer is excited, wagging his tail with the force of a jackhammer. They told me that he's made friends here. I'm glad about that, because that first month after James died was as rough on him as it was on me. He still looks for James when we go out onto the sidewalk and it fucking breaks my heart.

I head back down, sneaking in a few shots of nasal spray. My allergies go crazy when I ride with him.

Alverson has the backseat dog blanket stowed away in the trunk by the time I'm back at the limo. Between the nasal spray and weekly dog washings, I've been able to make it work, allergies be damned.

I drop my stuff off in my office and handle a few quick fires before heading down to the lab. I put on shoe covers, a head covering, gloves, and a sterile gown and I go in, resisting my impulse to walk quickly, to put all the confusion and mayhem behind me; some of these instruments are so tiny and sensitive, even air currents disturb them.

I stop by to see how some of my people are faring with the project that we're working on, which involves enabling the microrobots to scavenge power from surrounding vibrations in a novel way.

I'll miss this team. They'll be taken off this thing and reassigned. I don't like abandoning this project, but that's how it has to be.

I set up at my workstation, complete with vibration-isolation surfaces where sensitive instruments and projects are held up by air currents, or, as Francine would put it, *literally* held up by air currents, to guard against the ambient vibration of a city full of active subways and jackhammers.

I'm going at the same problem I've been going at all year—one tiny problem in a whole series of dominos.

People tend to get annoyed with me when I won't stop going at a thing, when I won't stop hammering at it. There have been many times where I've kept at things long after everybody else has given up. Usually it's wasted effort, I'll admit, but every now and then I'll get a result, just from pure dogged persistence.

This particular project will likely amount to nothing and no sane company would continue to fund it without results by now, but I feel like I can solve it, and I can spend the time. For now. That's one of the beauties of owning your own company.

Needless to say, I'm getting it out of my system; once I sell, I'll need to spend a year sticking to Protech corporate goals, and I'll have to work these kinds of projects on my own time and in my own space. I tell myself that I'll have the money after that to fund my own lab.

Though I do already have my own lab. That's the thought that's been creeping into my head ever since Francine pointed out my hatred of working for people.

It's funny—I'm constantly questioning assumptions in the world of robotics and technologies and nanoparticles, but I rarely turn that questioning toward myself or the larger picture of where I'm going.

James used to tease me about my lack of introspection. "You never stop and think about what you're doing or feeling, you just soldier ahead."

Maybe it's true. What I do know is that with his leadership abilities gone, selling is the logical next step. Yes, he was dead set against the sale when it came up, but he's not here, and I can't be both him and me. I can only be me.

Much as I don't want to work in somebody else's lab.

I get to work and the hours melt away; I don't even break for lunch. Suddenly it's four in the afternoon and my neck is aching and my body needs to move, so I leave the sterile cleanroom environment for the world of dusty shoes and bagel crumbs and uncontrolled humidity and temperature.

Aaron's outside my office when I get there. "You look terrible," he says, referring to my irritated eyes.

I blow him off with a grunt and lead him into my office, sneaking in a few discreet puffs on my inhaler.

"That shit's not good for you to take that so much," Aaron warns.

"It's fine."

"You promised you'd take care of him, not that you'd *personally* take care of him," he says, referring to Spencer, of course. Aaron's a big one for the path of least resistance.

"I'm not pawning Spencer off on somebody he doesn't know. It's hard enough on him as it is."

"You find him another nice owner and he'll never know the difference."

"He's a dog, not a fish," I say. "He'll completely know the difference."

Aaron grumbles his dissent.

I sit. "What's up?"

"Look, about that Protech dinner. The girl came through for us, I'll be the first to admit it," he says, though actually the last to admit it. "You were right to pull her in, but it's time to cut her loose. Every day that you don't sign those divorce papers is a day that we're exposed to her taking a piece of the sale. She could hurt both of us."

"It won't come to that," I say.

"What if it does? I don't trust her."

"If worse comes to worst, you said you could handle it. Did you not say that?" Not that it would ever come to that.

"Of course I could handle it," Aaron says. "Probably. She does have a claim, though. And she's playing some kind of game here, I can feel it in my bones. You need to cut her loose."

"That's not gonna happen until I'm good and ready," I say, firing up my monitor.

Aaron sniffs unhappily.

Aaron was angry that James was so against the Arcana Protech offer. Naturally, I sided with James.

Aaron is way too focused on his portion of the money, treating the sale like a done deal whereas it's anything but assured. Sales like this frequently seem to come together only to evaporate like clouds in the wind.

"In fact, I have her living at my place," I add.

"What?" he says. "Why the hell would you do that?"

"Because she's playing my wife," I say. "Because I can. Take your pick."

"Have you lost your mind?" he asks. "You'll give her a taste of the billionaire lifestyle and then send her back to her hovel? And expect her not to go after a piece of your fortune?"

"She won't," I inform him. "I doubt she even balances her checking account."

If anything, this deepens Aaron's distress. I suppose somebody who is so money-focused can have a hard time comprehending somebody as art-focused as Francine.

There's nothing profitable about a moment of beauty, and that's what Francine's gunning for. She would literally give up her freedom of movement—*has* given up her freedom for three weeks—because she wants to dance in front of some ancient ruins.

I think it's an admirable way to be. Inspiring, even. I've

spent so much time in the world of business, I've forgotten about the artist's mindset. It's a refreshing way of moving through life.

"Francine's main goal in life is to see this ballet come into being," I inform Aaron. "To create this moment in time. That's worth more to her than any tangible thing either of us could come up with."

"That's funny," Aaron says. "I thought Francine's main goal in life is to get free of you."

I shrug. He's not wrong about that.

"You don't think she's laughing at you?" he asks.

"I don't give a shit either way," I say.

"She's asked you for one thing and one thing only," he continues. "A divorce. And here you are, forcing this charade on her, going on about arty spectacles. Is this some kind of punishment? Some kind of test? Are you trying to prove once and for all that you're immune to her?"

"Francine's commitment is three weeks and it's my instinct to use them all," I say. "My instincts were spot-on last night, they're spot-on right now. Frankly, if my instincts hadn't been so spot-on for the past ten years, you wouldn't be riding around in the back of a Bentley."

"But most people who arrange a fake relationship do it for a specific event, like a wedding or a holiday or a black-tie event," he says. "What is this for?"

"I'm correcting bullshit rumors that the world seems to have about me," I say.

"You never gave a shit about those rumors before."

I give him an ice-cold stare.

He holds up his hands. "I'm just saying."

I wait.

"Fine," he says.

I pick up my phone and scroll, letting him off the hook, so to speak. As soon as the sale is over, Aaron and I will never lay eyes on each other again. Won't be soon enough for me.

"Legally speaking, though—"

I raise my eyebrows. This better be legal.

Aaron pulls an envelope from his leatherbound folder and slaps it on my desk. "I tweaked the boilerplate she came to you with. Made it a bit more ironclad in the area of claims to assets accrued...you'll see. The changes are marked in each case with purple stickers. Sign it, then have her sign it."

I grab the envelope, stuff it into my case and shut the top.

"Aren't you going to sign it?"

"I'll sign when I'm good and ready," I tell him.

"The sooner, the better."

"I think somebody's already shopping for oceanfront property, that's what I think," I say.

"Damn right," Aaron says.

FRANCINE'S STRETCHING on the living room floor when I get home the following evening. She's got her legs splayed out with an exercise band hooked around her small toe. Spencer is sitting next to her looking on contentedly.

She hasn't aged in the past ten years so much as grown into herself—that's something I've noticed over the past week. Her cheekbones are more majestic, her eyes blaze with intelligence; her inner confidence has grown. She challenges me just as much as she ever did, though. She gives as good as she gets.

The feeling of her nearness sometimes radiates across my skin. Though you could say the same thing about static electricity.

"She would normally do this in the workout room," she

suddenly blurts. "But Billionaire Bluebeard has forbidden her explicitly—"

"We're gonna take Spencer to the dog park," I grumble. "You'll grab something there if you haven't eaten."

"Is that an order? Part of my conscription?" she asks.

"It's part of your conscription," I say.

"And of course that overrides any stretching that I must do," she says.

"You're always stretching," I say.

She frowns.

It's true, though. Francine always stretched at random times, always working on the project of keeping limber—during blocking, during Beau Cirque meetings, waiting for her friends after our late-night cast dinners. She uses a band when she does toe exercises. They say dancers have strong legs, but it's actually all about the feet.

With a harsh look directed my way, she rises from the floor in a fluid motion not once using her hands. I remember her declaring back in the Beau Cirque days that getting up from the floor without using your hands is one of the best exercises there is.

"And is there some dress code? Since you didn't like my last outfit?"

"The dress code is no ridiculous outfits." I leave to find Spencer's collar. A few minutes later, Francine's at the door in shorts and sneakers and a T-shirt that says "Hedgehogs: Why don't they just share the hedge?" Because she pushes it. She always does.

We head out toward Twenty-Sixth past the galleries. She slows to look at the paintings and then catches up to us, a small rebellion.

"So are we playing happy married couple to any specific audience I should know about, or is it just the public at large?"

she asks as we wait for the light. "Is there some point where I should be smiling and laughing and looking at you so adoringly?"

"You should be looking at me adoringly all the time," I say.

"Are you being funny?"

"I feel like everybody should be looking at me adoringly, don't you?" I say.

She snorts.

"All the neighbors with dogs go to the waterside dog run," I tell her. "That's your audience." Not that I really care. I guess I don't know why I'm bringing her. Yet again I hear James's voice in my head: *What the hell?*

The light changes and we walk. Spencer's excitement ratchets up as we approach the green space. He knows what's coming. We head down past the willows, past people sitting on the giant stones. The water sparkles brilliant blue beyond the rail.

It's here I notice that she's limping, trying to disguise it. She always was an expert in the art of disguising her limps during our time at Beau Cirque. The dancers worked injured all the time, and they'd constantly be talking about their injuries; some of them even seemed to wear braces and wraps as hard-ass badges of honor, but not Francine. She didn't like to talk about her injuries, as if that might give them power and status.

Exactly how bad is her knee? Are there people in her life who know she dances injured? Would they confront her about choosing this tour over her long-term health?

Francine can get tenacious when she wants something, and not everybody has the spine to challenge her. She always fought to be taken seriously—I remember her talking about it on one of the interminable shuttle rides back and forth from the strip to the apartment complex where Beau Cirque put us all up. I don't know why I remember so many inane little details about her; it wasn't as if she was even talking to me when she said it. But Francine always had to be the center of attention, and like the loser I was back then, my antennas were permanently tuned in to her.

The point is, she doesn't know how fiercely she can come off.

Do they know she'd do anything to be on that tour, push through any kind of pain, risk any kind of damage? Even move in with Billionaire Bluebeard? But then again, it's not my problem, is it? Francine's a grown adult, capable of making her own choices.

"Spencer!" A couple of kids walking a tiny dog kneel to pet Spencer and Spencer sniffs their dachshund.

"You on your way?" the oldest girl asks.

"Yes, is it busy?"

She shrugs. "A little."

They head off.

"Spencer's popular," Francine says.

I grunt in agreement.

The dog park turns out to be not that crowded, luckily. We head in the double gates and let Spencer off his leash. There's a cool springtime breeze coming off the river, and an explosion of tulips all around.

The husband of a financial whiz I work with waves and heads over. "Showtime," I say under my breath.

"Friends of yours?" she asks.

"More or less," I say. Which is true. This circle of friends came with James when we got into business together, and the group still includes me, James's socially challenged business partner.

Aside from working with James and the team in the lab, I never fit anywhere. I never even fit in with my lively family, to the point where people would joke that maybe I was switched at birth, that maybe there was a family of somber, crushingly serious nerds who had a rambunctious, outgoing son they didn't know what to do with.

So this circle; it's not really that critical that they meet her, but it certainly cuts down on the questions. Best of all, once they meet her, she'll be valuable as an excuse not to do things.

And Aaron thought she'd outlived her usefulness.

"Alan!" I say.

Alan smiles. "Hey!" He comes over and we move our little group to the side of the trail. I introduce Francine as my wife.

"Nice to meet you, Francine," he says, trying to hide his shock. "So you exist after all," he jokes. But it's not really a joke.

"She has a busy ballet career, what are you gonna do?" I say. "Francine is one of the most dedicated dancers on the planet."

She looks up at me questioningly. Does she think I don't see it? You'd have to be an idiot not to see it.

"Not an exaggeration," I add.

"A marriage of workaholics," Alan says. "That's a convenient thing to have in common. You can both be shitty at work–life balance together."

"Yeah, right?" Francine says. "He doesn't get after me about living, sleeping, and eating pirouettes and I don't get after him for being single-mindedly obsessed with the microrobot takeover." She lowers her voice here. "You do know that's what he's up to, don't you?"

I smile. Her characterization is minorly amusing, I suppose. Without thinking about it, I settle my arm around her shoulder, and at that exact split second, she slides her hand around my waist, and then we smile at each other. Well, you have to admit, it's funny we had the same idea at the same exact time. You couldn't have choreographed us better if you tried.

Alan snorts. "Hopefully you'll put in a good word with the tech overlords when the time comes, Ben," he says.

"I'll think about it," I say.

"If I didn't pull Danielle off the stock tickers and news feeds for meals and sleep, she'd be comatose by now." Here he turns to Francine. "How long are you in town?"

"Two more weeks, and then I leave on a tour," she says, curling her hand around my waist. I'm highly aware of those fingers, highly aware of her shoulder under the flat of my palm.

Alan wants to know where the tour goes and she rattles off the cities—London, Paris, Seville, Istanbul, Stuttgart.

Maybe it's because we're flush to each other, but the pleasure she takes in saying the names reverberates through me, and not just that, but the warmth of her, the shape of her—willowy but made of pure steel, muscles ruthlessly honed to catlike strength, ready to spring into action with outrageous athleticism.

"It's not just a European tour," I say. "Francine's working with the famous choreographer Dusty Sevigny. She's a soloist in one of his original pieces."

"Congratulations!" Alan says.

Francine's beaming, radiant. She's happy.

Out of nowhere, this little voice comes to me—*Why not cut her loose? Why not give her the papers she wants and let her go back to her life?*

I push the little voice back down. Because this is good—Alan will tell people that he met my wife—nothing like an eyewitness. And folks at our income level frequently live on different sides of the country or maintain multiple residences in far-flung foreign capitals. Especially when they have busy careers.

If my past self were to see this scene—Francine and me in a dog park meeting friends—he'd die of excitement.

Until he learned I was forcing her to play this part, in which case he'd punch the shit out of me. But that Benjamin is dead and gone. That Benjamin had juvenile ideas.

"Well, if you guys can tear yourselves away from things," Alan says, "Danielle and I are having a rooftop cocktail party a week from Friday. Aaron's coming."

Francine and I exchange glances as if we're a normal couple.

I say, "Will your rehearsal—"

"Be happening? God, I hope not! We have weekends off unless Sevigny is freaking out on something." Francine smiles at me here.

Is she happy? Does she like this idea?

Francine does enjoy meeting new people. She loves to dig into people and learn all about them. Once she gets a thread of you, she'll pull and pull and pull—that's the beauty of her, but also the danger of her. And she has this devious sense of what threads to pull, the specific things to ask. She unravels you and makes you defenseless.

"Right," I say, nodding, like Sevigny's temperament is something I know all about. Is this what it would be like? Being married? Would we be these people? Invested in each other's careers, supporting each other like teammates?

"Honey?" Francine says.

I blink. "What?"

Alan's watching me, waiting. "Can you do it? You don't have a reservation on a rocket ship or anything, do you?"

"Oh," I say. "No, I'm thinking...no, it's good."

"I'll have our guy shoot your guy a text," Alan says. With that he takes off.

I spot Spencer with something dubious in his mouth and I go over and deal with it. Spencer runs off. I rinse my hands in a fountain, then wander over to the railing, staring out over the water. I need some space. I don't know why.

"He'll have their guy text to your guy?" she teases, coming up to me. "Do he and Danielle have a butler-assistant too? Do all of your friends have butler-assistants?"

"No, not all my friends have them, but Danielle is one of the most high-powered financial gurus around, and Alan's a bigshot graphic designer. It helps to have somebody managing household and admin. It just does."

I turn to watch Spencer and she mirrors me. We stand there with our backs to the water, watching Spencer play with a German shepherd.

She says, "So this is what it would be like."

"What?" I ask, as though I don't know what she's talking about, as though I didn't have that same thought. I like her by my side, but I know better than to let this feel too real.

"Us. If we were really married," she says. "And we walk Spencer and meet people we know and we have little exchanges. And they invite us over."

"Well, we are a married couple," I say.

"You know what I mean. A real one."

"We are a real one. In the eyes of these people. In the eyes of the IRS."

"Whatever you say, Poshface," she says.

"Seriously, I can't even begin to imagine the kind of tax trouble you're in, filing single all these years."

"Wait, what?"

"Tax trouble. The IRS."

"But I didn't know!"

"Ignorance is never a valid defense for breaking a law," I say.

She stiffens. "You think I'm in tax trouble?"

"You've been filing as single," I inform her.

She has the good sense to look alarmed. "Shit. A lot of trouble?"

"You need to fix it, let's just say."

"How?" she asks. "Ten years of tax trouble that I need to fix?"

"Get a good accountant."

"Right," she says. "Okay."

I cringe inwardly, imagining what kind of accountant she'd dig up. Francine may not be capable of identifying a good accountant. She'll get a shitty accountant if she gets one at all. Maybe she'll just apply her famous wishful thinking. Nobody's said "boo" for a decade about it, after all.

I imagine informing her that I've got it under control. I'd tell her I'll handle it, and she'd be standing there with this grateful gaze, eyes full of energy. Things like taxes are hard for her, and I'd imagine she doesn't get a lot of competent help out there for the endless binds she gets herself into.

She'd be so relieved.

This weird feeling of weightlessness flows through me and I look away. I suppose I still have some of that in me—that gullible, dim-witted kid who'd do anything for her. That kid isn't running the show anymore, though. Thoughts like this are sad artifacts, I tell myself, only useful in reminding me of how far I've come.

All Francine wants is a divorce. That's all she wants from me, now.

Spencer's come back around, panting. It's time. I put his leash back on and we head out back onto the sunny walk.

She really could end up in trouble. It really is mind-blowing that she didn't know. And god how she'll bungle it, trying to get out of it.

I could put people on it. I could.

The braid-haired twin sisters who sell tiny paintings off a bench near the dog run entrance call out to Spencer. Spencer is one of their favorites, though I imagine it all might have started because one of them might have been a favorite of James's. James was a fierce and idiosyncratic thinker who always went for the nose-ring beauties. With a painful hit of sadness, I flash on him flirting with a woman at a falafel stand, Spencer as his partner in crime.

The woman who I always think of as the leader of the two asks how Spencer's doing.

"He's great," I say, willing her to not say anything more, because I don't need Francine in my business now. Missing James is hard enough without having her playact compassion and make me feel worse. Having Francine in the mix will just confuse everything.

Too late—I can feel her attention on me. She senses she's being shut out of something.

"You're such a lucky boy to have him looking out for you," the lead sister says to Spencer massaging his neck. "You're gonna be okay, buddy!"

I roll my eyes, as though annoyed. Why can't people mind their own business?

I still feel Francine's attention. It's not just that she zeros in and pulls your threads; she makes you *want* her to pull your threads.

You're an awkward misfit and she's suddenly joking with you and pulling you into her world, and you want her to unravel you.

And then she does.

And it's the best thing in the world until it's the worst thing in the world. God knows how many hapless casualties she's left unraveled in her wake.

"I'm so glad," the other twin says. "You're a lucky boy! Yes you are, yes you are," she repeats as Spencer licks her face.

I finally pull Spencer away, getting us away from them.

"Was something wrong with Spencer?" Francine asks me.

"Nope," I say.

"Then what did she mean, asking how is he? She sounded concerned."

I shrug.

"Fine," she snaps, hurt now.

We keep walking. She can think what she thinks, feel how she wants. This is a transaction, not a kumbaya circle.

But I can't stop thinking about her taxes, now.

I could just put an accountant on it. Handle the whole thing. It would take half a day and some fines I'd never even notice. It would be a simple matter, but then I'd have to deal with her gratitude, as if I'm riding in there like a savior or something, all swelled up like an idiot.

"Hey, can we head up to the habitat garden after this?" She points to a sign. "We could just loop up there. It wouldn't be out of our way—"

"No," I say.

"Why can't we loop up there?" she asks.

"Because this is the route Spencer likes to go."

"But we could walk up after the dog park and then go down to your place after," she tries.

"Spencer doesn't like to deviate."

"So Spencer gets a say and I don't?"

"Yup."

"How is that fair?" she demands.

"That's how this marriage works," I say.

"Seriously? Man and dog are numbers one and two in our pecking order, and I'm three?"

"That's the pecking order," I say.

"So I'm the accessory," she says. "Been there, done that."

"That's not this," I say, because I won't be classified with her Vegas boyfriends with their casino flash. I want to say more, to make her see I'm not like them, but then I remember I don't give a shit.

"Was Spencer sick?" she asks.

"People ask after other people's kids and pets. It doesn't

mean anything." I pull Spencer away from a bush he was sniffing at.

"How about you just tell me that you don't want to talk about it instead of trying to gaslight me about there not being an issue with Spencer? I'm the help. I get it."

I feel my cool composure draining away. I'm bad at emotions. I'm bad at people. Why do I care if she's upset? I don't need to explain myself to Francine. It's ridiculous that I would want to. "It's not that," I say. "It's just...hard—"

"Wait." She spins around to face me. "Was Spencer James's dog?"

"Yes," I sigh. "I promised I'd care for him," I say casually.

There's this silence where I brace for her to accuse me of clinging to Spencer in some pathetic and hapless way. Or maybe some recriminations or expressions of hurt feelings.

"You're a very loyal person," she says.

I look up. That was the last thing I expected her to say. "It wasn't a deathbed promise or anything, but it's important to me." I say. "I didn't get the chance..." *To say goodbye.*

"I'm so sorry."

"But I did say I'd care for Spencer at one point," I say.

"Spencer really is lucky to have you," she says.

"I'm lucky."

We stroll on past tulips in riotous shades of pink, red, and yellow. New tree buds dust winter-brown branches with vibrant shades of green. There's something about early spring in Manhattan—things feel almost soft for a moment before the hot, smelly slog of summer sets in.

Her limp is pretty pronounced at this point. "Should we stop at a bench?" I ask.

"Why?" she says.

"You know why." I angle my gaze down to her knee.

"Oh, please," she says strolling on, more successfully concealing the limp now. Which probably taxes it even more.

"We're going to stop at that bench up there and call Alverson," I rumble, "and that's that."

"This isn't the kind of marriage where you can boss me around," she says.

"Actually, it *is* that kind of marriage," I say.

"No, it's not," she says. "As a matter of fact, this is a marriage where you hang on my every word and want to make my every dream come true," she says. "Including my cherished dream of walking home without your dumbass opinion."

"However, as your husband, I'm invested in your cherished dream of having dance in your future, as well as a stupid little thing known as walking around. So when I suggest we rest on the bench and wait for Alverson, you understand that husband knows best."

Spencer picks this moment to enthusiastically sniff a lamppost, and that brings us to a halt.

She turns to me, there at the side of the walkway, eyes blazing. People and bikes flow past. Somewhere in the distance, a folkie plays folk guitar, bright notes mixing with the din of traffic.

"Actually, this is the kind of marriage where you value *my* opinion," she says. "And if I say something's not a problem, you take me at my word."

"Except this is the kind of marriage where I happen to know that you can fool a lot of people, but you're not fooling me. And I know that you're hiding a very grave injury."

"A very grave injury, Benny?" she asks. "Have I been shot with a bullet?"

"You know what I mean—it's very grave...you know..." I almost say, very grave to your career, but I don't, because apparently I'm in the business now of protecting her wishful thinking.

"Grave enough," I amend, but it's too late; I can see the distress in her eyes.

I can feel my practiced smoothness draining away.

I want to make it better. I want to kiss her.

I'm sure that would be hilarious to her, to bring out the awkward, worshipful nerd in me.

It won't be happening. That kid isn't in the driver's seat. Not anymore.

TWELVE

Francine

"I KNOW MY LIMITS," I say to him, willing him to stop talking about my knee. I can blow off Kelsey's concern—she overtrains as much as I do.

Same with my fellow dancers—don't throw stones at glass houses and all of that. The company powers that be have no idea how bad an injury it is. And Noelle believes me when I minimize my injuries. And my parents on their Zoom calls from the back of the tourist shop in North Dakota—they don't know.

But Benny seems to have figured it out what with his weirdly intense way of zeroing in on people and things to the exclusion of everything else in the world. It's not just that though; his concern feels dangerous, and for whatever reason, I want him to believe it's okay. Maybe even need him to believe it.

"And like you told Alan," I continue, "we are both very focused on our own careers; you steer clear of giving opinions on my career the way I steer clear of giving opinions on yours."

A hint of a smile appears around his eyes, and the beauty of him takes my breath away.

He steps closer, and I know he's going to deliver some sort of gotcha, and I don't even care. I like having him near. Maybe I need my head examined.

"Like when you told me I was an idiot for selling the company and working for somebody else?" he rumbles. "Steering clear like that?"

I grin. "That wasn't an opinion, it was the truth, and you very much are an idiot in that respect, but I know that I can't save you from yourself, so I've stopped giving that opinion. Just as you know that you can't save me from my very grave tax troubles."

"Oh please," he gusts out, like I'm the peskiest person on the planet. "I'm gonna handle your tax troubles."

"What?" I say.

"You would just bungle it," he says. "It's excruciating—just absolutely vexing—to imagine how badly you'd bungle it. I shudder to think what sort of accountant you'd hire. It probably wouldn't even be an accountant. You'd go for an insane clown. You'd get yourself into more trouble by trying to fix it."

"You don't have to put things so diplomatically," I say. "Tell me what you really think."

"I have people sitting around waiting for me to assign them tasks like this. It would be maddening to know you're trying to handle it with ninety-three point five percent pure incompetence."

I get in closer to him, get into his face. "How much incompetence was that?"

"You heard me the first time," he says.

"What if I like it when insane clowns do my taxes?" I ask.

He draws in, near enough for me to be able to see the whorls of his tawny-brown brows. "Too bad."

"The insane clowns are donning their giant shoes as we speak," I say dimly, eyes falling to his lips. "Sharpening their water-squirting pencils."

As if he knows I'm studying his stupidly attractive lips, he forms the words carefully, dramatically, fetchingly. "You can't stop me."

And this burst of affection and happiness rushes over me.

And I want to touch him—*need* to touch him. To kiss him. To press into him. He's a magnet I must shamelessly glom on to. It's a physical need, but also emotional. I feel so close to him now.

Maybe it has to do with playing his wife all week, sarcastically calling each other "honey" as we pass back and forth between the penthouse and our busy lives. Fun little snipes here and there. Being surrounded by his things, his scent.

But it's more than that. It's confiding in me about Spencer. Trusting me enough to be vulnerable about it, to show his heart. The little he did, that's big for Benny. It makes me feel closer to the guy he was in Vegas, and that strange magic of us then.

And the idea of him helping me with my taxes—I really *was* worried about the tax thing. I'm bad at numbers-and-red-tape situations. And mostly there's my knee.

Spencer is back, threatening to tangle us in his leash, breaking the moment. "Well...thank you," I gust out, words ragged, as if all of my anguish gusts out with them.

"You're welcome," he says gruffly.

"No, really, thank you," I say again. "I don't know why I'm so emotional."

"How much does it hurt?" he asks straight out, apropos of nothing.

I shake my head, desperate to get off of this subject, casting around in my mind for anything else. I focus on Spencer. I need to say something about Spencer.

"That bad, huh," he says bluntly. Because he's a guy who sees the important things and, of course, he'll have some shit to say about them, because he has zero tact.

I can't look at him now, because it feels like my whole face is warm, like wet steam is taking over my eyeballs, tears trying to escape like horrible little prisoners. That's what a bundle of emo I am. Like all the bottled-up worry was waiting for somebody to ask. Emo at the gates, pounding at the gates.

"Fuck off," I breathe.

A finger on my chin. The shock of contact electrifies my skin. He turns my face to his. My heart pounds like a jackhammer. The feel of his finger—that one finger at the base of my chin—it's blowing me apart.

He adds another, a touch light as feathers, two fingers on my chin.

I stare up into his pale brown eyes, and he's studying my about-to-cry face or maybe I am crying—are tears actually out of my eyes or are they just bunching up in there?

Except my whole world is those fingers, now. I like them there, and I have the crazy impulse to turn my head so that his fingers would be on my cheek, too.

Maybe I'd turn my head some more so that his fingers would be in my hair or even my arm. I suddenly have all this empathy for cats with catnip toys, trying to rub their bodies all over something, all at once, because that's how I am with Benny's fingers.

And I feel like he sees everything, like he gets how much I care about my dreams. And he's beautiful and so very Benny with his vexatious fractional percentages.

Two hands move abruptly in to cradle my neck in a motion that is way more Vegas nerd Benny than suave Manhattan Benny.

Something in my belly melts. My gaze drops to his lips.

Abruptly, he clutches the back of my neck. "Francine," he

whispers hoarsely. The sounds of the park become hollow and distant compared to the whooshing in my ears.

"What?" I blurt.

Everything goes still for a moment. Brown eyes regard me with a million percent intensity.

And then he kisses me. It's not just any kiss, it's a feverish torrent, unpolished and true. He groans, fingertips tightening on me. I pull him to me, pull his magnetized self flush against my breasts. I need more of this kiss—the delicious Benny kiss that is so devoid of coolness, of suaveness, of any game whatsoever. I need more of him.

He rumbles in that low Benny rumble. It sets off explosions in the back of my head.

And then he pulls away.

My heart is racing, and I'm so not done with this kiss; like a madwoman, I grip his upper arm, thick with muscle and urge him back toward my nerd-turned-wolf-seeking lips.

Suddenly he's kissing me again—with more energy this time. He's claiming my lips with mad hunger. I'm gripping his shoulder while my free fist makes mincemeat of his shirtfront.

Kissing Benny is everything I love. I imagined it ten years ago, but the reality is so much better.

I pull him in more tightly. Like we're holding each other in place, in this swirling strange place we shouldn't be in.

His tongue is in my mouth, a wholehearted and passionate invasion of my mouth that I very much welcome.

Energy skitters over my skin. The sound of his rumbly groan reverberates through me. His mouth is so delicious. File this kiss under wrong, wrong, wrong. Also file under: amazing. So freaking amazing. The more I have of him the more I crave.

"Unnngh," I say.

He sucks in a breath and kisses me anew. He's definitely shed his well-practiced cool-guy veneer, and I love it.

I lean into him. Benny is kissing me and I don't know what anything is. We're panting, falling together through some kind of weird trapdoor of us, and I don't even care.

I'm practically grinding against him. I wish that we weren't in a place full of people, because I've never been so turned on in my life.

Does he feel the same way I do? Surely he does!

Then, as suddenly as he started, he stops. He seems to get his breath under control.

He's regarding me strangely and something changes in his eyes; it's as if a neutral expression has come over his face. His smile is sexy, but more cool than warm, now. Slowly, he slides his hand over my hair over my head, then he takes my ponytail in his fist, gripping it hard.

He tilts my head just right to come in for another kiss, and lord help me, I'm all there for it...except this kiss is different. It's not so much passion as technique. It's good technique—very good, actually—and I begin to get lost in it, lost in the feathery-light lip-nips mixed with masterful mashes.

But it doesn't feel like him.

He pulls away, looking all cool and smug. "Well, if anybody had any doubts about us, they don't now."

My heart drops through my socks. So the kiss was all for show? It meant nothing to him?

I pull away, straightening my spine, utterly crushed.

"Yeah, that was some Oscar-winning shit right there!" This I say breezily, like I'm not trembling down to my toes. "You spot a nosy neighbor or something?"

His gaze moves over my shoulder. "I've seen a few," he says.

This final confirmation is a cannonball through my belly.

"Not surprising, given that this is my neighborhood," he adds.

I realize here that we're a mere block from his place. So

that's it? Just one big faker party? "You were very enthusiastic," I say.

He brings Spencer to a bench on the side of the path and sits, pulling out his phone, casually scrolling.

I stand there, fists clenched, hating that it was fake.

I was so into it, and it was *fake*. Was he just messing with me? Trying different kissing styles on me and then tossing me aside? Was any of it even real?

I move to stand in front of him. "Very enthused," I repeat. Wishful thinking, maybe. I'm still whipped on this man.

"I work the stuffing out of my assets. It's part of how I got to where I am today." He scrolls his phone, scroll, scroll, scroll, leaving me alone with his words. "Alverson's nearly here," he adds.

"Forget it, I'm walking."

He looks up, surprised. "Francine," he says. "Alverson's not a block away."

I turn back to him and give him the biggest fake smile I can muster. "See you at home, honey!" With that, I head down the sidewalk, my knee flaring with pain. And wildly, stupidly, I know somehow deep down that it's hurting him, too.

God, I barely even recognize myself.

THIRTEEN

Francine

I RAISE MY HAND, signaling to the bartender that our side of the bar needs another round of drinks.

"Wait," Tabitha says, covering the top of her pink drink, "I'm good for now."

"I'm good, too," Noelle says. "In fact, I'm switching over to kombucha!" And then as if that weren't enough of a suggestion, she adds, "It's not like you to be drinking while you're in rehearsal mode."

I point a finger at her. "You think I'm schnockered?" It would've probably been good for me not to use a word that gives away the fact that I am a bit schnockered. "In fact, tomorrow's my day off." I turn to Antonio. "Dude. Another. You have to."

"Why not?" He does the weary-yet-sexy-Italian wave that only Antonio can do, indicating he will have another drink.

"Such a jerk," I say, continuing the analysis we've been having, which could be titled, "Why is Benny such a jerk to me?"

I told them about the fake kiss in the park, but not how intense and great it was, or how sure I was that it was real. I left out how stupidly upset I felt that it wasn't real. Sometimes I inspect the memory for clues that it was real. The way he sucked in a breath, the way he seemed to lose his suave control at first.

Antonio exchanges a full bottle of beer for an empty with the pretty bartender, giving her his million-dollar smile in the process.

The pretty bartender smiles at Antonio and heads to the other side of the bar.

Tabitha snickers and jabs him mercilessly in the side.

"What?" Antonio protests.

"Rhymes with corn dog," Tabitha says.

"*Mi uccidi con queste cose che dici!*" he exclaims. "You're killing me! You are!"

Jada is just laughing. Both she and Kelsey have had flings with Antonio but have remained fast friends with him. We all tease Antonio mercilessly about his position as most active and popular bachelor in Hell's Kitchen. What can he say? He *is* the most active and popular bachelor in Hell's Kitchen and he knows it. He doesn't even need Tinder; life is his Tinder, with women accosting him nonstop for him to swipe right or left on. His charm and great looks and sexy Italian accent are a bachelor superpower here in Manhattan.

I sit back and sip my new drink. "Benny's being such a bully."

I should tell them the truth about the kiss—these are my dear friends, after all. But I didn't even tell Noelle. I just feel so stupid for how into it I was. And then he turned out to be faking it. A show for neighborhood bystanders.

"And he thinks I'm so into him," I add. "It's the worst. Seriously, what kind of person does this?"

"Benny, apparently," Noelle says. "But really, couldn't you just reason with him? On this whole forced cohabitation arrangement?"

I shrug. "I haven't tried that hard, I guess."

"Interesting," Noelle says.

"Oh, please!" I say, but she has a point. I can't recall the last time I felt so alive, so optimistic. I feel this easy camaraderie with him in spite of our animosity—or maybe because of it. All of that sparring and that humor—I'd miss those sparks.

"Mr. Billionaire Bluebeard," Tabitha says.

"You don't know the half of it!" I slam down my drink, nearly spilling it. "He literally has a room I'm not supposed to go into, and it's full of mysterious boxes!" This gets everybody's attention. I describe the boxes piled up to the ceiling, all the same size. Just this massive jumble of boxes that I'm never to open or even to touch. People are fascinated and excited because it's deliciously weird. Benny is not like other guys. It's something I love about him.

"Do the boxes have any kind of writing on them?" Antonio asks.

"Nonsensical letters and numbers. SKU sort of stuff. And they're all the same size. Large. The size of a washing machine."

"So let me get this straight," Jada says in full gossip mode. "One part of the room is completely bare, all pristine floors with some workout stuff, and the other side is full-on hoarder madness?"

"Correctamundo," I say, shaking my head.

"Washing machine. In other words, human-sized boxes," Antonio says.

"But it wouldn't be anything psycho like that," I say.

"Because you'd smell it," Jada says.

"There's always mummified remains," Antonio says.

"Oh please, stop," I say. "He's not like that. I'm thinking

more like...maybe a failed invention stuff?" I say. "Benny is really sensitive, and he has exacting standards for himself."

"But he must need access to whatever is in there, or else why not put it in storage?" Tabitha says. "You don't buy a kabillion-dollar condo just to stuff it with boxes."

"Perhaps it's a great quantity of something he likes to roll in," Jada says. "Maybe hundred-dollar bills."

"Or maybe it's something incredibly endearing...like Toys for Tots donations," Noelle says.

"Or a product that got discontinued," Antonio suggests. "Invite me over and I'll get it out of him. I'll be sneaky."

"Antonio, don't even think it!" I say, laughing. Antonio is an amazing model and friend, but not the best actor. Though he is the best over-actor.

Jada turns to me. "Benny said that you can't set foot in there, but a friend could. You could stand in the doorway and a friend could look through the boxes."

"No way!" I say. I forbid anybody looking in Benny's boxes and the conversation rolls on to Tabitha's style storefront empire, as we like to call it. I listen, loving my friends extra hard.

But she's given me an idea: I promised Benny that I wouldn't ever go in that room, but I could stand in the doorway and teach, couldn't I? And Kelsey and the girls could be in there. Nobody would have to touch the boxes. There's enough room in there to rehearse without having to go near the boxes. It's such a brilliant idea!

I text Mac, instructing him to arrange it, complete with a link to the parents-and-guardian contact info on Dropbox. He can always say "no."

Rex arrives, kisses Tabitha, and proceeds to order several baskets of deep-fried tater tots for the group. Tabitha is just beaming, because that's how much she loves them—almost as much as she loves Rex.

"I understand congratulations are in order," Rex says to me.

"Uh! Don't get me started!" I say. "But I couldn't be more excited about the tots!"

I don't eat that kind of thing while in rehearsal mode—I have to worry about weigh-ins and bloating and keeping my energy level up, but I allow myself to have a few when the baskets arrive. And then a few more, because they are so delicious, they blow my mind.

And then a few more.

Eventually, I force myself out of my chair and excuse myself to go to the restroom to stop myself from consuming the whole basket. In-town performances start soon, and I have to be good.

I get in line behind a couple, thinking about the boxes, and suddenly I'm replaying the kiss, snapping back to the fierce gravitational force of the scene, every deliciously sexy, edgy, exciting moment of it.

I work the stuffing out of my assets.

I breathe in the memory of it, filling myself with the goodness of it.

And I know I think wishfully, but it really seemed like he was into the kiss for a while there. And for that matter, I still think he remembers "Alejandro." There's no way he doesn't, considering his amazing memory and how many times we all heard the song. Why would he lie about it? It's one of my favorite memories of him.

Argh!

I send a text to Benny.

Me: You're such a liar. You totally know 'Alejandro' still!

Which comes out as "Yours such a life" thanks to autocorrect and predictive text and me hitting the send button early.

Me: Scratch that.

Which comes out as "such that" due to those same factors.

I amend the text yet again with similar results, and suddenly my phone is ringing.

And naturally my attempt to send his call to voicemail ends with his voice saying, "Francine? Is that you? Where are you?"

I press the thing to my ear. "Screw you, you know that you still know 'Alejandro.' And so do I. We both know that you know 'Alejandro.' We both know that song perfectly well, that's all I'm saying."

I'm all about getting off the line, but he wants to know where I am and if I'm okay and with friends.

"Yes to all of the above. Your asset is well and good!" With that I hang up.

Why did I contact him? Why would I do that? How embarrassing is it that I'm acting like a besotted schoolgirl?

Several minutes later, I'm back with the gang. They've left a last tater tot for me, and it makes me feel weepy, so touched and tipsy am I. "You guys are the best. The absolute best. You would never think I'm an asset!"

"I think you're a wonderful asset," Tabitha says.

"You're an asset to this group, *stellina mia*!" Antonio says.

"Fine," I say, savoring the last delicious bite. "But I'm not convenient!"

Tabitha tilts her head, thinking hard about this.

"I'm not," I assure her. She looks like she wants to argue, but right then, Kelsey and Mia and their "Anything Goes" gang all arrive. There are hugs all around, and the sound level rises dramatically like it always does with an influx of theater people. They crowd around the bar; a few of them still have dramatic stage makeup on, a few just have intense eyebrows. The crowd at The Wilder Club is used to that kind of thing.

Max is suddenly there—he's telling some funny and highly entertaining story, and more drinks are ordered. Somehow I end up with a fresh drink, too, and I'm drinking it and losing myself in the scene. Kelsey can't believe I'm drinking more than one drink, and I'm telling Kelsey that maybe my punishing and spartan training regimen will benefit from some variation. She thinks I won't think that tomorrow, and I disagree.

"Dynamite" comes on and she screams that we have to dance. There's no dance floor, but that doesn't stop somebody like Kelsey—or Max or Mia, for that matter, and suddenly we're all dancing in the middle of the bar, all wild and free. Even in my drunken state, I know how to dance with mostly upper body movements, to have fun and protect my knee. Years of living with this knee pain on and off has settled that knowledge into my bones. Everybody is always telling me not to do this and that, but they are looking at the outside in. They don't see how I can make things work.

I take a break and grab some water and share a bubbly drink with Noelle while informing her that I really, *really* need to go. Instead I pull her back out into the dance area.

Two songs later, I feel Mia's grip on my arm. And people have stopped dancing even though the music is still playing.

"What?" I say.

"He's here," she says.

"What?" I ask, even though I heard her perfectly well.

"He's here," she repeats.

I don't need to look around. I can feel him. And then he's in my line of sight, pushing past people wearing his Wolf Benny face, coming in all hardass. My heart beats happily.

My friends let him through, but stay hovering.

"Francine," he says.

I narrow my eyes. "Shouldn't you be out dressed as people's grandmothers delivering things in baskets?"

"What are you doing?" he asks.

"Drinking, dancing. Tater tots were recently involved," I say.

He scowls, and it just makes me happy. I link arms with him and turn to my friends. "My husband is here!" I say it as a joke, but it feels nice—to the same idiot part of me that thought the kiss in the park was nice, anyway.

I introduce him to my friends as we all head off of the dance floor.

Antonio is acting especially chummy. "We're brainstorming strange collections to start," he says. "Do you have a favorite thing to collect, Benny? I bet a man like you has a collection of some sort."

Benny frowns. "Not really."

"Some people collect products that have been discontinued," Antonio says. "I know a guy who collects Smartwater!"

Benny nods. "Uh-huh."

I laugh, keeping his arm locked up in mine.

Antonio puts on a stormy and tragic expression, brow furrowed, very Shakespearean. "If they ever discontinued Barnabus light hair texture hair cream, I don't know what I'd do," he growls darkly. "I would want to buy it all."

"You must really love that hair gel," Benny says politely, mystified by Antonio's strange passion.

"I do," Antonio says. "And if it were to be discontinued..." He stares intently at Benny.

Benny nods.

I'm just grinning stupidly at him. My face has a mind of its own at this point. "Don't mind Antonio!" I say.

Benny gives me a strange look. "Somebody's boisterous tonight," he says.

"If that's a euphemism, then yes, I am boisterous," I say.

"Seconding boisterous," Kelsey says.

I pull Benny closer, so happy he came. "We are so deeply in love," I say to my friends. Then I turn to him and our gazes lock. It does something to me deep down. "He cannot stand to be without me. That is the kind of marriage that we have. He realizes his mistake what with the Swiss chalet. The Bluebeard workout room. The wifely conscription."

He gives me a warning look that may or may not be playful. It's so wrong to think he's sexy.

"He couldn't be without me," I continue. "So he came out into the night."

Menacing heat emanates from Benny's adorable face. Excitement skitters in my stomach.

"His penthouse feels empty without his sweet wife," I continue. "A house that is not a home."

The delicious heat beams on. I watch, lost in his eyes. My friends are chattering about something else, but all I can see is Benny.

He draws close, speaking softly. "I was just thinking, you know, what you told me about regretting staying out late. Athlete in training and all that."

I blink. He remembered?

"And Alverson said he had dropped you here, and I just wanted to make sure..."

"That is very gallant," I say.

"I am your husband," Benny says.

"True," I say. And he's acting like a husband, and I'm enjoying it. I appreciate him trying to bring me to my senses. It *is* late. I *am* an athlete in training.

Five minutes later, we're in the back of Benny's limo, speeding toward home. Streetlights strobe his handsome features in soft yellows and whites with the occasional red flame of a taillight. Benny's texting and scrolling. He mumbles something about morning in Europe.

I flash back on the way he walked in, so annoyed and determined.

"He couldn't stay away from his beautiful wife," I say. "No

matter how hard he tried, no matter what measures he employed."

He sniffs, still focused on his phone.

I smile.

Sculptors talk about chipping away at a hunk of stone with the sense that they are freeing the true form inside. I can relate. Benny is a beautiful, cold, hard statue that traps a beating heart that I very much want to touch.

I adjust his collar. "Thrice he visited the boxes," I continue. "Even that did not suffice."

"Are you going to make me regret coming to pick you up?" he rumbles.

"He sat upon the workout room floor surrounded by the boxes' unspeakable contents, regretting bitterly that he didn't sing 'Alejandro' to her when he had the chance. What, really, would it have cost him? He couldn't sing a simple song?"

He finally looks up. "When will you stop with the song?"

I grin. "Ummm..."

He watches me, still in his quintessential stone-statue mode. Everything about him feels achingly familiar, yet so maddeningly remote.

Suddenly he begins to speak: "He sat at home in his lonely study, wondering why she keeps asking. Why does she care? Is it something he should be worried about? Has she perhaps contracted rickets? Or scurvy?"

I close my fingers around his non-phone-arm. I'm near enough to his whiskery cheek that I can smell his spicy scent, near enough that I can feel the heat coming off his skin. I can even feel his pulse rise. Or maybe it's my pulse rising.

"She keeps asking because she doesn't understand why he says he doesn't remember when she's quite sure that he does." I do the rest as a stage whisper. "It drives her a little bit crazy."

"What you overlook entirely, however, is the fact that he likely has good reasons," Benny says.

"The fact that you used 'entirely' and 'however' in the same sentence so makes me want to kiss you," I say.

"I wouldn't advise it."

"Wouldn't you?" I ask, grinning. The more wolf-nerdy he talks and acts, the more I want to kiss him. "Would you entirely not advise it? Would it vex you?"

He glares sullenly ahead, as though he's enduring the unendurable. His eyebrows are slashes of brown over his tan glasses, which have tiny pale striations in the rims.

I slide a hand on up onto his lapel. "I won't give up on you, Benny."

He closes his fingers around my wrist—gently at first, but then his grip tightens. Maybe he meant to remove my hand from his person, but he just holds it there, pressed against his heartbeat.

Our gazes lock. Time stills. The energy between us swells in the small space of the limo.

Something new is happening. I'm a miner, sensing a crack in the unforgiving veneer of Wolf Benny. I want to wedge in and pry him open. I want to touch him, skin to skin.

I lean in. My lips hover at the side of his, desire beating in my veins. "She's going to kiss you now," I say.

He turns to me suddenly. Strong hands cradle my face. Harsh lips claim mine, pressing hungrily against mine. He's kissing me, greedy and frenzied with passion, fingertips practically vibrating against my jawline.

I groan, shot through with liquid pleasure. His kiss radiates through my belly, my thighs, my breasts.

He pulls back, then, staring at me in a feral way. His nostrils contract with a ragged intake of breath. I feel like the prey of the sexiest beast ever, paralyzed with excitement.

He kisses me again and I kiss him right back, tunneling my fingers through his hair.

I swoop my tongue into his mouth, feeling deeply connected with him—so much so that I can feel the shifts in him like the topography of a grade school map. Here he's thrumming with excitement, here he's ragged, here he's groaning.

Then suddenly he's smooth. All the wild energy is gone. The heart of him is gone, like somebody flipped the suave switch. Like he turned into Sexorator 2000 or something.

"Hey," I whisper. "Come back."

"What are you talking about?" he rumbles.

"You left. You were there, and you left. You were in with me and you left," I say.

He gives me a debonaire gaze, ever so amused. "If you don't like my kissing technique, just say so."

"I liked it for a while. Until you closed yourself off."

"Just as a reminder, the current charade is you as my wife; not my psychotherapist." He straightens his jacket, resuming his faraway stare out the other side of the limo.

"Well, if anybody had any doubts about us," I say, echoing his words from the park, "they don't now."

FOURTEEN

Benny

I HEAD for my study when we get home, knowing I'll be unable to sleep. Hating how I forgot myself back there.

I should've resisted the impulse to go and get her in the first place, resisted the urge to kiss her. Francine always wants what she can't have. She's a cat who hates a closed door, and like a cat, she'll lose interest the moment she gets what she wants.

Been there, done that.

When I come out a little bit later, I find her curled up asleep in the den with *Sleepless in Seattle* playing. She's in the loveseat next to the fireplace. It really is the best seat in the house—you can see the fireplace, you can see the TV, you can see the view out the window over the river.

But it's not the best for sleeping.

I stand there, annoyed on her behalf, unsure what to do. She didn't even choose the couch; she went for the small loveseat. She'll feel like shit tomorrow.

Our wedding night all over again. Though unlike tonight, I

was drunk, too—we were both lightweights back then, I guess. Unprepared for the tequila punch.

I'd kissed her that night—thoroughly and ravenously and over and over. And then again at the wedding ceremony; the moment they'd instructed us to kiss, we'd drunkenly and exuberantly obeyed. I had my wits about me enough to know we shouldn't sleep together, though. Francine was eager to, but I wanted us clearheaded. It was important to me. The whole thing was important to me.

Not so much to her.

She remembered at least some of that night—a lot of the fun parts, from what it sounds like, and still she took off. Never looked back.

She shifts and a lock of hair falls over her cheekbone. Maybe this charade needs to end. I need to give her the papers and cut her loose.

The first time I ever saw Francine was in the season kickoff meeting to 'Alejandro.' All the dancers and stagehands were gathered in the auditorium seats where the audience would normally sit, and the managers and directors took to the stage to go through the schedule and rules.

I noticed her right away. How could I not? She was the most beautiful woman there. The most beautiful woman in the world.

It didn't occur to me to talk to her. She might as well have been another species. I was too blunt on a good day; self-conscious about every little movement. My awkwardness only got worse when I was excited about something; I'd come off intense, angular. Annoyed.

When I was interested in something, people thought I was glaring. They assumed I was annoyed when I wasn't. Yes, I'd get annoyed from time to time. I'd get annoyed when people would act illogically or when they'd refuse to grasp the most obvious of things. I'd get annoyed when people made assumptions about my annoyance, an unfortunate feedback loop.

I was fine as a loner.

Until Francine.

She struck me as very nearly magical in the way that she breezed through rehearsals, nailing the choreography with minimal effort, drawing people into her enchanting sphere of charm.

At the same time, she had this curious quality of being outside of the herd, though it was impossible to put my finger on exactly how, because she was the center of attention. I slide my fingertips against each other, remembering the feel of her face.

I remind myself that a woman like her always has to be the center of attention wherever she goes, even if it's two people in a limo.

Still I should move her. It would be best if she was in a bed.

I consider getting a blanket and a pillow, and then maybe sliding a pillow under her head. I stand there, vacillating intensely between being annoyed and concerned. Though when I'm honest with myself, my annoyance is mostly concern.

She shifts in the chair, frowns. Troubled. I really should bring her to the bed; she'll feel shitty enough as it is tomorrow. She'd hate that she's sleeping like this.

It's here that I make my decision. Gently, I scoop her up, lifting her slowly into my arms and pulling her into my chest. I head silently across the living room and dining room, down past the river in nightscape, flashing here and there where spangles of waves catch the moon.

She's light and warm in my arms; frail, even, though I know that she's anything but. A dancer is an athlete with the explosive core strength of a wrestler.

The dancers came from different dance backgrounds and dance traditions; a few of them had come out of gymnastics and circus arts, but when they'd compare notes, it became clear that none of them had even an iota of the background and discipline that Francine had. Yet she acted like she was on perpetual vacation.

Francine was the girl who wanted to stay out the latest, to have the most fun, to eat the most decadent foods, to date the flashiest guys. It baffled me because getting to her level of ability took extreme practice—I was a manically dedicated person myself, and knew another maniacally dedicated person when I saw her.

I head down the hall, walking smoothly, taking care not to let her feet brush the walls.

We were all forced to dine together after shows and rehearsals—some weeks even with assigned seating. Those in charge thought it would inspire camaraderie between the dancers, the stagehands, and tech crew. I found these meals to be a torment and an exercise in delineating just how acutely I didn't belong, but at least I came to understand a lot about dancers in general, and Francine in particular.

She started dance at three, and by ten years old, she was boarding at an elite academy, hundreds of miles from her home on the plains, putting in ten-hour days of workouts and stretching and drills and dances. There were strict dietary regimens, lots of yoga and physical therapy, magnesium baths for her muscles. When her day was over, she'd drag herself up the ladder to the bunk bed she shared with another dancer who was also far from home, and start her school studies.

I settle her into her bed and go in search of a warmer blanket than what she has. I don't know where anything is. Why should I? I never have guests. I try the linen closet, but it's just sheets. I send Mac a text and wait alone in the silence of my hallway.

The almost monk-like nature of her preteen and teen years

became even clearer to me when I realized how unfamiliar she was with the workings of a normal high school; she'd never snuck out of the house, she'd never gone to a party or football game or a music festival. I hadn't either, but it wasn't surprising in my case. Francine would've loved those things.

In the world, but apart from it. Like a fairy tale creature.

The night we were married we told each other everything. Francine confessed how shut out from her peers she felt, like an alien from outer space. And being the youngest of a large rural family, her parents and siblings treated her as the permanent baby. Nobody believed she could hack the dance world. People didn't think she had grit.

They couldn't have been more wrong.

Before I could stop myself, I was telling her how awkward I always felt. I would act too intense and put people off. I told her about my high-energy, outgoing, tech-challenged family and the jokes that I was maybe switched at birth. You'd think a family like that would've made me more socially adept. It didn't. We joked that we were aliens who'd found each other.

By her own admission, she remembers a lot of that night. Not all of it but a lot. Enough.

Mac gets back to me: ottoman blanket storage, another feature for guests that never gets used.

Mac was adamant I keep guest amenities just in case, and I went with it, more to placate him than anything. Because what the hell do I need with guest amenities? I only have business visitors, and if and when I would ever have a non-business visitor, I would put them up at a hotel, including my parents, though they never visit. The few holidays I ventured back to Michigan, I always stayed at a hotel. We're not close like other families.

I bring her the blanket and then I go back and get the water and the aspirin and I bring it in and I set it on the bedside table where she'll see it. I decide that's everything I can do, so I head back to the kitchen to make a bagel.

I stuff the two halves into the slots of the toaster, watch the wires turn red.

The Monique and Igor thing was the first time I'd ever engaged in any kind of joking or humorous interaction whatsoever, though I would have never admitted it. What kind of person doesn't joke? It sounds psychotic. It's not that I couldn't recognize or appreciate humor—I always have appreciated humor and I laugh when things are actually funny—a rare occurrence, but it happens.

However, Francine's Monique and Igor thing was one of those rare instances when something was actually funny, though I seemed to be in the minority about it. Cast members would smile politely as if her fake daughter stories were simply odd, but really they were hilarious. The one thing that was missing from those jokey humblebrag stories of hers was a competitor for Monique. With that, Igor was born. Unexpectedly. A surprise baby like me.

Suddenly I was telling an Igor story, putting it up against her Monique story.

And suddenly we were having fun.

Me. With a sense of humor. It had everything to do with Francine; we clicked invisibly. Synergistic operating systems under the surface. Two fake children, uniquely ours.

The night that we got married, she described the picture she had in her head of Monique, which looked suspiciously like her. And the picture that she had of Igor looked like me. "Igor is brilliant and misunderstood like his papa," she'd said, "though one must overlook the tragic little teapot performance incident."

———

WHEN I GET up the next morning, there's coffee made and the cutting board has a little puddle of juice from an orange sliced into six sections.

I flip Pandora on the penthouse-wide sound system, assuming she took off, but when I wander into the den, she's on the couch with Spencer. Her hair is down, glossy as a mirror. She's in a T-shirt and pajama pants, one leg outstretched with the pants leg rolled up. She's pressing an ice pack around her knee, forming it into a semicircle.

The Beau Cirque dancers used to do that, trying to press the ice or the heat all the way around their sore joint. Usually they preferred pressing it for each other, so that the person with the injury could focus entirely on relaxing it. That seemed to be the gold standard—somebody else doing the pressing while the injured person relaxed.

But of course, I've ripped her away from all of her girlfriends who would probably do this sort of thing for her.

"Good morning," I say.

She looks up. "Thanks for the aspirin." I can read everything from her tone. She feels angry. Shut out.

The heat pack is draped over on the back of the couch, probably having cooled off. That's the dancer technique from Beau Cirque—ice-heat-ice-heat-ice. They were always very specific about beginning and ending with ice. It was considered a bad sign when a dancer was ice-heating a lot.

"What?" she asks.

"You want me to heat that?" I ask.

"No."

"Is that a yes?" I ask.

She looks up. If she thinks that's funny, she's disguising it well. "No."

I stand there, frustrated. I want to heat up the heat pack for her. And what about this injury? A picture pops up in my mind of her confiding in me about it. Maybe I can help her think this thing through or find resources for her knee. I want to protect her wishful thinking. I want to pick her up and carry her across the condo again—not to her bedroom, but to mine. I try to look annoyed while I fight like hell to get my reactions to her under control. There's a first—me *trying* to look annoyed.

"I'm standing right here. I may as well."

"You don't get to be a cold and remote captor one minute and then a caring husband the next. I'm your show horse that you need for whatever reason. I'm a convenient employee for the next two weeks. Do you go around getting ice packs for your other employees?"

"You're being ridiculous," I say, frustrated. "It'll ruin the whole process if you have to get up and walk all the way back to the kitchen. Lest you forget all that time I spent in the auditorium. Why not maximize all of the tools that you have at your disposal?"

"Like you did with me?" she asks.

"That's right." I grab the heat pack and head to the kitchen, tossing it in the microwave, stopping at every ten seconds to get it just the right temperature—just bearable to the touch. That was always the goal. When it's just right, I take it into her.

She holds it, evaluating the temperature. "Perfect," she says.

"Move over."

"Just give it to me," she says.

"I'm right here. Let me."

"I have these things on the ends of my arms, you see." She holds up her hands.

"It's better for somebody else to hold it and you know it," I say. "You can concentrate on softening the joint." That's what dancers always used to say.

"Leave me alone. Let's just get through this thing, okay?"

Get through this thing. What the hell am I doing? I should

tell her she can have the papers. They're still in my briefcase. All I have to do is sign them and give them to her to sign.

"Move over, come on."

I see it in her face when she's about to relent. I feel it in my chest. We're too connected, or at least, I'm too connected to her, a woman who discards people as easily as peanut shells.

She rolls her eyes and scoots over. I settle in next to her and she puts her legs over my lap, wincing briefly. I don't like it. Her pain tugs on something deep inside of me—some primal need to protect her, to find a solution.

Fuck.

I hold the heat pack in a concave manner so that it gets all the spots at once. She leans back, eyes closed, finally relaxing. "Thank you. I guess this is nice," she says.

"You guess," I say.

A smile lights the corners of her mouth. She smells like spicy flowers—even the shampoo she uses is her specific Jasmine. A melodic song is playing over the sound system. Something sweet and old by Bowie. I'm glad it's not something annoying.

Her legs feel fucking amazing on my lap. I could so easily lean down, press my face to her PJ—pants-clad thighs. No other woman has ever inspired the urges in me that she does. Even her flaws are sexy—her impulsiveness. Her fanaticism. Her pigheadedness when it comes to injury—even that makes me want to kiss her.

But I keep it objective. I've seen guys lose their objectivity over a woman and it's not pretty. She ripped a hole inside me once before and I won't be that besotted kid again, twisted up in painful knots of one-sided love—or what he thought was love.

"That's the problem with palatial penthouses," she says. "Everything's far away from wherever you're sitting. Extreme wealth really is so inconvenient."

"Oh yeah?" I say.

"In little apartments, the microwave is just a few steps away from the comfortable living room chair. Way better."

I keep the contact light and present, nearly all the way around to the back of the knee.

It's strange. In my long-gone juvenile ideas of us together, it was always her dazzled by me in some way; it was never anything so human as this. One person caring for another.

"You have good friends," I observe.

"I do. I'm really lucky—I absolutely lucked into that building. And then my roommate moved out, and I was so sad, but this shy, rural girl answered my ad and we were instant best friends. Noelle—you met her."

"The mail carrier," I say.

"Mm-hmm."

"I've been here for years and I don't even know my neighbors," I say.

"Most people in the city don't. I think part of it is that a lot of us are just so passionate about the things that we're passionate about, and that connects us. I have friends who are artists or in the theater or starting their own little businesses...they all get what it's like to be giving up a lot of your life to chase a dream, and not everybody understands that. Not everybody understands when you're not automatically free to watch a football game on Sunday or go out on the town. Not everybody understands when you say you won't be free for the next six months. But my crew at 341 understands that. You understand it."

"I certainly do," I say, shifting the pack.

She gazes out the window. "When you live in the same building, you can walk down the hall and have a twenty-minute visit with a friend without blowing up your whole day. In rehearsal season, I'm so busy, I'd only see other dancers if I didn't live there."

I think about James and this twist of sadness moves through me. Though it did help to talk with her about him. I didn't expect that.

"You were friends with the gang at Beau Cirque," I remind her.

A fleeting smile touches her lips. "And you were so over them. You were your own little island with a keep-out sign."

"Hardly," I say. "It was the reality that I had in front of me, that's all."

I feel her gaze snap in my direction. "You would've changed it if you could have? Even with the Beau Cirque dancers? You wanted to be chummier?"

"Well, I would've settled for not making them nervous. I didn't want to have resting annoyed face."

She narrows her eyes. "You mean, like resting bitch face, except you looked annoyed?"

"Exactly."

"You're telling me you weren't annoyed all that time?"

"Not *all* that time," I say.

A smile touches the corners of her lips. "I don't know, Benny," she says. "I think you were annoyed some of that time."

"Fine. Some of the time. I'd say it was only fifty percent of the time that I was annoyed. The rest of the time I only *looked* annoyed."

She's just laughing now. Only Francine would laugh about this. "I don't know if that helps your case!"

"What?" I protest.

"Annoyed only half the time. Please, folks, don't get the wrong idea. Benny's only annoyed about half the time, lest you think he's annoyed all the time."

"There are a lot of annoying things out there," I say.

"And vexing," she adds.

"Many people are far more easily vexed and annoyed than I

am." I form the pack over the part that is the traditional pain point, pressing gently.

"That feels good," she says.

This puffs me up ridiculously. But lest things go too well, the Dave Matthews Band comes on.

The Dave Matthews Band does not feel good. It feels like nails, in fact, scratching on a chalkboard. I stare longingly at my phone, just out of my reach on the side table. What the hell! Why does that keep happening? If only the phone were nearer, I'd zap that song to high heaven.

She's staring at me, wide-eyed.

"Sorry, I hate that band," I say.

"It's okay if you want to get up and change it. I would totally understand."

"That's okay, I'll pour bleach in my ears later," I say.

"You're not gonna change it?"

"This is a very delicate procedure with your knee here," I say.

The way she looks at me, it's like I turned into Mother Teresa or something, just because I don't want to leave my post of knee-pack holding, even though turning off the most hated music on the planet could only be helpful. She may not hate the Dave Matthews Band the way I do, but it has to be doing something destructive to her on a quantum level.

The strains of Dave Matthews go on. It blows my mind, because how can a band pack so much insipid annoyingness into one song? Teams of musicologists could work around the clock studying it and never figure it out.

"Dude, change it! Every fiber in your being is itching to change it!" she says.

"Maybe Sloan-Kettering can give me a lobotomy later," I say.

She smiles and I feel this rush of affection for her that I quickly tamp down, because I know better. She pushes my hands from her knee and lifts her legs. "Grab your phone and change it already! It's like you're being boiled to death right before my eyes!"

I twist to the far side of the couch and lunge for my phone, stabbing a decisive thumbs-down.

I settle back in and she flops her legs back down onto my lap like it's the most natural thing in the world. I carefully press the ice around her knee and we sit in companionable silence. It feels good to be with her.

"I still need to get those Dave Matthews Band tickets for us and Juliana," she teases.

I give her a dark look.

She pets Spencer's scruff. "So how's the sale coming?"

"The negotiation of it is done. We've met each other. There are a few more details to handle, but the next step is to finalize the terms and then close the deal."

"And that happens when?"

"In five days, supposedly."

"Supposedly?" she echoes.

"Well, there's the reality of working for somebody for a year," I say. "It's a year of my life."

"Oh my god, are you rethinking that crazy plan?" She sits up. "Are you coming to your senses on that?"

"It's not as simple as coming to my senses," I say. "A lot of things would have to change if I nixed the sale. I started the business with a friend who had a similar vision, and that friend is gone."

"Right," she says softly.

"Being in the trenches with a best friend like that, solving problems, getting ideas, weathering defeats, having each other's backs, it was a once-in-a-lifetime thing."

She doesn't rush to fill the silence that follows. I look up and she's watching me, and I feel her kindness, her compassion.

"Six months," I add, meaning, that's how long he's been gone. "People have moved on. Rented his home. Filled his chair. Closed his memberships. Like he's erased."

"*You* remember. Spencer remembers."

Of course she gets it. She sits there silent, a warm presence on my lap. Maybe I can't trust this easy feeling between us, but I'm eating it up.

"Was he into robotics like you?"

I sniff. "Was he as big of a nerd as I am? Is that your question?" I ask.

"Maybe."

"Yeah, though you wouldn't have known it from the outside —he looked like he belonged in the Rocky Mountains more than subway cars, but he knew his way around a lab. We loved having freedom to pursue crazy ideas. Solutions to impossible problems. We gave each other a lot of shit. We played a lot of ping pong."

"A friend like that is everything, Benny."

I shift the pack. Her empathy feels real and I don't know what to do with it. I don't want things real with her. I don't want to be unraveled. Those things belong in the past.

"To find a counterpart in that way," she adds. "Will Juliana's firm allow you to continue those pet projects at least?"

"No, they're all in on the microrobotic cleaners."

"Well then why sell to them?" she asks.

"Because I can't run the firm alone. Big-picture thinking is not my thing," I say. "Don't forget, I'm the microrobotics guy."

She gazes up at the ceiling. There's a skylight up there, and you can see fluffy white clouds sailing slowly across the bright blue sky.

"My roommate, Noelle, and I used to eat chocolate chip cookie dough ice cream," she says. "The only good part was the chocolate chip cookie dough. So, whenever we'd have it we were both always angling to get the bites with chocolate chip cookie dough. One day I found a package of just chocolate chip cookie dough. And I was like, why are we not getting this? So we got it."

"It was better?"

"Much better. So my question to you would be, what are the chocolate chip cookie dough parts? Is there a way that you can arrange your company so there are only chocolate chip cookie dough parts?"

I shift the pack. "How did I skip the chocolate chip cookie dough section in my business courses? I can't imagine how it happened."

"Seriously!" She pokes at my thigh. "Tell me the chocolate chip cookie dough parts."

I'm watching her, mind spinning.

"What?" she says.

"What?" I ask.

"You're looking at me funny."

I adjust the ice pack. It's a good question she's asking. Simple. "Chocolate chip cookie dough parts," I say. "Working with the team in the lab. I'm not good with people—"

"Wuuuuut," she jokes.

"Right?" I say. "But when we have a project between us, a natural thing to orient around, then I enjoy a team."

"What would you work on? If you had that year and that team. If you weren't in Juliana's lab."

Before I can stop myself, I'm telling her about microrobots scavenging vibrations for energy. She thinks I'm making it up. I'm laughing, going on and on, fed by her amazement. At one point I notice she's beaming at me. "What?" I ask.

"I love how intense you are about it," she says. "When you're in that lab, you probably give it your whole soul."

"My whole soul! Let's hope not," I say, and she snorts.

I don't know what to do with her affection, her help, her kindness. This marriage is a mirage and I'm dying of thirst.

"I mean, can't you get a team like that?" she asks.

"I have one, but I can't run the business without James."

"Can't you find another James? And you go, here's some money, please steer this thing and leave me alone in my lab? Aren't there headhunters and things?" she asks. "Don't you deserve to be happy?"

That question, I don't know what to do with it.

I sit there with her legs in my lap like the sexiest keyboard in the world, my hands formed around an ice pack, trying to still the thundering in my chest.

I'd meant to keep her at arm's length, but I'm doing a shit job of it. Things are feeling real now, and I'm feeling raw.

I need more of her. And I also need her to stop.

I lower my voice. "Are you even concentrating on relaxing your muscles?"

Her gaze rivets to me. The low voice affects her—I noticed that earlier.

"Or are you worrying about my business?" I rumble, brushing her thigh as I adjust the pack.

"I can do both at once," she says.

I draw a finger up her shin bone, up to where the pack covers her knee. Her skin feels like warm silk.

A wary light appears in her eyes.

"I can't have my show horse limping around, can I?" I lower my voice to an even deeper rumble. "It simply won't do."

She sucks in a breath. "You mean, your *magnificent* show horse?"

"I can't have my magnificent show horse in anything but peak condition."

Her voice, when it comes, is throaty. "Because of how you like to work your assets?"

I slide my hand down her calf, taking full control of the situation. "I like to work my assets wickedly hard."

She gasps as I slowly push a sock off her foot, then I bare the other. I'm not a foot guy, but I'm not above going with the flow. I let her feel the weight of my hand, let her feel like I'm in control here.

Even this slight touch overloads my senses, threatens to crash my control. Which tells me that I shouldn't be doing this—I really shouldn't, but I can't seem to stop myself. It's the feel of her skin. It's her heated expression. It's her Francine-ness.

"With your wicked ideas?" she asks with a mischievous gleam.

"That's right," I say.

She tries to sit up but I settle my other hand on her belly, push her back down. "Stay there," I say. She's threatening to steal all of my practiced control just by lying there—I don't need her hands on me, sending me over the edge.

She watches me, belly quivering with arousal.

Carelessly, I toss the ice pack.

A grin touches her lips.

I lay an arm lazily over her calves, holding her there while I creep my other hand down, down from her belly to the tie of her pajama pants. Slowly I loosen them, watching her watch me, aroused, which is a total turn-on. I'm hard as rock under the perfect weight of her legs. I can feel my pulse clear into my cock.

Francine reaches for me. "Let me—"

"Not a word, not one word," I say, pressing my hand down to the wetness between her legs.

She lets out a surrendering groan.

I pull her pajama pants clear off.

"Your shirt," I rasp. "Off. Now." I say it almost as a warning, letting her know that this is my show.

Her skin looks alive, cheeks darkened with excitement. Shaky hands move down to the hem of her shirt, then she pulls it clear off her head. Her sheer bra does nothing to disguise the sexy brown coins of her nipples. How many hours had I spent wondering what she'd look like?

I reach up and graze a hand over one perfect breast.

She tugs at my shirt. "I'm feeling a bit of clothes inequality here," she says.

"And you'll continue to feel it," I say, kneeling on the couch between her knees, efficiently stripping her bottom half bare, exposing her perfect mound, just a strip of dark hair that I have big plans for.

"If you think you're doing Sexorator 2000 again..." she says.

I don't know what she's talking about. All I can focus on is how badly I need to taste her.

Roughly I hoist her leg—the non-injured one—over my shoulder, struggling not to lose my senses in the face of her hotness, her spicy scent.

"Benny—"

"If you don't have that bra off in the next two seconds..." I turn and place a kiss on the inside of her thigh.

Her lips part, forming a soundless "o." That fucking "o" is everything. I kiss her thigh again, struggling to maintain control. "If you don't have that bra off in the next two seconds."

In my days of polishing my sex technique, I found it best to give commands. The more unreasonable, the better. I'm not bossy by nature, but when I learn a thing, I learn it well, and right now I'm learning her. One of us will be losing control and I plan for it to be her.

"Now. If you want to keep going..."

There's a torn look on her face. She wants this but she doesn't quite know what to make of me like this.

I kiss higher, a bit nearer to her sweet spot.

Her rib cage rises and falls. "God, Benny," she says, voice hoarse with wonder.

And then, wide-eyed, she does it—she pulls her bra off, revealing perfect breasts, smooth and perfect as the rest of her. I groan. I'm so fucking horny, I feel like my skin might rip apart from the inside.

I kiss my way up her inner thigh as she pants, rocks with need. I plant a kiss on that strip of hair. "Open your knees. Wide—wide for me."

She complies and I push my tongue clear into her hole. She gasps. I shove it in more, fuck her with it, and then I fuck her with my fingers while I drag the flat of my tongue clear up her pussy.

Small hands fly to my hair, gripping the strands as I lick her.

My name gusting out of her lips is the hottest thing I've ever heard. I take her folds into my mouth and I suck, letting her feel the inside of my mouth. I suck her and then I lick her some more. And then she's coming, crying out, sex pulsing under my merciless tongue.

"Oh my god," she says as she comes down. "What..." she asks, breathy, unable to form whatever question flew through her mind.

My hands are on her breasts now, and I'm kissing them. For the first time since we started, I let myself really take in this situation. It's Francine—fucking Francine!—sprawled out on my couch, naked and dizzy from an orgasm that I just gave her.

And everything in me swells, so much so that I'm in danger of rocketing right out into space.

Her hands are on my hair again and she pulls my mouth up to hers.

I get back ahold of myself and kiss her expertly, smooth with just the smallest edge of hunger showing, the perfect amount of tongue.

"Oh my god," she says into the kiss, wriggling under me like the pleasure is still radiating through her. My cock might never go down again. And then her hand is on my belt.

"Off," she says, giving me back my command. And I comply, clambering off the couch. I pull off my shirt first, because we're doing things my way. Her nostrils flare as she looks me over. She trails lazy fingertips down my stomach, my six-pack.

"Mmmmm," she says, and all of those hundreds of daily crunches in the workout studio are worth it, hundreds of crunches, reps upon reps of every muscle workout possible, all fueled by imagining just this moment.

Except not quite this moment.

It was a product of my juvenile imagination after Vegas nine years ago. It involved Francine being filled with remorse for having cast me aside like she did. It was her lusting after me, bitterly regretting her mistake, filled with lust and so freaking sorry. And I'm of course indifferent to her. I've gone on to bigger and better things. She has no more chance with me for anything but a quick tumble.

As one year turned into two, I grew out of that ridiculous fantasy, stopped orienting around her, stopped even considering her, though I kept up the workout regime.

I unbuckle my belt, yank it off with a flourish and toss it.

Francine slides her hands up my jeans-clad thighs, up to my fly. "Let me," she says. "I want to..." Pressing a palm over my impossibly steely erection. "I want to go all kinds of crazy on you, Benny!"

I'd imagined her saying things like this, but more generic.

And I wouldn't be affected the way I am now—I'd feel nothing but cold victory, the triumph of showing her what she'd never have, somebody so far beyond all of those losers in limos that she dated. I saw myself looking down dispassionately as she closed her lips over my cock. And then I'd grab her head and pump right into her.

Reality, needless to say, is radically different.

The high, excited hum she makes when my cock springs free kills me. She kisses the side of it, making Francine sounds.

I can barely function enough to shove my garments off my legs.

She looks up with a lusty smile. "I am going to so..." She doesn't finish the sentence because she's Francine.

She kisses the other side of it and I shove my fingers into her glossy hair.

I think my skin might peel off from sheer desire. "I am going to so..." And then her mouth is over me, finishing this sentence. I'm stroking her head, spinning so hard with pleasure it's a wonder I can keep standing.

I come with a guttural cry.

She waits for my dick to chill out before pulling her mouth off me, because that's how physically in tune she is with me.

"That's one way to punctuate a sentence," I say.

"Sometimes an exclamation point just won't do."

I'm laughing in spite of myself.

She beckons me down next to her, and without thinking, I go, squeezing in next to her on the small couch.

Francine only wants a divorce in the end. The sooner, the better.

Even so, I pull her head to my chest, wrap my arms around her head. I don't want to let her go, but I don't need to be face-to-face. I don't want a divorce, but I don't trust her in some essential way. I want to be free of the past and that kid that I was, but it's all around me.

Her scalp is moist with sweat against my pounding heart.

"Are you a cuddler, Benny?" she asks.

"No," I say.

I can feel the shape of her cheeks change, as if she's smiling. She doesn't believe me.

I'm not smiling. I'm looking up at clouds through the skylight, all puffy and fluffy and weightless against that technicolor blue. They look fake.

FIFTEEN

Francine

I'M STILL COMING BACK to planet earth, nestled in his arms. We're cuddling. I don't care if he wants to believe it's something else; that's what we're doing.

For a while there, I felt so connected to him and his vexatiously cogitating ways. It felt like we were being real together. I loved it. But then the next minute, he was Sexorator 2000, cool and smooth and uber-confident, the sexiest and most confusing being ever to walk the face of the earth.

Even so, it was hot. I'm still vibrating from the things he did to my body. And I pulled him off of it in the end. Sexorator 2000 is awesome, but Benny's better.

I turn and look up at him. I slide my palm over his cheek. He seems so somber. "What is it?" I ask.

"Nothing," he says.

He's not big on introspection—James definitely had his number there. There's clearly something on his mind, but you can't pull it out of him. He likes to stay remote.

I'm glad he had a friend like James. There are not a lot of people in this world who can look past that resting annoyance face to see the true beauty of Benny, but James obviously did.

And the fact that Benny's madly loyal surprises me not at all.

Will he ever find a home for Spencer? Maybe he doesn't want to let that connection to James go. Maybe he plans to ride out his allergies. There is so much I want to ask him but I don't want to push it and make him shut me out all over again.

"You want a snack?" he asks.

"Does it involve cheese and crackers?"

He's off the couch, pulling on his clothes. "It does now."

"Yay!" I say.

He disappears, and I reassemble myself, trying to put the least pressure on my knee, which is feeling nice and loose and nearly normal for once.

SIXTEEN

Francine

BENNY LEAVES for the office after that, and I do a recuperation day, taking full advantage of the semi-spa nature of the bathroom.

Afterwards, I head to 341 to pick up some more clothes; I stick around to hang out with Noelle up on the new rooftop garden that Malcolm created. She shows me her new planters. She has big plans for berries.

I don't go into the full rundown of what happened between Benny and me on the couch, meaning the story gets pretty vague after him holding an ice pack on my knee.

Even so, she's amazed. "I think he's into you," she says.

"It definitely seems like that at times, but I don't know if he'll ever forgive me for acting like a freak and making a pass at him and then ghosting him," I say.

We're leaning over the railing, staring at the building across the street, trying not to look in people's windows. That's the deal you make in New York. You see, but you don't look.

"I tried to apologize to him," I continue, "but he doesn't like to talk about the past. I think he will never really trust me."

"Yet he makes you play his wife," she says.

Luckily, there is big drama at her work, and I'm happy to hear about it, to get my mind off of the strangeness of Benny.

I don't see him that night at all.

The next morning when I trot out to the kitchen to grab coffee and a quick snack, his favorite mug is on the counter.

I put my hands around it. It's still slightly warm. I think about his hands on it. His lips. I run my finger all around the rim. Is he avoiding me now? Is he going to be an asshole again?

There's a knock at the front door. I go, thinking it might be Benny, and feeling happy about that, but it's Mac.

"You have to knock?" I ask. "I thought you just came in and out." *Like a butler*, but I don't say that.

"I always knock before I come in, but I do then let myself in if I have work here to do," he says, breezing past. "And I have tons to do to get ready for your class."

"Wait, what?"

He goes on to inform me that my class is all set for five o'clock after I get home from the dance studio. He had waivers signed and plans to have some chairs set up and parking figured out for those who need it.

"Parking..." I say.

He's going on about how there's probably only room for ten to view from inside the workout room but he'll set up a lounge just for the parents in the den. There will be snacks.

"Wait, back up, Mac! This class can actually happen?"

"You requested it the other night," he says. "Have you changed your mind? You said the class needed more practice times and that you wanted to use the space and have me make it happen. I've got two times worked out, but there's a possibility for a Saturday one. I was able to use the class roster you forwarded to interface with the parents and get everybody's a-okay."

"And Benny's okay with it?" I ask, stunned.

"He's good with it. He says this is your home, too."

I feel...elated. The girls need more practices. Adding another class time or switching class time by even ten minutes is traditionally half a day's headache, and here Mac has achieved the feat of scheduling entirely new class sessions. We won't be able to do barre work without a barre, but I'll take it!

"Okay," I say, practically backing away lest he change his mind, and also I'm running late at this point for the studio. "It's decided. They'll be here."

I lose myself in company class, working like a demon at the barre, letting the music wash through me.

It's hard not to keep going back to everything that happened. Center work begins, and I watch my colleagues in their grand pirouettes as I rehash the emotional roller coaster of being with Benny. I am really and truly falling for him again.

It's been ages since I've felt close with a man. It's just that guys don't ever seem to measure up, and somewhere along the line, I got too busy for the whole dating thing. Not hard when you're in a professional ballet company.

Eventually Annie and I are up for grand pirouette combinations. I use my heel to guide my rotation as the ballet mistress counts to eight, over and over again.

Class wraps up and I go down to the pocket park at the end of the block, thankful to spot an empty bench. I grab it in between bites of banana and give Kelsey a quick call to tell her the news that Mac, butler-slash-household manager extraordinaire, has worked his magic and put in a class tonight.

"Oh, I know. He called me too," she says.

"Oh," I say. "Well... Wow."

Kelsey is just laughing. "Not only that, but I told everybody at 341 that you've got a butler helping to manage our class now, and we all laughed at how easily you're sliding into your hated billionaire lifestyle. Mia told me to tell you to pass her the Grey Poupon."

"Boy, you really don't want me to send that limo to pick you up now, do you?" I say.

"I don't even know you right now," she says.

Of course I do send Alverson to pick Kelsey up, because I might as well enjoy the perks of being Mrs. Benjamin Stearnes while I have them. Up in the penthouse, Kelsey and I help Mac set out waters and a cheese-and-vegetable platter for the guardians. I'm about to say he doesn't really need to do any of it, but he seems to have worked hard on it. I also don't say yet again how shocked I am that Benny would be okay with it.

The students and their parents and guardians arrive. Everybody is stunned by the new practice space. "It's just temporary," I explain. "I don't really live here."

"If you lived here, you probably wouldn't be teaching dance classes," one of the mothers says.

"Oh, I'd still do it," I say, and it's the truth. I'd teach the girls for free.

We get the girls all herded into the space and Kelsey and I start the gang on their warm-ups, going from fast walking to backwards walking to the dreaded bear walks.

Mac's been busy. The heavy bag has been hoisted up and he pushed the weights to one side. A row of chairs at the far end creates a natural barrier to the boxes. I'm glad. Making sure the boxes and their contents remain private is important to me. Maybe it's ridiculous that I have this sense of protectiveness over him and his weirdly private ways, but I do.

The fact that I have to stay in the doorway and not set foot into the room doesn't stop the class from being awesome. The space is bright and full of light, and the girls feel like they're on stage a little bit, and they glow with pleasure. The girls just never stop being fun.

What's more, my being trapped in the doorway doesn't stop Kelsey and me from doing our usual routine of acting like we're having fun, power-lounging and inspecting our nails while we put the girls through the rigorous and punishing warm-ups. It's our special ritual, and the girls love being screamy and complain-y while we act like we're having fun watching them toil.

There's one point where I'm just laughing, and the girls are dancing, and I'm looking at the scene from outside of myself, in a way, and I realize that working with this troupe is peak fun, peak creativity, and peak happiness—professionally, anyway.

I'm shocked.

Is it truly possible that I'm the most fulfilled when I'm teaching this class? I get tons of energy from it. I love it. I look forward to it. When did class start being more fun and fulfilling than my work on stage? I try to think back...a year? Two years?

I love performing, and I love company class with my colleagues, but it has felt like a dark cloud in my life because of my knee. All the worry, the pain, the anguish.

I always imagined myself hanging on as a performing dancer for as long as possible, but do I need to reassess that? It's a shock even to ask myself the question.

"So," Kelsey says, breaking me out of my reverie. "You're settling into Chez Billionaire like a boss!"

"Stop!" I say. "Quite the opposite."

"Gonna need more than that," Kelsey says. "I need an update. And by update, I mean me and everybody else at home. You had definite strange chemistry the other night at Wilder. We all saw it. Don't deny it."

"Okay, it's going intensely and vexatiously confusing. Will you accept that as my answer?"

Kelsey's studying my face. "No."

I clap and call out a direction change.

"Maybe you guys should be...at least dating maybe?" she tries.

"He's making me play his wife. I think the tell-me-your-favorite-hobbies phase is moot at this point," I say.

"Guys," Kelsey grumbles. She goes out onto the floor and models a move, something I can't do being banished from the hardwood flooring, but that just lets me hang back and enjoy the girls and think about my life.

Nobody asks why I stay in the doorway.

The ballet is based on a Netflix show that these girls are wild about; it was decided by the group that this would be the theme and we did the choreography together. It's exuberant and fun like a ballet should be—far more fun than the Sevigny ballet.

Is this where my heart is?

They're leaping when Kelsey comes back to stand with me.

"So what's his deal, really?" Kelsey asks. "Is he using you to make sure that every woman he has a tryst with in the future understands she will always be the other woman? Is it a simple case of being a commitment phobe?"

I yell out another few commands, trying to ignore the weird way this sits with me. Benny with another woman. Having sex with women that he doesn't even like. Having sex with any other women at all. Even as Sexorator 2000.

"I don't know about him being commitment-phobic. I think he only gives a slice of himself," I say. "He gives you a slice of himself at a time but he'll never let you into the whole pie."

"You would hate that," she says. "You of all people would hate that! You always want to know everything."

"Are you calling me nosy?" I tease. "I mean, please!" I sweep a hand at the jumbled-up wall o' cardboard mountain looming on the far side of the otherwise spartan workout space.

"Good point." The song is over. "I got it." She grabs the masking tape and sets up a few little markers for the next part of the number while I pull up the next song on the phone.

The girls are excited and keyed up and distracted with the new space—they don't want to buckle down, but we threaten more bear walks and that gets them concentrating.

Mac comes up and stands next to me at one point, reporting on the mood of the parents in the den. Apparently they're enjoying the new class lounge. He asks how the space is working, and I tell him that there's a wild group leaping run we can't do, but other than that, this amount of space is more than workable. I cannot thank him enough.

He insists that he's just doing his job but I can see that he's pleased. He heads back to monitor the parents' drinks and things.

Soon after, my skin prickles with awareness, and I turn and there's Benny, coming down the hall wearing a business suit and an annoyed look, but it's not his super annoyed look; it's more like his bemusedly annoyed look. They say that the Inuit have dozens of words for different types of snow. I could give you just as many words for Benny's annoyed looks.

"Welcome to Forty-Second Street Twirlers," I say.

"Dance classes in the penthouse," he grumbles. I follow his gaze to the small mass of girls, all of these beautiful, high-spirited girls bursting with life and fun like a bright tornado.

"I really appreciate your allowing us to hold the class here," I say. "Thank you."

"It's your place, too, right now," he says.

Kelsey comes over. "You're really gonna make her teach from the doorway?"

"Better than the ceiling," I say.

"What? No, you can go in." He's shaking his head. "Go on. Go on in," he says.

I don't need to hear it twice. I go in there, clapping my hands, rounding the gang up for another run-through from the top.

They're doing a great part of the routine, running and jumping. I want him to see them, to see how beautiful and amazing those little girls are. And so talented. Maybe it's stupid, but I want him to see.

SEVENTEEN

Benny

THE KIDS ARE ninety-nine percent pure mayhem, and Francine, directing it from the center, is right in her element, surrounded by crazy preteen energy, laughing and dancing and throwing out compliments. She seems taller in a strange way. Happier, maybe. Full of generosity. Creative generosity. Generosity of spirit.

She demonstrates a move and my breath catches in my throat. It's been so long since I saw her dance—all of that grace and heart and vulnerability. And god, the hopeful longing. I never knew anybody so full of longing, so full of dreams.

At one point she twirls around, demonstrating something for them, and I'm back on the couch in the den, hands eating up her skin, tasting her, reveling in her. I loved the way we seemed to fit, and how every second was hotter than the last. It was a struggle to keep from unspooling with lust, to keep from devolving into the panting dog I once was. I could barely maintain control, to resist my impulses to worship every inch of her.

I shove my hands in my pockets as if that will somehow force away the images of her.

Yeah. Good luck with that.

I forgot what it felt like, to desire a woman like this.

As if she can feel me thinking about her, she turns and looks at me and smiles.

I bask in it like a schoolboy. I remind myself that it could just be that she's grateful for the use of the space. Thankful. For a second though, I have the illusion that it's for me.

It was my own private struggle to light that stage production of "Alejandro," to follow the lighting design set forth by the Beau Cirque powers that be. I knew how to run tech across the ceiling and along the apron, how to get the angles. I knew how to follow the scheme to make the lighting braid in with the music, but in truth, I really only wanted to light Francine. She wasn't the star, but she was the best thing up there, no question, and I lit her beautifully. She was all I'd see. She'd dance her heart out, and I'd tweak the lights. A one-sided collaboration.

Kelsey comes and stands by my side. "We could power half the air conditioners in Manhattan with that energy, huh?" she says.

The kids. She's talking about the kids. "Quite a handful," I say.

"Yup." I can feel Kelsey watching me, wanting to engage me, but I can't quite tear my gaze from Francine out there. Even when she has to stop the class and scold the misbehaving rebel of the group, she does it with love. I never saw this side of Francine. There's so much I don't know about her.

She claps and asks them to circle up. She's whispering excitedly, hands on her hips. I'd give anything to know what she's saying.

"Really, dude," Kelsey says after a spell of silence. "What are you doing?"

"I never knew how into working with kids she is," I say. It's not an answer. I don't owe anybody answers. I don't need to explain myself—not to her, not to anybody. It's one of the beauties of being me.

"This is her thing for sure," Kelsey says. "This age, especially."

We watch Francine hassle the kids for being lazy. Teasing, but always with kindness. "She has such a good way with them."

"This whole wife thing, though," she says. "What's up with it?"

"It works for me, that's what's up with it."

"Why, though? Because if you're out to hurt her, to use her in some way—"

"Nope," I say.

"What's the endgame?" she asks.

"I have this wife nobody sees. May as well let people get a look at her and—"

"Oh, I'm sorry, I should've clarified; not the bullshit explanation, please," she says. "The real one. Why make her play your wife? It's weird as fuck, dude."

I turn to her. "I wanted to."

"That's not a very complete reason."

"She came for a divorce and my gut said no," I tell her. "I always go with my gut."

Kelsey snorts. "Is that what the kids are calling it these days? Your gut? You mean the one that lives below your belt? And sometimes thinks for you? Because I'm gonna tell you, I think you're angling to get into her pants."

I give her a stern look, though really I'm impressed by her directness, and surprised that Francine didn't say anything about what happened between us, just because I know she and Kelsey are extremely close.

I like that she kept it private. Something just for us. Way

back when, she didn't seem to care about anybody else's feelings but her own. But that hasn't seemed true these past two weeks. Do I need to update my perception of her?

I changed, after all. I left the past behind.

Kelsey's watching me, wanting an answer.

"I follow my instincts," I tell her. "They know more than the brain."

"Hmmm," Kelsey says. "I'm going to remember that the next time I need a bullshit reason for something. It's very good."

"I'm not playing you," I say. "Once I decide something, I do it."

"Fine. You got it in your *head* and you went with it."

"It's true," I say.

She crosses her arms and looks out over the class. "She did say you're the most single-minded person ever."

"She said that?" I ask, surprised.

"Oh, yeah," Kelsey says. "She said that once you're on a thing, you hate being torn off from it. Like really hate that, and you scare people a little, but they don't get that it's just your passion. Apparently people have you really wrong in many ways."

Francine said that? To her friends? "Wow," I say.

"Yeah, she thinks you're so misunderstood," she says. "But apparently she understands you."

"Yeah?"

"Oh, yeah," Kelsey says. "Furthermore, contrary to public opinion, you have a sense of humor; in fact, Francine says you're hilarious. I don't know if I see it, but..." She makes a weird face. A new song starts and she runs back out there and picks up the class from Francine.

Francine sits on the floor across the room, clapping to the music while the girls do some sort of balancing exercise under Kelsey's direction.

She really said all of that about me? Is this more proof that I need to update my perception of her?

It's not easy.

Distrust of Francine is embedded so deeply in me, it's a reflex, no different than pulling my hand away from a hot flame, except the hot flame of Francine is made of pain and humiliation. It might be a decade old, but the memory is as acute as if it had been yesterday.

Reflexes exist to protect you. But it doesn't mean that they always do. It doesn't mean that they're even needed.

Francine bends down to talk to one of the girls. She looks tired. She's probably hungry. We should have dinner after this. A nice dinner like a normal couple—not that that's what I'm trying to be. That window is shut.

Still.

Mac has his hands full with all of these unexpected guests but I have a phone, don't I? Both Francine and I need to eat.

Before I can think better of it, I'm ordering up a whole feast. Back at the Beau Cirque buffet table, she was a big one for loading her plate up with coconut shrimp. She seemed to like baked brie things and tofu spring rolls. It's not a very thematically coherent meal, but those are foods she liked, so I order them up. Of course I have bubbly water on hand already. I arrange it all on my phone while I'm standing there watching her clap.

I've been viewing her as a woman who'd use and discard people, not caring for anybody but herself. Not seeing anybody but herself.

Spending this time with her over the last two weeks, something's been shifting. And the way she is with the kids, and the kind things that she said about me, it's all chipping away at the picture I had of her.

Yes, she *did* walk out without so much as a word or even a

goodbye ten years ago, refusing to answer so much as a text. She discarded me after using me to heal her bruised ego.

But maybe she's changed. *Maybe...*

Something tightens in my chest at the thought of it. Can I believe this new Francine? What does it mean to let go of my old image of her? Why is it so fucking unsettling?

Of course, it means I'm the asshole for putting her through all of this. It means I might be falling for her again. It means I'm putting my heart on the table again. It means I'll be like that kid again.

This dark feeling grinds inside of me. I'll never go back there. Not ever.

I turn and get out of there. I can't watch class anymore.

For now, we'll have dinner.

EIGHTEEN

Francine

I GET out of the shower to find a text from Benny. Dinner is served.

I look at it for a long time. Really? Dance class and then dinner? Can this man be more confusing?

Though I *was* just going to scrounge around in the kitchen. I'm absolutely famished, no doubt about it.

I throw on a T-shirt and a skort, then I decide that looks like I'm trying too hard so I change it to yoga pants. Then I decide that I felt better in the skort, so I change back to the skort.

The smells coming from the dining room are unbelievable.

I head in, crossing the kitchen. His ubiquitous Pandora mix is playing, and I'm hoping Dave Matthews Band doesn't come on. I need to tell him what I did. He'll probably think it's funny.

I walk under the dining room archway and am stopped in my hungry tracks by the sight of this table loaded with food and lit candles. Benny's already sitting there, unbelievably handsome in a light brown button-down shirt that matches his eyes and skims his broad shoulders.

"Dude," I whisper. "I think a man wants to have sexual relations again," I say. Okay, it might be a woman who wants that.

"A man can't feed his wife dinner?" he protests.

"Oh, a man certainly can." I take a seat. There's a tall glass of fizzy water with a twist waiting for me. He thought of everything. I help myself to several spring rolls and a coconut shrimp. "This looks amazing."

He just sits there all remote and mysterious. I don't know what to make of him. It would be so much easier if I didn't care, if I didn't feel so happy around him.

"Seriously, though, what's the occasion?" I ask.

"No occasion." He toys with his spoon. He seems to have something on his mind. Is he going to let me off the fake wife gig? And is that what I want?

"You looked hungry," he says.

"Um, thanks?" I say. "You know, usually the wine-and-dine thing goes *before* the marriage."

He shrugs. "You know me."

There's also an elaborate charcuterie board, and some sort of risotto dish. I point to it. "What is that?"

"It's a baked Brie and asparagus risotto."

"What a strange and delicious dinner," I say.

He frowns. "It seemed like something you'd like."

"It's everything I like!" And nothing that's going to blow weigh-in—not after the athletic day I had. "I don't know which to eat first," I say.

He lowers his voice. "Does my sweet wife need a suggestion?"

I point my fork at him. "At your own risk! I'm telling you, I could eat a horse."

"I'll take that as a compliment."

"You do that." I load my plate up with a little bit of everything and start eating. Completely famished.

Benny feeds Spencer a bit of meat from the board.

I dip a spring roll loaded with veggies into a little thing of peanut sauce and take a bite. "Mmm! Tofu spring roll alert!"

He's concentrating on his water. Sometimes it's like he doesn't want to let himself be too happy around me.

"Look at us having dinner as a fake married couple," I say. "Or a fake real married couple. I kind of don't know what we are."

"Maybe we're something that doesn't have a name," he says.

"How very mystical of you."

"Definitions are rooted in the past." He tears apart a hunk of bread. "I'm focused on the future now. The past is in the past."

I study his hands as he spreads butter over the steamy bread. I love his hands almost as much as I love his lips. He wipes his fingers on his napkin and folds it just so, lips pressed together with Benny-ish attention, and I want to get up and go over and kiss those lips and then I would kiss his Benny-esque nose, and I would sit on his lap and take off his glasses.

Maybe we're something that doesn't have a name.

He's definitely still every inch the fierce and idiosyncratic thinker he was back then. He's a man who wants to change the world. He *is* changing the world, I suppose.

"Past in the past. Works for me," I say, because I still feel ashamed for how I was. "However—" I point at him with my fork. "You must never undo your past decision of having bought this condo. Because it is perfect. If I had to make up a setting for a real-slash-fake marriage, this is where I would want it to be taking place."

"Mmm," he says strangely, stuffing a bite into his mouth.

Mac comes by to announce that he's leaving for the night.

"Thanks so much for arranging everything with that class," I say to him. "That was completely amazing and hard to do."

Mac smiles. "No big!"

"And this dinner is inspired! You managed to assemble all the best foods."

"Benny did it," he says. "Oh, and by the way, there's a delivery that came for you during class. I put it in the foyer."

"A delivery?" I ask. "To me? Here?"

I look over at Benny, who shrugs. "Not from me."

"Weird," I say.

"It's big," Mac says. "Addressed to Mrs Benjamin Stearnes. Hold on." He disappears, returning moments later with a giant rectangle that looks to be nearly four feet tall and three feet wide, like a large bulletin board or something, all wrapped in brown paper. With that he takes off for the night.

I stand and go over to it. "Wow!" I grab the envelope off the front of it and pull out what looks like an invoice.

"What is it?" Benny asks from somewhere behind me.

"Uhhhh..." For a second my eyes aren't able to make sense of what I'm seeing.

I hear Benny getting up, coming around the table.

"What the hell," I breathe, because what I'm looking at is an invoice for seven million, made out to me for something that I apparently ordered ten days ago. And then it hits me. It's the painting that Vicky was talking about. The fake seven-million-dollar painting she was going to have made.

I didn't know she was really going to do it!

"What the hell?" Benny says, which tells me that he's caught sight of the invoice. He snatches it from my fingers and examines it more closely. "What is this?"

"It's not what you think," I say.

Thick brown brows furrowing handsomely. He's way more annoyed than I think I've ever seen him.

"It's hard to mistake a seven-million-dollar invoice," he says. "Seven million. It's plain in black and white. You ordered whatever this is...on the credit card I gave you?"

Like I'd ever!

I'm surprised. It's as if he wants to believe the worst of me or something!

Just for that, I decide to wait to tell him it didn't cost millions. I pull the brown paper wrapper off to reveal a giant portrait of me. It's actually pretty good. I'm standing next to a Grecian-looking column wearing a ballet tutu and a diamond tiara with actual cubic zirconia bits affixed to it, sparkling like diamonds, and apparently they had extra cubic zirconia, because there are what looks like diamonds in the air surrounding my face. Like I'm enchanted. Or surrounded by really bright gnats.

I love it!

"Seven million dollars?" he growls.

I frown. Seriously, he thinks I'd do that? Now I'm annoyed, too. What kind of person does he think I am?

"You don't think it would look good above the mantel?" I ask. "You don't want to honor your beautiful wife?"

"You can't order that kind of thing!" he says.

"Why not? I'm your wife. You said to go crazy."

"Not seven million dollars' worth of crazy!"

"Is this our first fight? I can't believe you don't like it!" I take the picture and carry it into the living room. He has a beautiful, tasteful photo over the fireplace mantel. I lean the picture of me over the photo. "There!" I say.

He looks pale.

I stand back and link my arm through his. "Don't you think it's pretty? Do you like the way the diamonds shine?"

"No, I don't like the way the diamonds shine."

I snort.

"What?" he demands.

"It's not what you think," I say.

"This is an invoice for seven million," he says, waving the paper. "And that's a picture that has little diamonds stuck to it."

"Benny," I say, deciding to put him out of his misery. "It's a joke. Those aren't really diamonds. You didn't pay seven million. Nobody paid seven million."

He looks bewildered. "It's a joke?" he asks.

"You might have paid a thousand—tops."

He narrows his eyes, cogitating.

"It was this silly something my gal pals cooked up to make you regret this whole wife thing. It seemed funny at the time. Frankly, it still is..."

The color is finally coming back into his face. "Jesus Christ." He shoves his hand through his hair in the old Benny way, and this rush of lust fills me.

"You totally thought I was going to make you pay seven million for a picture of me?" I grab his arms. "I can't believe you think I would order a picture like that! What kind of person do you think I am?"

Something flashes across his face, like the question hits him strangely.

I draw closer, heat pooling in my belly. "You think I am one of the legions of gold diggers that are constantly after you?" I hover my lips near the fleshy lobe of his ear. "Is that what you think? And I'm soooooo enchanted with myself that I must have this portrait?"

He winds my hair lazily around his fist. "I think you have some freaking nerve, that's what I think," he says.

"Bring me an artiste! I want the grandest picture of me, me, me! Is that what you think?"

He pulls our faces near, staring into my eyes.

"Maybe next time they'll be real diamonds," I whisper. "You

never know. Mrs Benjamin Stearnes likes only the finest things."

Some emotion crosses his face—affection mixed with desperation. Blunt fingers grip my arms more tightly; I can practically feel the energy vibrating through him. My pulse skitters.

He seems to give in to something and he kisses me hot and hungry.

I wrap my arms around his neck, pressing into him, needing to be touching all of him. "You think I'm a gold digger," I mumble into the kiss.

Protest rumbles in his throat.

"We can get a matching portrait of you," I tease.

He growls and steals another kiss. His fingers play along the edges of my T-shirt, making scorching contact with my midriff. My breath quickens as confident hands pull my shirt up over my head.

Not to be outdone, I pull open his shirt, which has pearly snap buttons, much to my delight.

"We'll have to invite our dog park friends over for hors d'oeuvres," I continue. "Won't they be surprised!" I kiss his bare chest. I love his chest. I love the light smattering of hair. This man drives me crazy. "Mmmm."

"Don't forget Monique and Igor," he says, relieving me of my bra while I go after his pants. We're just a frenzy of nonsense talk and clothes getting pulled off at this point.

I reach down and press my hand against his hard cock, clad only in boxer briefs.

He groans.

"This," I whisper. "So wet for you."

"Fuck," he breathes, sliding his hands over my ass.

Sensation shivers through me as he grinds me into him.

"I want to feel you inside me," I say to him. "I need to feel you in me. Please, Benny."

He just rumbles, all low and sexy. He grips my ass even harder, and then he hauls me right up off the floor.

I wrap my legs around him as he walks backwards, walking me toward the daybed at the corner of the place.

He lays me down. There's a hard gravity in his gaze that sends heat blooming through my body. I touch his steely thigh as he skims his palm over my belly, down, down, down to my core. He slips a finger inside of me, then another.

Gasp!

"I like you like this, laid out for me like a feast," he says.

He leans down to suck my breasts while he does me.

I grab his hair and hold his head in place, rife with pleasure at everything he's doing. He's plundering me like a marauder, and I'm here for it!

I maul his muscular shoulder with my free hand.

"Please tell me you have a condom," I gasp. "I'll die if you don't. I need you to have one right now, specifically *on* you."

He pulls away with a feverish look.

Without a word he disappears. When he comes back, he's ambling back cool and slow, cock jutting out from a tawny bush of hair. He's a sexy sculpture, hard and beautiful. He stands over me, slipping it on himself—slowly—possibly even making me wait.

"Take your time why don't you," I say.

"I plan to." Rough fingertips glide over my body, making me burn with need. He seems to know everywhere to touch.

Suddenly it comes to me—he's doing the Sexorator 2000 thing.

But he keeps touching me, stoking the quicksilver sensation between my legs higher, and an evil little voice inside me asks, *do you really want to stop now?*

I don't want to stop! I need to get Benny back.

"Come here." I reach up and pull him to me, pull him over me, and he obliges.

He climbs over me and slides his hand over my shoulder, over my breasts, over my belly. "You are so fucking beautiful."

His fingers are back between my legs, doing more magic there. I rock my hips as he strokes me. He gets up a rhythm. I'm gasping and panting and forgetting to be anti-Sexorator 2000.

"Please!" I beg, arching up toward him. "Need you inside me!"

He nudges my legs apart and seats himself between them. The fat tip of his cock presses against my opening. Holding my gaze, he pushes into me.

A strangled sound escapes my throat. Pleasure courses through my veins. I'm kissing him, digging into his back, meeting his thrusts.

He adjusts his angle. "This?"

"Mmm." I skim my hands over the hair-roughened steel of his chest and then I press my lips to the sheen of sweat on his neck. "More," I say into his neck.

He obliges, going a little harder, a little faster. "This?"

"You taking requests or something?" I ask.

He grabs my hands so that we're palm to palm. Slowly—ever so slowly—he presses them over my head, onto the back of the couch. "Anything," he says.

"Now slower," I say.

He slows, grinding against me. Bright waves of pleasure roll over me. It's so crazy sexy...but not quite Benny-ish.

"Now...be more awkward and intense," I say.

"What?"

"Like you're unself-aware. Like you're carried away. And a little unsure..."

"What the hell?" He slows. He doesn't seem to like this request.

"You said I could request anything."

"I think you suck at being the boss." He lets go of my hands and puts his attention on my pussy. One ruthless and all-knowing finger massages my way-too-ticklish clit while he fucks me.

It's everything.

I'm breaking up into bits of pleasure. Thoughts of Benny-vs-Sexorator 2000 evaporate, because Sexorator 2000 has sex tricks, and my libido is all in for those sex tricks.

I'm teetering on the edge, panting and teetering and then—suddenly—orgasming.

He loves that I'm coming—I can tell by the way he groans, by the way he begins to piston into me. Finally, here at the end, he's somewhat losing himself.

We come very nearly together. I collapse. He collapses next to me.

I trail a finger over his muscular arm. Maybe it's nothing for a man like Benny to stay remote, even during sex.

But I want to be close to him, not just get off, great as that is.

But maybe that's all I get as fake wife. Random slices of him while his heart stays off-limits in a granite sarcophagus.

NINETEEN

Benny

ALAN AND DANIELLE'S rooftop is a 10-story-high world of festive lighting, luxury outdoor amenities, and outrageous greenery, including potted palms and massive outdoor topiaries, most notably a seven-foot-tall rabbit with twinkling lights woven all through its leaves. Guests are abuzz with speculation on how they got the massive plants onto the roof, because they certainly didn't grow them up here. They couldn't have brought them up the stairwell.

The sunset blazes over the river in the distance, painting glass building faces orange.

But the real wonder of the rooftop is Francine, casually elegant in a black-and-pink flowered dress. Her hair is down around her shoulders in loose waves that look unbearably sexy.

"What do you think?" she asks when I bring her a fresh bubbly water. "Are you cogitating on the topiary?"

I tuck a stray bit of hair behind her ear. "I won't play."

"What do you mean?"

"Its only purpose is to get people talking," I say. "I don't want to play."

"I so want you to, though," she says. "Do you think it was a helicopter? They're saying this isn't a proper helipad for that."

"All the better," I say. "What a bore it would be if this was a proper helipad."

"You are so obstinate!" She tugs on the lapels of my suitcoat. "Tell me."

I smile like I know. Which I do. It drives her a little bit crazy and she begs some more. I love the sound of her begging. It's a drug that I'm quickly getting addicted to.

I should tell. Then again, I should do a lot of things. Like let Francine go. I need to do it. I've been in denial of that fact, but what the hell? She's in the most difficult rehearsals of her life. She needs to relax when she's not rehearsing, to baby that hurt knee.

I'm starting to suspect that I really am the asshole here.

"Please?"

I lean in. "Heavy-lifting drone."

Her eyes widen. "You think so?"

I nod.

"Hah!" She links her arm into mine, pleased, and it does something to me. "Nobody guessed that. But then, a drone is just a big robot, isn't it?"

"Entirely," I say.

She beams at me.

"What?"

"Helicopter. Whatevs!" She pulls my arm in more tightly, pleased and proud—of me, of us as a team in the world.

Here I am, her captor. If I were her, I wouldn't show me anything, but Francine shows her emotions, sparkling with feeling, sensitive to the vibrations of the world, all brightness and flow and beauty.

I spent so much of my life trying to contain my emotions—unsuccessfully. I get so full of curiosity, so consumed with the drive to make a thing work, that my world can sometimes collapse to a single point. I'd go at things with too much intensity. I fall in love too desperately.

A few people come over; it's more of James's network that adopted me, the sullen nerd that James inexplicably elevated to best friend. Like everyone, they're curious about my long-lost wife.

We tell our origin story for about the fifth time that night. People have a hard time believing that I was ever even peripherally in the theater. She's describing elements of the show in humorous terms—the swans, the gunfight expressed in acrobatic ballet. I remind her of other details, and she takes them up and spins them. The show really was ridiculous. Nobody knew that better than us cast members.

She hooks her arm into mine. "If you get him drunk enough he'll sing 'Alejandro.'"

"You never give up, do you?" I say to her.

"No way does Benny sing 'Alejandro,'" somebody says.

"He totally does," she says, smiling.

She was happy when I sang it. She'd be delighted if I sang it again. It's such a little thing. What would it cost me to sing it? Nothing. The mechanical action is simple—the mouth forms consonants and vowels.

The problem is that it feels like more than just a song. I've resisted singing it for the same reason I've resisted saying so many things. The vocal cords vibrate. You string words into one honest sentence. You follow it up with another honest sentence. It should be so easy, but it feels like moving mountains.

Telling her about James was hard like that, though it did feel good after.

People are arguing about what 'Alejandro' was really about. Some say it was about Lady Gaga's old boyfriends. Others say it's about her gay friends. Still others claim it's about the civil war in Spain. The talk flows as freely as the champagne fountain, another topiary-involved creation.

Eventually the iPhones come out.

We wind up in another group where people are talking about the park construction project—some of our favorite paths are going to be closed. Fitness classes will be canceled. Francine is telling them about something called bear walks, and also how important it is to be able to get up from a lying position without using your arms. She's telling them about the study that she loves to quote where elderly people who can get up from a lying position without using their arms live longer.

A few people try it—right there on the rooftop—and discover that it's harder than it sounds. We exchange glances, laughing. Francine would normally be demonstrating, but she doesn't. It's her knee.

Later, she grabs another bubbly water from the open bar and wanders off to the far side to look over the railing, looking out at the lights, looking so sad. And I know she's thinking about her knee.

She should be home, resting it.

I go over. "If only Igor and Monique were here. They would show them how to rise without using their arms."

A grin spreads across her face. "They would laugh at everyone too much," she says. "They can be merciless."

"Igor is so good at everything, he doesn't understand," I say.

"Monique, too," she says, fixing my collar. "She's so gifted. Igor helps her understand what it's like to have issues."

"That's funny, because I find Monique helps Igor in that respect," I say.

"Who are Igor and Monique?" It's Jeff, another neighbor.

Francine is smiling. "I brought Monique to the marriage, and Benny brought Igor. They're both nine, and it's sad because Monique speaks three languages and is an international personage while Igor is still having trouble with 'Little Teapot.'"

"Well Igor doesn't like to show off. It's important to Igor to make Monique feel special."

"I'm sure she doesn't notice," Francine says, "what with her artwork being on display in the Louvre."

"The Louvre?" Jeff's wife is here, now, confused. People are wandering over, Aaron among them.

"Our children, Igor and Monique, have been about nine years old for the last decade," I say.

"It's been hard on them what with our jet-setting ways," Francine adds. "Perhaps that's why they're so over-achieving."

"Igor is applying to colleges these days," I say. "Sometimes I think he is just far too serious for a nine-year-old."

Francine grabs my arm with a look of concern. "He thinks he's applying to colleges? Oh, how sweet!" This she says in a pitying tone. "Like an Easy-Bake oven, but colleges."

"You're correct in that he's not truly applying. He's been invited to quite a few of them. I don't know if he'd really have to apply, so you were right in that it's not really applying. I'm sure they would consider Monique if it weren't for the Victorian ailments."

"A few things are starting to make sense with you two," Danielle says. "Suddenly this entire weird relationship is starting to make sense."

"Oh my god, you guys," says a neighbor. "I was like, they have kids? They named one Igor? Who names a kid Igor?"

Francine snorts. "People who love Igor Stravinsky. Did you know that one of his ballet pieces caused a riot in the streets of Paris? The man's a badass."

I'm beaming at her proudly. Then I catch sight of Aaron, standing there with a fake smile that's very much like a dreadful rictus. He really doesn't like Francine, ever since she reminded me how much I hate working for people.

I haven't stopped thinking about that. I haven't stopped thinking about our chocolate chip cookie dough discussion, either. I've reached out to a few people, in fact. Exploring ways to edge Aaron out. To take on a new partner. It turns out there are ways I could do it.

After James was killed so suddenly, I was in survival mode, doing all that I could to interact with the fewest people. I just wanted to be in the lab, my comfort zone. Now I'm thinking bigger—figuring out how to arrange things the way that I want instead of just reacting to them.

Chocolate chip cookie dough ice cream. Who knew?

"This is what it would be like," I say as soon as we're alone.

She turns to me. "Yeah, right? Where they all think we're sadly weird."

"But we don't give a crap," I say. "That's the kind of marriage that we have. And it's a good example to set for Igor and Monique. They'll have trouble in life if they worry too much about opinions."

She's grinning. There's this feeling bubbling in my chest, and I don't know what it is.

Until I realize it's happiness.

God, our marriage is such a mirage, and I'm drinking it all in. I'm splashing in it. I can't stop. I lean over and brush my lips over hers.

Her hands curl around my lapels and she pulls me to her.

"Oh, I'm sorry!" A voice. Aaron.

We pull apart.

"Didn't realize it was showtime," he mumbles.

I give him a hard look.

He turns to Francine. "Monica and Britney want suggestions for ballet schools. I told them that you'd know. They're talking about sending their girls to *Ballez Over America* or something like that?"

"Oh, no. No, no, no," she says. "That's a scam!"

"Not what Monica says."

"Oh, man!" She heads over, leaving me with Aaron, who has some bullshit to say about Juliana. Moving up the signing.

"What are you doing?" I bark. I'm not a moron; he deliberately interrupted that kiss.

"What?" he asks, blue eyes wide and innocent.

"Fine." I walk off. Another beauty of being me is that I don't have to make excuses when I leave. I grab another beer.

What's up with Aaron *trying* to intervene? I've always known he was manipulative, but did I have my head buried so deeply in my ass I didn't see him trying to manage me? Is he trying to hasten the sale to Juliana because he doesn't want me to think it through? To think about the larger picture?

Alan, our host, comes up. "You know what I don't understand?" he asks.

"Topiary transportation?" I ask.

"You two," he says. "You have such independent lives, but when you're together, anyone can see the sparks fly. Do you have a secret of some sort?"

"If you're asking for relationship advice, you're in the wrong place," I say.

"Am I? Plenty of people I'm looking at right now spend less than half the year with their spouses. Some of them spend zero time at all. But they're not like you two. It always seemed extreme that you didn't bring her around, that you led such separate lives. But it's not the quantity, it's the quality, isn't it? You have chemistry, but also this friendship. You like each other. You laugh together."

Francine's the one laughing. Over across the roof, she's laughing, gesturing, pointing north, probably in the direction of whatever ballet school she's recommending. I think to tell him it's a charade. But even if I was in the mood to let him in on the secret, it's not entirely true that it's all a charade. We have chemistry. We have friendship. We have history. We're attracted to each other. We laugh together. We lead separate lives, yet we're married.

"Or do you work well as a couple *because* you're apart so much?" Alan asks. "Do you wish you were together?"

I stare across the rooftop at her, bathed in the festive lights strung overhead like giant stars.

Yes. I wish we were together.

The thought forms before I can think better of it. I'd risk it. I'd risk the hurt. The pain. I'd risk all of it.

The thought hits me like a sledgehammer.

Eventually she's back and Alan takes off to do host things. I coax her to a couch. She needs to not be standing.

"You remembered my mania about the whole 'getting up from a lying position without your hands' thing," she says. "I didn't even remember that."

"I remember. Every time I do it."

She pokes at my abs. "I'm sure it's easy for you, what with your hardbody weightlifting ways."

"That's right," I say.

"I can't anymore," she says, meaning she can't get up without the use of her hands. Because of her knee. "Not now."

"I'm sorry. I didn't mean to put your mind back on it again."

"Like I don't freak out about it twenty-four seven already," she says. "Running every doom scenario possible. Go ahead. You want to ask me how bad it is."

"I don't need to," I say. I already know. It's bad.

"Teaching that class yesterday in that beautiful space...I had this realization that that's where I'm happiest, even the most fulfilled."

"Wow! That's massive," I say. "Isn't it?"

She sighs sadly and looks out over the chockablock buildings, all muted grays and browns except for where the sky reflects. The sun is gone, but there's still brightness. For now.

"Isn't that a valuable insight?"

"No. Because I don't know who I am without that goal. This European tour, dancing in front of the ruins, being this international ballerina, it's what I've been dreaming of all this time—it feels like all my life. Striving and striving. When I think of letting it go...it makes me want to weep."

I curl my fingers around her forearm. I'm not the kind of man who's good with people or who knows what they need on an emotional level. I barely know my own mind, but I want to show her that I'm with her. I am with her. Or I want to be.

"I know what you think," she says. "I know you think I shouldn't do the tour because of my knee. You think I'd mess it up even more. I'd let down the whole company."

"It's not my decision," I say. "I'm the last person to suggest you stop being extreme."

This gets a smile from her.

"How about you tell me this," I say. "What are the chocolate chip cookie dough parts? Of the ballet tour? And what's the boring ice cream?"

"I think you're being sneaky," she says.

"What parts?"

"The whole thing is chocolate chip cookie dough," she says tersely. "That's the problem."

"Come on, you know that's not true. Tell me."

She touches the buttons of my sports jacket, one and then another, then adjusts my lapels. "The chocolate chip cookie dough is very plentiful. Dancing in front of the ruins, obviously. Being specifically chosen for this prestigious tour out of a large pool of hopefuls. That's chocolate chip cookie dough, dude. A European dance tour! Fabulous hotels! Dream come true."

"So dancing in front of the ruins, accommodations, and having been invited. What else?"

"What else..." She adjusts my collar. "Kind of, that somebody thought enough of my skills to literally pay for me to fly to Europe in order to dance for people."

"That's a restatement about having been invited. What about the dance itself? The ballet itself."

"It's an original creation of Sevigny's." She shrugs. "It's very challenging technically, and I'm proud to be nailing it. But Sevigny's not really thinking about the ruins on an artistic level. The ruins are just one stop on a tour that's all about showcasing his choreography."

"Like how?" I ask.

"This feels like an exercise in frustration," she says, swinging around so that her legs are on my lap.

I settle my hands lightly over her knee, wishing I had ice, wishing I could trade knees with her. "Tell me how the dance would be different if it were pure cookie dough."

"If I had my way, the dance would be done in complete response to the ruins. It wouldn't be as polished. I'd want it more exuberant, the way the girls dance. A less breakneck tempo. Better costumes."

"So the cookie dough parts of your upcoming tour are being invited in the first place, which you've nailed. Being able to do a technically difficult dance, which you've nailed. And the accommodations."

"And being on a worldwide tour as a ballerina," she insists. "Going down to have a café au lait in a café on the ancient streets."

I slide a palm over her calf, down to her sock and back up. Why is she knocking herself out for something she's not a hundred percent on? She's barely twenty percent on it.

"So you like it in theory, just not in reality," I say.

She raises one brow. "You'd better not be suggesting I blow off this tour. Because then we'd have a problem."

"You hear me suggesting that?" I protest.

"I think you're thinking that I should do my own damn tour. Maybe with the girls. Make that my whole thing. I think that's what you're saying."

"I said all that?" I tease.

She pokes my chest. "I think you should screw off."

I grab her finger and brush a kiss on her knucklebone.

"Not this again," she says.

I move on to the next knuckle.

"It's a lifelong dream," she says. "My dream since I was a kid. And you want to act like it's boring ice cream parts."

"I think you fought for it," I say. "I think you are the most tenacious person on this rooftop."

"No, you're the most tenacious person," she says.

I brush my lips over another knuckle. "It's a thing we have in common."

"Who knew!" she says.

A rush of déjà vu hits me. The memory of a conversation from the night we were married.

"What?" she asks, tilting her head. Her silky hair catches the light from atop a nearby building. "I can see those gears in your mind turning and churning. Tell me."

She's waiting, really wanting to know. She so hates being

the last to know things. And somehow, I can't resist. One brief trip to the past. "We knew that night."

"We talked about it?" she asks.

"We talked about being tenacious that night. That people get it wrong, like they take it weirdly personally. We talked about being both outsiders."

"I hate that I forgot so much of it," she says. "And I hate so much of how I acted."

"It's past. We don't have to talk about it." I glide my palm along her calf, soft and cool. "Don't worry about it."

"Maybe you don't like to talk about it, but I want to know. Tell me what else happened," she says. "I know you remember."

"For one thing, I had no idea that you were such a lightweight."

"*Such* a lightweight," she says.

"I wasn't used to drinking either, but—"

"But at least you remember our nuptials!" she says.

"We were acting in...an uncharacteristic way," I say.

"Like how?"

I shake my head. I shouldn't be going back there. The level of happiness I had that night is what made it hurt.

She's looking at me now, eyes piercing. "I want to know. And don't say it was tequila. Tell me really."

"One highlight," I sigh, "or possibly a lowlight, was us holding hands, running down the strip. And at one point, skipping."

"Wait, what?" Her eyes go wide. "No. Are you making that up?"

"Sorry to say, I'm not."

She fake punches my arm. "No way!"

Skipping. That's what she did to me then. "It was a little bit ironic, but not entirely." It was actually ecstatic. She opened me up and unraveled me and made me feel so much joy.

"Us. Skipping," she says. "Holding hands and *skipping*. You are so shitting me!"

"I've tried to suppress that part." Which is true, but not because it was dorky. Because it was good. We were both drunk on tequila, but I was drunk on impossible things, and that's a far more dangerous drink.

"Skipping," she says, stunned.

"Hey, don't shoot the messenger."

"No, it's..." She sucks in her lips, staring at a giant bush that's shaped like a duck. "What else? How did we...get the idea to you know, get hitched?"

"We were doing this whole thing with Igor and Monique. Something about giving them a stable family life. We were on a side street by this run-down chapel. They posted the marriage certificates the way restaurants post menus, all in different styles. You found one that had little birds holding banners, and a place to put names of children that would be members of the blended family. It was all bordered in gold foil. Calligraphy, etcetera. You were like, 'We have to get this!'"

"The wedding was my idea?" she asks.

"Well, you really wanted the certificate showing we were a family. And we didn't even keep them. We taped them up on a lamppost outside the Bellagio to announce it to the world. You felt that it was...beautiful and ephemeral," I say. "Those were the words that you used."

"Wow," she says.

"It seemed like a good idea at the time," I say, trying for lightness.

Seemed like a good idea at the time. Understatement of the year. She was the only thing worth having in the whole entire universe.

"We went back to my place because I had chocolates." I straighten her socks so they line up with each other. They're white with black smiley faces. Francine will go elegant, but she always reserves some part of her outfit for fun. Always the little rebel. "You ate every one of those chocolates before crashing on my bed. I crashed on the couch out in the living room. When I woke up, you were gone."

"I blew town," she says sadly.

"You blew town."

"And we were married," she says. "Why didn't you let me know?"

"I thought you'd find me when you figured it out," I tell her. "When you were ready."

"And I had no idea." She sighs dolefully. "I acted like such a complete and utter asshole. I'm so sorry."

"The past is in the past."

"I know, and I know you don't like to talk about it, and I don't blame you for not wanting to, but Benny—" She swings her legs off my lap, sitting up, like she wants me to get this. "I want you to know, I loved the thing we had going. I loved it even before that night. You were this bright spot in everything, this genuine person in a land of fakery. And I had to go and ruin it by making all those unwelcome passes at you. I felt like an ass."

"What are you talking about?" I say.

"When we got back to your place. You were right to reject me."

I frown, not sure what she's apologizing for.

"*You* know. Me kissing you and trying to unbutton your shirt, and you were like 'Francine, no, we can't.' The few good things I remember from that night are blotted out by my awful behavior. I had to ruin it, you know? I was so screwed up back then. And I behaved so shamelessly with you, and then I compounded it by ghosting you the next morning instead of staying there and apologizing."

My mind is reeling. What?

She presses a fingertip to my lips. "Let me get this out for once. You texted me," she continues, "and you were so sweet. I felt so ashamed, you have no idea. I couldn't face you, even through texting! Of all people, it's you I made a fool of myself in front of. I would think about it over and over, wishing I'd acted differently."

TWENTY

Francine

BENNY'S WATCHING ME, surprised. As if this all is news to him. Maybe he's just being nice.

"I had such a crush on you, but that's no excuse," I say. "If only I'd pulled my head out of my ass sooner on the guys I dated. But I'd decided I needed to be with a rich, flashy boyfriend and have everything be glittery and pretty dresses and limos and nightlife—that was my stupid plan of how I'd fit all of the life I'd missed into one summer."

"I had no idea."

"And of course you were annoyed at least half the time and focused on robot things. And then that night...I was so inappropriate. You were being nice to me, and I felt so ashamed for getting drunk and forcing myself on you."

He studies my face, baffled. "You didn't do anything wrong."

"Don't candy-coat it," she says.

"That's why you left? Because you felt bad for trying to kiss me?"

Laughter erupts from the far corner. People are having fun on this beautiful spring night, creating a soundtrack that's utterly wrong for the conversation that we're having. "And I was too immature to know what to do," I add.

"You do know we kissed at the wedding ceremony, right?"

"We did?"

"Enthusiastically," he says. "I was all there for it. But by the time we were back at my place, we were obviously both too drunk...I didn't want to do anything we'd regret. You shouldn't have felt bad." He frowns. "So...*that's* why you left?"

"Well...yeah," I say. "And I want to officially apologize already."

"You don't have to," he says strangely.

I feel this weight come off my shoulders. "Okay." I smile. "Wow." I feel like we just cleared something up, but Benny doesn't seem happy. Does he truly not forgive me? "What is it?"

"Ummm...I just had it wrong too, I guess."

"What?" I ask. "Did you think I got temporary amnesia or something? Abducted by aliens?"

"No..."

"What, then?"

"Nothing. I had it wrong, that's all."

"No, tell me!" I grab his shirt sleeve and tug on it playfully. "Now you have to tell me. We're confessing all."

"It's not important."

"It is to me! Don't not tell me," I beg. "Don't shut me out."

"I thought it was all just...maybe some sort of a joke. Or a game for you," he says.

I stiffen. "What do you mean?"

"Well, you'd come off that relationship with that jackass casino guy, and I thought you needed maybe...an ego boost."

My throat feels tight. "Like I was just using you? Maliciously..."

"Not *maliciously*..." He shoves his hand through his hair.

"But you thought I was using you? Like I was toying with you? Did you think I left the next morning because you'd served your purpose? I discarded you like a used paper towel?"

"Well, I don't think it *now*," he says.

"But you thought it up *until* now?" I ask.

His hesitation is all I need to confirm the worst.

I feel crushed—I can't help it. "So all this time, that's the kind of person you thought I was?"

"I got it wrong. What does it matter? I see I was wrong," he says.

"Why would you want me to play your wife if that's what you believed I was capable of? Why would you want me around? Was it...payback? I've been completely falling for you all this time, and you've been secretly harboring this dark thought about me? And when I tried to apologize about the past, you wouldn't let me!"

"I had you wrong," he says. "I wasn't thinking it through in that way."

"And you made me stay as punishment. Did you think it while we were having sex, even?"

He sucks in a ragged breath. He's lost his cool, suave-guy demeanor. I finally have old Benny back—too bad he thinks I'm the moral equivalent of Godzilla. "We need to rewind this whole conversation."

I fling up my hand. "I don't want to rewind anything." There's a sob trapped in my chest, clogging my lungs.

Monica breezes over just then, smiling, setting candles for the nearby table. "How's it going? We're bringing a cake out in five."

I stand. "I'm so sorry I'll miss it," I hear myself say. "I have to get going, but Benny will stay." I plaster on the best fake smile I can manage. "Later, honey," I chirp.

Somehow my feet are working. I'm heading toward the door, wearing my serene face—it's one of my ballet faces, serene and placid, when all I want is for the ground to swallow me up.

I somehow make it to the place where the elevators are and I get in. I have to be away from him.

Back home I'm packing in my servant wife quarters. I don't know if he'll give me my papers now. Will I even go on the tour? I don't know anything that's going to happen, but I do know that I can't stay. It's like I've been living in a sandcastle and now it's all collapsing along with little pieces of my heart.

Fake wife, fake sex.

He thought I was a horrible person. And this charade is my punishment.

I'm so stupid. So naïve. I was wrong to ghost him, yes. But for him to concoct this elaborate punishment?

I hear him come in. "You have it all wrong," he says.

"I don't know, you were pretty clear about what you thought about me!" I toss a pair of yoga pants into my bag and spin around. "I always felt like I knew you, and like you knew me, like we were outsider peas in a pod, even before we hooked up, but that isn't at all the case, is it?" I bunch up some socks and throw them in. "You thought I used you and ghosted you and you were pissed off. I think you never knew me." I zip up my bag with a loud *zrrrrp*.

"I wasn't pissed off, I was devastated," he says.

I sniff my disbelief and head into the bathroom. He follows behind. I grab my toothbrush, shove it into my travel bag.

"That night in Vegas was the best night of my life," he says. "You were the most amazing woman I'd ever met, the most beautiful woman I'd ever seen. When you left without so much as a word, when you seemed to have forgotten all about me, I was devastated."

I shove my makeup pencils into my makeup case.

"But I figured out that you'd have to be back. Sooner or later, we'd have to deal with this marriage that you clearly didn't want. This was a few months after Vegas. By that time James and I had started the company, and it was literally money falling from the sky."

"And that matters why?" I grab my shampoo from the spa tub area and catch sight of him in the mirror. He seems to be groping for words, looking around as if someone's going to appear and give him his lines.

Such a Benny way to be. My heart cracks a little.

"I told myself that I wanted you to feel sorry for walking out," he continues. "That you'd come back and regret what you did. That's what I wanted."

I throw my razor in the bag. "So you plotted your revenge? Lying in wait?"

"That's not it."

"You just said it!"

"Fine. You want to see the revenge I plotted?" he asks. "I can show you."

"You can show me?" I ask suspiciously. "I don't think I want to see the revenge you plotted."

"I want you to see."

"Too bad," I say.

"Jesus Christ." He snatches up my phone and heads out of my room and down the hall.

"Hey!" I say, following after him. "Gimme that!"

He keeps going. "I will."

"What are you doing?" I say.

"I'll give it back, don't worry," he says, turning the corner, heading straight for the workout room.

He pushes open the door. I follow him into the empty space. A band of yellow moonlight streaks up hardwood. He flicks on the lights, sets my phone on a ledge, and heads straight for the boxes.

Is he going to show me what's in the boxes?

"Stand back," he says.

Stand back? What the hell?

I grab my phone and take a few backward steps.

He pulls a box away from the base of the mountain and a whole bunch of them come tumbling down.

I'm watching, mystified, thinking that whatever is in them must be light as feathers. He keeps pulling them away from the far end of the workout room, digging through them. His movements are abrupt, all harsh angles, familiar in the most painful way.

I wrap my arms around myself. Is there some specific box that he's going for?

One of the boxes that tumbled down is only a few feet away from me, flap partly open. I go over and give it a shove with my foot. It's almost as if there's nothing inside it.

"What's in there?" I ask.

"Nothing," he says. "There's nothing in the boxes. There never was."

"What?" I don't understand. "Why store empty boxes?"

He keeps tearing down the wall.

"As revenge schemes go, it doesn't seem that effective," I say.

He's pulling more of them away from the wall, baring something, maybe.

And then I see the mirrors. Floor-to-ceiling mirrors. My belly swoops. More boxes come away

A ballet barre stretches all the way across.

I'm standing in a *ballet studio,* not a weights room. A gorgeous ballet studio in the most beautiful building in all of Manhattan.

Shivers slide over my skin, my scalp.

He's standing in the middle of the space now, surrounded by boxes, hair mussed, unsure. Cool, suave Benny is nowhere to be seen. "I wanted you so fucking bad," he grates out.

My pulse is racing. "All this..."

"I loved you in a hundred crazy flavors that I didn't have words for! And when you ghosted me..." He flings a hand at the mirrors, the barre. "I told myself this all was about making you sorry. I was young and still reeling, and I thought if I had enough money, if I got fit enough, if I bought a place in the kind of building that you would love to be living in, that the day that you came back asking for the divorce, you'd regret what you did. You'd regret that you couldn't have me back. But that was just bullshit that I told myself. Feeling angry is so much easier than feeling a broken heart. I never wanted you to be sorry—not really. I just wanted you. I wanted to be the kind of guy you wanted, to help you envision this life we could have together."

"You made this whole ballet studio."

"I know. It was..." He throws up his arms as if exasperated. "You never showed. I pretended to myself that I didn't care, but I was getting worried. I knew you didn't give a shit about paperwork, but it was extreme even for you."

He turns around to look at the far wall. The thing that makes this place a true dance studio. Our gazes lock in the mirror. The window behind me blazes with lights and stars and pale clouds sailing across the night sky.

"A year later I looked you up," he says. "I was surprised that you were living here in New York, just living your life. That's when it hit me—you weren't giving us or Vegas a second thought. You probably hadn't thought about me at all, and there I was building this elaborate nest. What the hell, right? It was a little..."

"Extreme?" I whisper. If he hears the adoration in my voice, he doesn't show it.

He turns back toward me. "I forced myself to stop thinking about the past altogether. The business was doing great. I focused in on microrobots. I was determined to put the past in the past. I put up the boxes."

"And then nine years later I show up to ask for a divorce," I say.

"I'm sorry I jerked you around. I just wanted you, but I pretended to myself...I don't know." His tone softens. "Maybe I didn't want you to leave again. It's no excuse to force you into this charade, though. Of course your papers will be ready in time."

I go to him. "This all...was for me?"

"In an entirely bonkers way."

A smile takes over my face. "How did you know I'd love this building?"

He slides a strand of hair off my shoulder. "How could I *not* know? Look at it! It's you, it's how you dance. It's how you live."

My heart squeezes. It might be the most beautiful thing anybody's ever said to me. "I love it," I say.

"You do?"

"So love it." I say. "So love *you*."

"What?"

"You heard me."

Three tentative fingers touch my cheek, warming my cheek. He's studying my eyes like he's not so sure.

"I so love you," I say. "How could I not?"

His breath comes out in a whoosh. Hungry lips come over mine. He grips my shoulders, fingers harsh with passion.

I clutch his shirtfront and pull him to me. We're a mad chaos of kissing and clutching, like all the passion is coming out of us in a rush. Rough lips slide to my ear. "Say it again."

I cradle his cheeks, breathless as he presses against me. "My husband is so amazing. Most guys would just send roses. How pathetic would that be?"

"Fuck." He wraps me up in his arms, kissing me like he can't stop himself. He's all Benny now. Benny who I'm mad over. "God, Francine," he says.

I'm pawing off his sports jacket while pressing into him. I don't know who's humping who at this point, but it's the best activity ever. We're furiously pulling each other's shirts off and it's wrong and funny and the most sexy thing ever.

He walks me backwards and flops me onto this stack of weight lifting mats.

"Ungh," I say, bouncing.

His voice seems to rumble up from deep inside of him. "Sorry, I can't..."

"Be fake?"

He lowers himself over me. There's fire in his eyes. His breath is uneven. He kisses down my body, down my bare torso, devouring me with his mouth. My hands are on his head, fingers plunged into his hair, urging him on in all his jerky, untutored abruptness. He comes back up and kisses me some more.

"Yes," I say. I never want to stop this. I reach down and grip his cock, huge and silky.

A groan of pure need twists up from his chest.

"This," I whisper.

"That?" he says.

"Mmm."

Two harsh hands slide up my skirt, pressing it up over my

waist, bunching it up. His muscles flex with the wild urgency of his movements. "I didn't know it could feel like this," I say.

"It's everything." He slides his hand over my hips, my belly, roving hungrily all over me like he's desperate to touch me everywhere—not to control me this time, but to be with me. I squirm with pleasure.

Searching fingers slide over my mound, grazing my inner thigh. A tremor curls through me. Suddenly he's tearing off my underwear with furious movements. He's ruining them, and it's so hot it blows my mind. I want him to shred them, and then he does. I hear this rip.

"Oh my god, sorry," he says.

"The only thing I hate about what you just did is that you can't do it again. I wish you could do it again and again. I want you to rip my clothes forever. Shred them to mincemeat!"

"If I spent my time on that, then I couldn't do this," he says, and he's pressing my thighs apart with an iron grip and devouring my sex—there's simply no other word for it. His oral sex technique—or as he'd probably term it, cunnilingus technique—is raw and hungry and hot as hell. Not like when he was being suave.

For the record, out-of-control Benny is completely wicked.

I'm fisting his hair, gone with pleasure. It's not even about the orgasm; it's just Benny being so Benny between my legs—so intense, so single-minded. "Ungh," I pant.

"You okay?" he halts long enough to ask.

"Ohmigod what? No! Don't stop! It was more than okay just keep—" I push his head back, and he's devouring me again, nearly sucking on my whole pussy.

My eyes might be rolling backwards in my eye sockets. My brain might be rolling backwards in its brain socket. My entire person might be rolling back in its personhood socket. My soul might be sprawling backwards into its soul socket, surprising the entire spiritual realm.

And I'm coming hard all of a sudden, clutching at his head, at his hair. His ears are in there somewhere.

He crawls up over me, staring at me with a kind of wonder. He dips his head down to kiss my breast, then my other breast, then the first one, and then he's up to my lips. And then he pulls back and he's just staring at me.

"Come here," I say.

"I am here," he says.

"No, here." I urge him nearer and grab on to his cock. I slide my hand up, enjoying the specifically Benny topography of veins and velvety softness. I grip a little tighter. The way he sucks in a breath, you'd think nobody's ever done this before.

"Want you like crazy," I say. "Just like how you are right now. You are so you and so sexy I can't even." I kiss him and stroke him. "We need to go to my servant wife room."

"We do?"

"Bring me," I say.

He hoists me up and I'm kissing him wild and free all the way down the hall.

Back in the room, I go into the little zipper pouch that has the travel pack that Tabitha made for all of us one Christmas. Sewing kit, moisturizer samples, condom!

I pull it out, holding it up like a trophy. I go to where he's kneeling on my bed, him and his hard curves and corded muscles like a map of his tenaciousness, his cock rigid as a flagpole.

"She's going to put this on you now," I say, unwrapping it with a crinkle.

He grabs my hair, rasps right into my head. "And he is going to fuck her so hard."

"So hard," I say. "She wants it so bad." I roll the condom onto him. "She wants him inside her so bad."

"He will so oblige, so much."

I let out small incoherent whimpers as he enters me. It feels like the first time, us together, rolling around.

I come in a white-hot storm of bliss, followed by him gripping my ass, crying out, artlessly ecstatic.

TWENTY-ONE

Benny

SHE'S MAKING breakfast in the kitchen the next morning, wearing my shirt, hair up in a high ponytail. I have this strange sense of déjà vu; not the kind of déjà vu where something once happened and now it's being conjured back in some way. This is déjà vu from years of fiercely imagining a scene like this.

But it's not me alone here with my secrets, trying to keep them walled off, trying to keep my pain walled off.

I let her in, and it makes everything feel new.

It's not about great sex or Francine's fun sense of humor or how generous and fascinating she is, or even the easy fit of us. It's the feeling that I'm home.

Now that she's here, I'm home.

"Are you trying to figure out if I'm basking in the afterglow?" she asks. "Magic Eight ball says yes!" She turns back to her eggs, ponytail swinging. She's never looked more beautiful.

I go to her and slide my hands around her waist and nuzzle the back of her neck. "Come back to bed."

She shakes me off, laughing. "I have to get to the studio. If I don't eat now, I'll collapse! Is that what you want?"

"Will it get you back in bed?"

"Screw off!" She shoves me away and grabs toast from the toaster. She puts more slices down and heads back to the pan with her spatula.

"Do you always eat half a carton of eggs for breakfast?" I ask.

"We burned off a lot of calories last night." She turns and gives me a quick kiss. "Tempting as your offer is, me collapsing and being brought to bed by you and all." She's buttering while tending to the pan.

I grab a cup of coffee. "I bought that kitchen table imagining us at it. It only sounds ninety-two percent psycho."

"I'd say eighty-seven percent," she says.

"Oh, thank you," I say.

My thoughts go to James. I wish he could have met her. He would've like her—a lot. And she would've liked him. James knew about the whole Vegas marriage. He'd seen inside the ballet studio room before I'd blocked it off with boxes. He teased me about my invisible wife, and I teased him about playing hacky sack. We trusted each other. We protected each other's weirdness.

It's one of the things that I have with Francine. We're inside looking out. Together.

She grabs a sip of coffee. There's a faraway look in her eyes.

"Is something on your mind?"

"I have an important mission. Probably. But right now it's eggs," she says. "I didn't even ask if you want any."

"I never eat this early," I say. "I'm sharper if I wait."

"Maybe you're sharper because it's your hunger instincts kicking in. Your body is giving all your fuel to your brain, desperately hoping you'll help it find food, but instead you're putting your energy toward that robot takeover. Psych!"

"Right?" I say.

"I could never skip breakfast," she says.

She arranges four perfectly buttered pieces of toast on a plate, flips six eggs over them, and brings it to the table. I sit next to her and watch her eat. She's thinking about something, but she'll tell me when she's ready. We have time now. She'll go on her tour, but that won't be the end of things.

She takes care to get a specific amount of egg yolk on every bite of toast. She's always been a deliberate eater, liking to portion things. It's something I can definitely understand.

She feels me watching her and looks up.

"I want to never shut you out again," I say.

"It's okay if you shut me out of some things. Let's not be a married couple that tells each other about their poop."

"We can't stay a married couple. Your tour—"

"I've made a decision about that." A serious look comes over her face. "I'm going to the studio this morning, but not to attend class. I need to talk to Sevigny. I'm pulling out of the tour. I've been thinking about chocolate chip cookie dough."

I barely understand what she just said. My mind spins with questions and concerns. "Pulling out?"

She just looks me square in the eye and says, "Yeah."

"Francine," I say, touching her arm. "Are you sure?"

"I am."

"You know I'm behind you either way."

"Of course I know that." She turns to me, holding her fork. "But for real, what am I doing? With my knee like this? Who am I fooling. Sure, maybe I could make it through the tour, but at what cost?"

I nod and wait, knowing she's not looking for answers from me.

"I've been going after this specific vision of a ballet career for so long, it's all I know," she says. "It's everything that I've molded myself to be. I've never questioned it because it's what my brain wants and it has been forever, like I have five fingers on each hand and I'm gonna be an international ballerina. But what if it's not what my heart wants? What if this ballet tour is like an instruction manual I wrote for myself fifteen years ago, and I've just been blindly following it all this time, never questioning it?"

"It's always good to question."

"I was thinking last night—what if I can make a dance at the ruins happen without Sevigny? If I can do it on my own terms? What if I blended my desire to dance at the ruins with teaching the class? What if I made it a class goal to do this amazing choreography based on the ruins, to get grants, to raise money, to make it happen? I feel like I can teach these girls dance, but also, how to do a big thing. It would be pure chocolate chip cookie dough."

"A hundred percent," I say.

"I always feel like everything has to be a struggle," she says, "but why can't my goal just be to have the chocolate chip cookie dough parts? I know I gave you that lecture, but I don't apply it to myself all that much."

"I love that vision," I say.

"Right? It's scary though. A sudden about-face like this?"

"Maybe that just shows it's right," I say.

"I know it's right. Even so, I feel sad and even scared about it."

I touch her arm. We're in it together. That's what my touch says.

She looks down at her plate and assembles another bite—a square of toast, a blob of bright orange egg yolk. "You helped inspire it all. Our conversation about your Juliana sale."

"I'm definitely rethinking it."

"Wait, what? You seriously are?"

"Yeah. Am I truly willing to trade a year of my time working in somebody else's robotics lab just to get more zeroes in my bank account? Because who cares? I already have more money than I'll ever spend. And it's a *year of my time.* Misery was an okay trade-off for a little more money before, but...I'm going to nix the sale," I say. "Juliana and the gang are going to be unhappy, but nothing was in stone."

"You'll keep the company?"

"I'll make it into what I want," I say. "I have some big plans. Radical plans. I've been thinking about restructuring things. Spreading the profit around. Raising everybody's salary and cutting my own. Creating a foundation to unload some money."

"Wait, what?" Her eyes go wide.

"My wife is not into billionaires, and it turns out I'm not either," I say.

"Oh my god," she says. "Are you serious?"

"Entirely," I say.

"Aaron is going to be so upset," she says. "Aaron is going to flip out."

"Yes, he will. He's definitely going to try to stop me," I say. "But I don't owe him anything. He'll still get a lot of money. Not as much as he wants but..."

"And a year is precious," she says. "We could do so much in a year."

We could. We. Us.

She grins.

"I love this," I say.

"Me too."

We haven't talked much about the future, but it feels infinite now, and full of possibilities.

I go around behind her and pull her hair free of the hair

binder, kissing her on the neck where she loves being kissed. "I feel like we've done everything backwards, getting married before anything. But maybe we could take the very huge step of dating. If you would do me the honor..."

"And make you the happiest man in the world?" She spins around and kisses me. "I'm in."

"We can see where this goes. We can make it up as we go along. You live in a place that you love with all of your friends and that's great. But it goes without saying, the studio here is all yours. It always was."

"Oh, Mr. Stearnes."

"We'll figure it out as we go along," I say.

"Hell yeah," she says. "We can apply the chocolate chip cookie dough test to everything. If it's not chocolate chip cookie dough, screw it!"

"If we had to do our wedding vows over again, that would be mine, Francine. All chocolate chip cookie dough from now on, starting with you."

Her eyes gleam. "So we're doing this. We date. I'll dump the tour." She stands and extends her pinky.

"Pinky shake?" I ask. "You know guys don't pinky shake, right?"

She forms her beautiful lips in a little pout.

I grumble and grab her pinky with mine.

"I'll call Aaron and Juliana," I say.

"YOU CAN'T JUST PULL OUT," Aaron says when I call him.

"I can absolutely pull out," I say. "This whole month was our getting-to-know-you phase and I know I'm not interested in the sale anymore."

"But this is the deal we've been waiting for!"

"You're not the one who has to work in somebody else's lab for a year," I say. "I'm no longer willing to do that."

"Is it the price? Are you looking to get more money?" he asks.

"I've been reevaluating things. What I really want, when I really think about it, is the freedom to pursue the ventures that I want to pursue."

"And with the money that you'll get, you'll be able to do that!" Aaron insists. "Arcana Protech is the only game in town."

"It's not the same," I say.

"Have you been negotiating with someone else?"

"I'm just rethinking a lot of things," I say.

"Does this have to do with Francine?" he asks. "She's a gold digger—"

"Which just goes to show that you know nothing."

"She's the most dangerous kind of gold digger there is—the kind that convinces you she's not."

"I don't owe you explanations, Aaron. I'm nixing the sale. I'm going to exercise my option to buy you out."

"Hold on here," he says. "Can we think this through? We need to think this through."

"I don't need to think this through," I say. "I know you were counting on a payday. You're still going to get an enormous amount of money relative to the hours that you've put in."

He's got a lot of legal arguments for me, but I've done my research. There's nothing he can do if this is my decision.

"Let's discuss this. Before you make any moves, can we just discuss it? Think through all of the options?"

"I've made up my mind. There's no world in which this sale to Juliana and her people happens, so there's nothing really to discuss."

"Just humor me?" Aaron pleads. "Have you had lunch? Let's meet at Brandenburger. You haven't had lunch yet, right?"

I roll my eyes. He thinks he can change my mind. He thinks he can tempt me with zeros and spreadsheets. Maybe he'll even sweeten the deal for me. It's not going to happen.

"For old times' sake," he says. "James would hear me out."

I groan inwardly. I hate that he's invoking James. James *would* hear him out—it's true. James was all for being diplomatic.

I sigh. I'm in love with Francine and she's in love with me. I can afford to be generous.

I agree to meet him at three. I can give him an hour more of my time, and then we're nixing this deal and I'm buying him out.

It's dizzying.

"Can we make it three forty?" he asks.

I don't know what the difference is, but I agree.

Brandenburger is a neighborhood restaurant down two blocks and over. Burgers, chili, that kind of thing. There's a ton of construction out front that's been hurting their business and I'm always trying to take meetings there, to support them.

I'm texting, walking under the massive scaffolding shed on the block before the restaurant when I see Aaron up ahead, waving.

"Hey!" he says.

I walk up to him. "Is everything okay? Were there no tables or something?"

"No, it's fine, I just wanted to have a quick word before the restaurant. I wanted to show you something." He's noodling on his phone.

Did he pull the Protech people together for this? I wait, feeling annoyed, leaning on the gap in the barrier. Hammers ring out above us. Workmen shout from somewhere in the distance. Traffic whizzes by behind me, the screeches of massive trucks and busses, honking horns.

"Is this honestly something that we can't handle in the restaurant?" I ask, impatient. "I'm taking this meeting as a courtesy. My mind is made up. You won't change it. Neither will Juliana."

"This is really important," he says, holding his phone up, screen faced toward me.

I take off my glasses and squint; I can't see it. "What is this?"

"I'm sending it to you. Check your mail. It's critical."

I pull out my phone and open my mail. "I don't see anything."

"I just sent it," he yells over the screech of more traffic.

I'm squinting, looking for whatever ridiculous thing he wants me to see. The mail hasn't come through. The next thing I feel is pressure on my chest. Two hands shove me backwards—into the traffic.

My phone flies from my grip. I can't get my balance.

Time seems to slow. I'm aware of a massive hulk of steel barreling down on me. The last thing I see are Aaron's crazy eyes.

TWENTY-TWO

Francine

HE WON'T WAKE UP. They don't know when he'll wake up, and they don't know *why* he won't wake up. It's a head trauma—that's the word they keep using. He lies there, motionless. His head is bandaged and his leg is in a cast, elevated by a sling that hangs from the ceiling. Tubes snake into his arm.

I'm in some sort of shock. I've gone completely numb. Everything seems unreal, almost translucent and far away.

I hold his hand in the folds of the sheets. I trace a soft finger over his beautiful lips, over his forehead. "Come on, Benny."

He's been unconscious for four hours now. I heard somebody use the C word: coma, and something about it being a bad sign if he's unconscious for more than six hours.

I tell him everything that comes into my mind. I want him to know I'm here. I try to sound bright and chipper, but I'm so scared. We just found each other—how could this have happened?

Waves of disbelief move through me, over and over.

Sometimes I lean over and just put our cheeks together. I don't want to jiggle the machines or anything, but I want him to feel me, to feel my skin, to feel my heart near his.

It's unbearable to see him so motionless. Unresponsive. Unable to ward people off with his scowly demeanor. Unable to be his intensely private self. He'd hate these tubes. He'd hate these lights. He'd hate so many strangers.

His nurse arrives. "It's a good sign that your husband is breathing on his own," she reminds me.

She's a woman of maybe forty with close-cropped brown hair, and she used to be in the Army. We talked a little bit about that on her last time through.

"He doesn't need a ventilator. It's a very good thing." She's hooking up something orange to the tube in his arm—an antibiotic of some sort. Apparently his blood pressure is good as well. They sometimes tell me he's lucky, considering he was hit by a bus going at full speed.

He needs to wake up.

Thank goodness we're married. I don't think they'd let me in to see him otherwise.

I was preparing our celebration dinner at his place when Aaron called me. Apparently they were to meet at a restaurant. Aaron was waiting, and when Benny didn't show up, he started walking toward the penthouse. There was all this commotion in the street—cars stopped. People gathered around. Apparently Benny had stepped out into some traffic.

Benny's phone was found nearby. He'd been immersed in his email and tripped or something. It's hard to believe he'd be so careless. It's true that when Benny puts his attention on something, that attention is total, but he's lived in the city for years. He knows you don't go bumbling into traffic while you're looking at your phone.

I tell him about my meeting with Sevigny, and about quitting the tour. Sevigny was upset, but people in the dance world get it about injuries. "I'm helping my understudy, Daneen, on my part," I say. "Of course my colleagues are upset, Benny, but I feel like it's right. I know it's right. We can do so much together now!" I squeeze his hand. "Right? Annie and the whole company, they deserve somebody who's operating at full capacity for the tour."

I scrub away a tear.

He just lies there, face ashen. I pull out my phone and put on a playlist that I made and downloaded, based on all of his favorite music. The nurse said it was okay as long as the phone stays in airplane mode.

"Your favorite music, Benny," I say, letting the tunes roll.

Nothing.

I leave it playing while I go to talk to Mac in the waiting room. He's distraught. "Benny's a good boss, a good guy. The best."

"The best," I agree.

"He'd hate this," Mac says. And I just nod. Mac says something about having called Benny's parents in Ann Arbor. There's been discussion of travel arrangements.

"He won't be unconscious for that long," I say. "I can feel him right there. I know he'll be fine. He just needs to wake up."

Mac nods. "Of course." I can't tell if he's placating me or if he really believes me.

"Hey, will you do something for me?" I ask. "Will you go back home and get his favorite robe and his slippers? We're supposed to have familiar things around him."

Personally, I'm planning on getting *Spock Must Die* on my ereader so that I can read it to him when I run out of things to say.

"I'd be happy to grab anything," Mac says, "but visiting

hours are over in twenty minutes. They're going to kick you out."

"No!" I look up at the clock. Shit. "I can't leave him!"

Mac shakes his head. "You may not have a choice."

I go to find the nurse who's working with us and beg her to let me stay over. "Aren't the first few hours of a coma critical? He needs to know I'm there!" I tell her.

She informs me that rules are rules.

I rush back to Benny's room, and I'm surprised to see Aaron there sitting in the bedside chair. "What are you doing here?" I ask him.

"Seeing Benny, obviously," he says. "What do you think I'm doing here?"

"I thought it was next of kin only," I say.

Aaron smiles. "I've got connections."

A queasy sensation spreads through my stomach. It's his smile. It's the way he said it. It's that he has no business being here! Benny certainly wouldn't want him here. "I'd like for you to leave so that I can be alone with him."

Aaron looks up at the clock. "Sure." He disappears.

It suddenly occurs to me: isn't it kind of suspicious that both of the owners of TezraTech would be killed in the same span of six months?

My pulse is just racing. My antenna is up so high, it's a wonder there are no holes in the ceiling.

Didn't Benny say that James was dead set against the sale of the company? And then he's run down on his bike? And then Benny turns against the sale and *this* happens?

Is Aaron in control of the company now? Does he get the money or something?

"What happened to you?" I ask Benny. "You have to wake up. You're right here—I can feel you." It's true. I can feel him. He's so close.

I look up at the clock, thoughts racing.

Could Aaron be responsible for this accident? Is it possible Aaron pushed him into the traffic? I feel this grip around my heart just thinking of it. The horror Benny must've felt. The pain.

And how did he even get in here to see Benny? He's not family! Did he bribe an employee? Will he be able to get back in when I'm gone? Will he return in the middle of the night and finish the job?

It feels crazy to think these thoughts, but I can't stop. It all just seems obvious now.

Benny was going to meet Aaron when this very mysterious accident happened.

Why? He'd resolved to call him and tell him the bad news—not meet him in person. Did he call Aaron and tell him he's nixing the sale? Did Aaron convince him to meet somehow? And then...

Am I being paranoid?

Benny's main nurse comes back in.

"You have to let me stay with my husband," I say. "I feel like he could be in danger."

"He's being monitored closely," she says. "If anything happens to him, he's got the best care in the world."

Not what I mean.

"I need to stay," I announce. "I'm not leaving."

"I'm sorry, you don't have a choice." She's checking the machines, hitting buttons on her handheld device. "They'll get security."

"They let Aaron in and he's not even family. So obviously the rules are not that ironclad."

"Your husband is in good hands," she says. "He's safe."

I grab Benny's hand. One of his favorite Spoon songs is playing. "I need you to wake up," I say to him. "I need you to wake up, Benny!"

The nurse gives me a wan smile and leaves.

At five minutes after seven, they still haven't kicked me out, though they've certainly made plenty of announcements about visiting hours being over. Maybe they're giving me a little extra time.

When the door opens next, I'm sure it's them coming to drag me out, but instead it's Aaron.

"Visiting hours are over," I say to him. "And you're not family, anyway."

"If visiting hours are over, what are you doing here?" he asks.

"Staying." I squeeze Benny's hand. I turn up the music. Lou Reed. Another of his favorites. "Come on, baby."

Nothing.

I look up and glare at Aaron.

The nurse comes in.

I point at Aaron. "This man is his soon-to-be ex-business partner and shouldn't be allowed in," I say to her.

Aaron looks surprised. "Ex-business partner? What are you talking about? I'm his current business partner. We were about to negotiate a big sale."

Right here I know he's lying. Benny was going to call him and tell him the sale was off. Benny does what he says he'll do. "Benny doesn't want to sell," I say. "But I think you know that."

"I think you might be overwrought," Aaron says. "Because I know of no such thing."

"He's not selling," I say.

"It's already in motion. It has been for weeks."

"You're both supposed to be out of here," the nurse says.

"Come on, then." Aaron holds out a hand. "We'd best get out of here."

My pulse is racing. “No,” I say. “If you won’t let me stay, I’m signing him out.”

“You can’t sign a vegetative patient out of the hospital,” Aaron says.

“He’s not vegetative,” I snap. I turn to the nurse. “As Benny’s wife, I demand this man be removed.”

“If you both don’t leave, I’m going to have to get security,” the nurse says.

“Get them,” I say. I’m looking around for something to tie myself to the bed with, or chain myself into the room somehow.

Aaron gives me a smile that curdles my stomach. “You’ll be able to visit him tomorrow.”

The air whooshes out of my stomach. “Get out.”

He gives me this innocent look. “It’s okay. I understand that you’re distraught.”

Another song, another favorite, comes on my Benny playlist. If only he’d wake up!

And then I get an idea. I grab my phone and take it off of airplane mode. I’m searching a music app.

The nurse has had enough. I hear her voice, “I need security in room 354.”

I find the one thing that I know will rouse Benny out of that bed.

I hit play and crank the volume up. It’s “Alligator Pie,” a Dave Matthews Band song.

Aaron frowns. “What are you doing?”

A different nurse bursts in the door with a goatee and a grim look. “Turn that off!” he says. “It’s absolutely forbidden to be playing music at a volume like this! Visiting hours are over.”

I stay right there, clutching my phone. They’ll have to carry me out.

My heart sinks when I look down at Benny. He’s unresponsive.

It's not working

"She's just distraught," Aaron says.

"I'm not leaving," I announce over the drone of the song.

When I next look over at Benny, I think I see his lip twitch. I perk up. "Did you guys see that?" I ask.

"You need to turn that off," Aaron says.

"Benny! Listen! Oh my god, what is playing? Can you even?"

Aaron sighs, like I'm so ridiculous. I glare at him. He has his smug smile, but then he looks down at Benny and the smile is gone. His skin goes chalk white.

I look down at Benny and my heart leaps. Benny's eyes are still closed, but his entire face is scrunched up, as if he's in excruciating pain. I've never seen such a beautiful sight!

I put the phone nearer to his ear. "What is this, Benny?"

This seems to annoy Benny even more.

"He's trying to move his arms!" the nurse suddenly exclaims. "He's in some kind of distress!" She calls for a doctor. She tells me to turn off the music.

Aaron is white as a sheet. "Turn it off," he barks.

"Screw off," I say.

Benny's groaning. "No...no..."

A new nurse comes in pushing a cart. Then two men come in who don't look like medical staff at all—obviously security. One of them is huge.

"He's trying to move his arms!" Benny's main nurse tells the new nurse.

A doctor rushes in, assessing the situation. "Somebody turn off that music! And get these people out of here!"

The nurses are rattling off numbers and medical terms.

Aaron comes toward me, holding his hand out for my phone. "You need to shut that off or I will."

"Get away," I say.

"What's going on, Benjamin?" the doctor asks. "Talk to me."

"No," Benny says more audibly. "No more!"

"Can you tell me what's going on?" the doctor asks. "Where does it hurt?"

"Dave...Matthews!" Benny croaks.

"Who's Dave? You want to see Dave? Is that it?" the doctor asks.

"Make it stop. Hate...hate Dave Matthews."

I'm grinning. I'm laughing. Tears might be streaming down my face.

Aaron's out of the room like a shot.

I've turned the music down but not off. Benny's eyes are slit open. Our gazes lock. My heart nearly bursts from my chest.

"Please," he mouths.

"Okay, baby." I shut off the song. I go to his side.

"You trying to kill me?" he asks.

The doctor is doing something medical on the other side of him.

I take his hand, trying not to squeeze the stuffing out of it. "You had us so scared," I say.

"Aaron," he says. "He pushed me."

"Oh my god." I suspected it, but it still shocks me.

"Police. File...a report," Benny rumbles.

I look up at his main nurse. She looks horrified. "The man who was just here?"

"Yes. His soon-to-be ex-business partner," I say.

The nurse with the goatee heads out the door, followed by the two security guys, presumably to get the cops.

The main nurse tells me it's a good sign that he's awake, and that his thinking seems clear.

I hang back as they work. They seem to have forgotten about visiting hours being over.

I grab something to eat when the police arrive to question

Benny. They find me in the waiting lounge afterwards and question me. I don't have much to add, aside from the fact that I believe Benny probably called Aaron and told him about his decision to sell. Somehow Aaron got to him. The police tell me they're looking for Aaron now.

The nurses won't let me back into Benny's room after that. The nurse with the goatee informs me that Benny's resting and shouldn't be disturbed. I decide to camp out in the waiting room. I doubt Benny's in any danger from Aaron, being that Aaron's the subject of a manhunt and all, but where else would I go?

Mac shows up an hour later with a bunch of my stuff and things for Benny. We wait there, camped out.

BENNY'S nearly his normal self the next morning. By which I mean, looking annoyed and exasperated with all the people breezing in and out of his room.

The police have Aaron in custody. They've reopened James's case, too—it's now a possible homicide with Aaron as the main suspect.

I can't stop touching Benny. I stay for hours. When I run out of things to say, I read *Spock Must Die* to him. Spock really doesn't die in it, or more, there are two Spocks, and one of them must die. I'm hoping the real Spock lives. The best Spock.

"I can't believe you let your old copy with all your marginalia go," I say after yet another chapter.

"I still have it. In storage," he says. "I socked away a lot of my old stuff from that time."

I smooth my palm over his two-day-old beard. "It's an amazing book-it deserves to be out on your shelf. Maybe it could even be up on the fireplace mantel, underneath the grand portrait of me," I say.

He's smiling. He's urging me toward him. I climb up on the bed with him. "Are you trying to get fresh with me, Mr. Stearnes?"

"Yes, I'm trying to get fresh with you," he says.

"Do you think that you're going to get a hand job right in this hospital bed?" I ask him.

"I do now," he says.

I'm just laughing. Definitely not happening.

A few days later, he gets something better than a hand job: a clean bill of health, or as much as he can have with a broken leg, two broken ribs, and a head injury.

The doctor rattles off facts about bones and she assures us that there's no reason he can't be 100%. I inform her that Benny would prefer to be 100.5%, and I'm sure she thinks Benny is glaring at me after that, but I know better.

Mac and Alverson and I get him home and set him up in his room. We take turns caring for him, though by day two he's the world's worst patient. Spencer stays by his side. It's not ideal for Benny's allergies, but Spencer makes him happy.

The two of us watch a ton of Netflix shows and every single one of the Marvel movies. I start experimenting with gourmet popcorn toppings; I mean, I really get into it. I always had to use salt in moderation because I had to keep my performance weight down, but not anymore. Benny sometimes teases me about how much salt I like on my popcorn, but hey! Making up for lost time here!

He's up and around on crutches by the end of the next week —a difficult endeavor what with his not-yet-healed ribs, but there's no reasoning with him.

I spend an afternoon at the rehearsal space giving Daneen

pointers on how to navigate the strange choreography. She'll do a great job with my part.

I'm finally getting physical therapy for my knee, and it's feeling better. The prognosis is good—way better than if I'd gone on that tour. I officially resigned from Gotham City ballet, of course. I'll always be able to go to classes, and I may go back in the future, just for those classes, but I'm on a different track now. I'm sad when I imagine my company doing the tour without me, but it's the right thing to do. For them. For me.

In the meantime, Kelsey and I conduct more dance classes in the now-proper dance studio. Sometimes I dance there alone, and every single time, I can't believe he made it for me.

As the weeks pile up, we're fitting into each other's lives more and more. Marriage, dating, and then we'll think about living together maybe—that's the joke we make to people.

When he's fully mobile on crutches, he comes over to 341. We hang out on the rooftop with Kelsey and Jada, and sometimes Antonio shows up. We also go on a few double dates with Noelle and Malcolm. One time we go out to eat with Lizzie and Theo, and that's the real revelation. Theo and Benny bond like freaks on science topics.

It's hilarious.

"You've created a monster," Lizzie says during one of our interminable dinners. "A two-headed billionaire monster."

I twirl my stick around in my bubbly water. "Benny's not a billionaire anymore. He's off of that," I say.

Lizzie snorts. "You guys are so weird!"

I love how she says that. *You guys.* We don't even take a car around anymore. Alverson has gotten into buying rental properties.

Kelsey and I are starting to plan for a girls' dance recital at the ruins. "Anything Goes" will be on hiatus the year after next, and that's when we'll do it. We're showing the girls pictures of the Roman theater and starting to imagine a dance that would go with it. We're also starting to raise funds.

Aaron is charged with first degree murder and attempted murder. He pleads guilty in exchange for a reduced charge of thirty years in prison. The New York Times runs a picture of him being led away in handcuffs. He looks small and angry in his orange jumpsuit, and I find myself wondering if he's sorry.

I bring my phone to show Benny, who's camped out on the couch with Spencer. He holds it in his hand and looks at it for a long time.

"Thirty years," I say.

He doesn't have anything to say to that. He hands it back to me and pets Spencer's scruff.

We take Spencer to visit James's grave a day later. Benny drops flowers in front of the gravestone while I hang back, holding onto Spencer's leash. It's a hot, sunny day—hot even in the shade that we've found. Benny balances on his crutches up there, talking in low tones. I'm thinking he's telling James about Aaron paying for what he did.

It feels like a chapter being closed, even though Benny will probably always keep James close in his own way.

I don't know what the future will bring for Benny and me, but if we ever have a kid, and that kid turns out to be a boy, I know what I want the name to be.

Benny's coming back, broken leg swinging between crutches. "Ready?" I ask.

"It's time," Benny says.

We take an Uber to Vicky and Henry's place and wind up standing all together in their sprawling courtyard watching Spencer and Smuckers tear around like puppies.

"They are so out of hand!" I say.

Spencer is a medium dog—quite a bit larger than Smuckers

—but Smuckers definitely holds his ground as they chase each other around.

"Can you handle this much energy?" Benny asks.

"No, but Smuckers can," Henry says. "He needed a brother."

"To tire him out!" Vicky says.

Benny watches the dogs with an annoyed look that's really happiness. It means everything to him that Spencer is getting a good home, and that he'll still be able to see him.

"And you'll be able to breathe now," I say.

"Breathing is good," Benny agrees. "And I'm sure that Spencer will learn to love that bow tie...someday?"

I chuckle. Vicky made him a bow tie to match the one that Smuckers wears.

"Dude, he loves it already," Vicky says. "Look how proud he is to be wearing it!"

"You don't want Spencer to feel left out," I say.

Hors d'oeuvres come out, we sit and snack, watching the dogs. Benny and I are telling them the story of when the portrait of me arrived—the supposedly diamond-encrusted portrait that supposedly cost seven million that Vicky's friend at the makers studio made.

"She puts it up over the fireplace," Benny chimes in. "I didn't know what to think. Seven million?"

"You were having a heart attack," I say. "It was so hilarious."

"You were making me suffer!" he says.

I sit on his lap. "I would never make you suffer."

EPILOGUE

Three months later: *Benny*

IT'S a gorgeous night in Mérida, in the west of Spain. A whole group from Francine's apartment building are traipsing down a walkway past ancient stone buildings under tropical trees. We're following Theo's sister, Willow, who's sure the restaurant she found for all of us is just around the corner. Antonio is complaining loudly.

I'm walking behind with Theo, spinning theories about the intersection of chemistry and microrobotics. Francine is constantly teasing us about having a bromance. I don't know about that, but he's definitely a friend now. It was through his connections that I found a new partner. We're doing interesting things and even considering some collaborations with Theo's company, Vossameer.

Kelsey and Jada and Mia and Francine are walking behind us, talking about the show we just saw at the Roman theater, the ancient-ruins theater that Francine's been dreaming about all her life. It sounds like Kelsey and Francine got tons of ideas for the choreography. I have to admit that it really was breathtaking, being there in person.

Noelle and Malcolm catch up to us. Malcolm is sure the restaurant's the other way. There's a lot of good-natured arguing. Eventually phones come out. I can see why these people are so important to Francine. It's really like a family.

We're technically here helping to celebrate Noelle and Malcolm's engagement, but they picked this place and made this vacation happen for the benefit of Kelsey and Francine. "Because why not?" as Noelle put it.

I have no doubt that the 42nd Street Twirlers will dance here. Francine and Kelsey are going to meet with a local girls dance troupe tomorrow—they're hatching a sister dance troupe exchange scheme that everybody is excited about. It's kind of brilliant. If all goes well, they'll be hosting a dozen Spanish girls at a fabulous New York theater after they do their thing here.

Willow leads us through some creaky iron gates into a magical courtyard restaurant full of fountains and pine trees and sparkling lights. An entire corner is reserved for our group.

Francine claps. "I'm just so excited! You guys, I can't believe this is even happening!"

"It's not happening for a year," Kelsey says.

"I don't mean our girls' performance," Francine says. "I mean all of us, being friends, meeting in this beautiful place."

"Weepy speech alert!" Jada screams. "Do I need to start filming?"

"No, I just wanted to say that!" Francine insists. "And also, love you all!" And then she looks over at me. "Especially you!"

"Double weepy alert!" Jada says.

I go over and kiss Francine. "I love you."

The party gets underway. Max, the consummate entertainer of the group, has ordered everything on the menu, and also every form of alcohol, apparently. Antonio is speaking to a smitten waitress in fluent Spanish, because he's the kind of man who can romance a woman in every language. Jada is poking him in the back, giving him shit, and I make a mental note to ask Francine about their history.

Later on that night, back in our hotel room, Francine and I are stretched out on the bed, exhausted from some semi-frenetic after-a-huge-dinner sex.

"Your friends are awesome," I say.

"I'm so glad you think that. It's so important to me that you like them." She lays her head against my chest, and I know that I will never tire of this fascinating woman.

"I want to discover everything about you," I whisper. "And I want to discover everything in life with you."

"Same," she sighs. "I feel like everything good is happening now. Like everything is chocolate chip cookie dough."

I agree. Except...

"There was one thing that you wanted very much that you never did get," I remind her.

"What do you mean?" She sits up and turns to me. "What would that be?"

"Well, if you don't remember, maybe you don't want it that badly," I tease.

"Tell me!" she says. "You have to tell me."

"You know how I love to hear you beg, though," I say.

Her lips part in shock.

Of course I never could resist her.

I begin to hum the first strains of 'Alejandro.'

Her face brightens. "Oh my god! What am I hearing?"

I sing her the song using the weird voice that she liked so much that night in Vegas.

She nestles her head back against my chest and hums along.

~The End~

THANK YOU!

Thank you sooooo much for reading the tale of Francine and Benny—it means everything to me! I hope you had as much fun with them as I did.

Each book in this series stands completely on its own—check my website (annikamartinbooks.com) or your fave bookstore to find the others.

Watch for more from the gang in the future!

ACKNOWLEDGMENTS

I am so crazy grateful to my many talented co-conspirators—you all lift me as an author...really! I would be a word-mumbling heap on the ground without you! In the order of appearance as angels of awesomeness for this book, I want to thank Jenn Stark for conducting the fun and fateful author tarot reading that kicked off the discussion that led to this idea, and Toni Anderson for adding her own twist (and a critical late read omg thank you), and Rachel Grant for the mind-blowing plot whispering—this plot was a gift, and I'm just wildly grateful to you for it. I'm also madly grateful to Molly O'Keefe for lots of handholding and brilliant insights that made this book—your friendship and generosity is everything to me. Joanna Chambers, you read this book and helped me weave straw into what is hopefully gold—you always see things so clearly, I sometimes don't know how I'm an author without you. Thank you to Crisshasart for drawing the fun cartoon figures. Jess Lourey, your friendship means everything, and our pandemic writing bubble and walks and discussions this past year added richness to this book and defo saved my sanity. Deep gratitude to Terri Whitman, Elizabeth Andrew, and Marcia Peck—I love our group so much, and the artistry you bring amazes me. You saw things and brought ideas to this book that elevated it immensely. And all the love and gratitude to my husband Mark— your constant willingness to go over the plot and your insightful reading and your freak-out-time hand-holding and willingness to pick up the household slack and general cheerleading has been a gift I can barely comprehend. And Sandy Waters Bredin, thank you so freaking much for the Italian assist and sweet friendship to the books! I'm massively indebted to Melissa Gaston—you are always there with savvy advice and the best help—where would I be without you? And Sarah Piechuta! Thank you for making me look spiffy out there. I'm super grateful to Nina Grinstead and the entire team at Valentine PR for the amazing work and support—you all rock! Thanks also to Kelly Reynolds for the help and support —I'm so grateful to have you on my team. Deep thanks to Peggy Schnurr and Judy Zweifel for beautiful proofreading...any lingering mistakes are my own because I cannot stop changing my books. And OMG Courtenay Bennett. You are a magical punctuation and prose whisperer, and I'm so lucky to be connected with you. I'm lifted by so many other book world friends that I can't thank you individually, but OMG the generosity of my peeps in this genre makes my world go 'round. Finally, all the love to my ARC gang – your support inspires me more than you will ever know. My heart bursts when I see what you do out there! And to all you readers out there—thank you for taking a chance on these crazy billionaire books!! Your friendship to the gang at 341 is everything. Heart eyes to you!!

ALL THE ANNIKA DEETS!

Annika Martin is a NYT bestselling author who loves reading fun, sexy books, doing yoga, taking pictures of her cats, helping animals, and consuming boatloads of chocolate suckers. She can be found hanging out in Minneapolis coffee shops with her awesome writer husband and sometimes tending her crazy bee-friendly garden.

newsletter:
http://annikamartinbooks.com/newletter

Facebook:
www.facebook.com/AnnikaMartinBooks

The Annika Martin Fabulous Gang:
www.facebook.com/groups/AnnikaMartinFabulousGang/

Instagram:
instagram.com/annikamartinauthor

website:
www.annikamartinbooks.com

email
annika@annikamartinbooks.com

Thank you for reading!

xox Annika

CPSIA information can be obtained
at www.ICGtesting.com
Printed in the USA
BVHW042009040921
616082BV00017B/222